Shakespeare's Problem Plays

Shakespeare's
Problem Plays
by William Shakespeare

Contents

All's Well That Ends Well

Dramatis Personae

KING OF FRANCE
THE DUKE OF FLORENCE
BERTRAM, Count of Rousillon
LAFEU, an old lord
PAROLLES, a follower of Bertram
TWO FRENCH LORDS, serving with Bertram
STEWARD, Servant to the Countess of Rousillon
LAVACHE, a clown and Servant to the Countess of Rousillon
A PAGE, Servant to the Countess of Rousillon
COUNTESS OF ROUSILLON, mother to Bertram
HELENA, a gentlewoman protected by the Countess
A WIDOW OF FLORENCE.
DIANA, daughter to the Widow
VIOLENTA, neighbour and friend to the Widow
MARIANA, neighbour and friend to the Widow
Lords, Officers, Soldiers, etc., French and Florentine

ACT I. SCENE I. Rousillon. The Count's Palace
Enter Bertram, the Countess of Rousillon, Helena, and Lafeu, All in Black

COUNTESS: In delivering my son from me, I bury a second husband.

BERTRAM: And I in going, madam, weep o'er my father's death anew; but I must attend his Majesty's command, to whom I am now in ward, evermore in subjection.

LAFEU: You shall find of the King a husband, madam; you, sir, a father. He that so generally is at all times good must of necessity hold his virtue to you, whose worthiness would stir it up where it wanted, rather than lack it where there is such abundance.

COUNTESS: What hope is there of his Majesty's amendment?

LAFEU: He hath abandon'd his physicians, madam; under whose practices he hath persecuted time with hope, and finds no other advantage in the process but only the losing of hope by time.

COUNTESS: This young gentlewoman had a father- O, that 'had,' how sad a passage 'tis!-whose skill was almost as great as his honesty; had it stretch'd so far, would have made nature immortal, and death should have play for lack of work. Would, for the King's sake, he were living! I think it would be the death of the King's disease.

LAFEU: How call'd you the man you speak of, madam?

COUNTESS: He was famous, sir, in his profession, and it was his great right to be so- Gerard de Narbon.

LAFEU: He was excellent indeed, madam; the King very lately spoke of him admiringly and mourningly; he was skilful enough to have liv'd still, if knowledge could be set up against mortality.

BERTRAM: What is it, my good lord, the King languishes of?

LAFEU: A fistula, my lord.

BERTRAM: I heard not of it before.

LAFEU: I would it were not notorious. Was this gentlewoman the daughter of Gerard de Narbon?

COUNTESS: His sole child, my lord, and bequeathed to my overlooking. I have those hopes of her good that her education promises; her dispositions she inherits, which makes fair gifts fairer; for where an unclean mind carries virtuous qualities, there commendations go with pity-they are virtues and traitors too. In her they are the better for their simpleness; she derives her honesty, and achieves her goodness.

LAFEU: Your commendations, madam, get from her tears.

COUNTESS: 'Tis the best brine a maiden can season her praise in. The remembrance of her father never approaches her heart but the tyranny of her sorrows takes all livelihood from her cheek. No more of this, Helena; go to, no more, lest it be rather thought you affect a sorrow than to have-

HELENA: I do affect a sorrow indeed, but I have it too.

LAFEU: Moderate lamentation is the right of the dead: excessive grief the enemy to the living.

COUNTESS: If the living be enemy to the grief, the excess makes it soon mortal.

BERTRAM: Madam, I desire your holy wishes.

LAFEU: How understand we that?

COUNTESS: Be thou blest, Bertram, and succeed thy father
In manners, as in shape! Thy blood and virtue
Contend for empire in thee, and thy goodness
Share with thy birthright! Love all, trust a few,
Do wrong to none; be able for thine enemy
Rather in power than use, and keep thy friend
Under thy own life's key; be check'd for silence,
But never tax'd for speech. What heaven more will,
That thee may furnish, and my prayers pluck down,
Fall on thy head! Farewell. My lord,
'Tis an unseason'd courtier; good my lord, advise him.

LAFEU: He cannot want the best
That shall attend his love.

COUNTESS: Heaven bless him! Farewell, Bertram.
Exit

BERTRAM: The best wishes that can be forg'd in your thoughts be servants to you! *To Helena* Be comfortable to my mother, your mistress, and make much of her.

LAFEU: Farewell, pretty lady; you must hold the credit of your father.
  Exeunt Bertram and Lafeu

HELENA: O, were that all! I think not on my father;
And these great tears grace his remembrance more
Than those I shed for him. What was he like?
I have forgot him; my imagination
Carries no favour in't but Bertram's.
I am undone; there is no living, none,
If Bertram be away. 'Twere all one
That I should love a bright particular star
And think to wed it, he is so above me.
In his bright radiance and collateral light
Must I be comforted, not in his sphere.
Th' ambition in my love thus plagues itself:
The hind that would be mated by the lion
Must die for love. 'Twas pretty, though a plague,
To see him every hour; to sit and draw
His arched brows, his hawking eye, his curls,
In our heart's table-heart too capable
Of every line and trick of his sweet favour.
But now he's gone, and my idolatrous fancy
Must sanctify his relics. Who comes here?
  Enter Parolles
Aside One that goes with him. I love him for his sake;
And yet I know him a notorious liar,
Think him a great way fool, solely a coward;
Yet these fix'd evils sit so fit in him
That they take place when virtue's steely bones
Looks bleak i' th' cold wind; withal, full oft we see
Cold wisdom waiting on superfluous folly.

PAROLLES: Save you, fair queen!

HELENA: And you, monarch!

PAROLLES: No.

HELENA: And no.

PAROLLES: Are you meditating on virginity?

HELENA: Ay. You have some stain of soldier in you; let me ask you a question. Man is enemy to virginity; how may we barricado it against him?

PAROLLES: Keep him out.

HELENA: But he assails; and our virginity, though valiant in the defence, yet is weak. Unfold to us some warlike resistance.

PAROLLES: There is none. Man, setting down before you, will undermine you and blow you up.

HELENA: Bless our poor virginity from underminers and blowers-up! Is there no military policy how virgins might blow up men?

PAROLLES: Virginity being blown down, man will quicklier be blown up; marry, in blowing him down again, with the breach yourselves made, you lose your city. It is not politic in the commonwealth of nature to preserve virginity. Loss of virginity is rational increase; and there was never virgin got till virginity was first lost. That you were made of is metal to make virgins. Virginity by being once lost may be ten times found; by being ever kept, it is ever lost. 'Tis too cold a companion; away with't.

HELENA: I will stand for 't a little, though therefore I die a virgin.

PAROLLES: There's little can be said in 't; 'tis against the rule of nature. To speak on the part of virginity is to accuse your mothers; which is most infallible disobedience. He that hangs himself is a virgin; virginity murders itself, and should be

buried in highways, out of all sanctified limit, as a desperate
offendress against nature. Virginity breeds mites, much like a
cheese; consumes itself to the very paring, and so dies with
feeding his own stomach. Besides, virginity is peevish, proud,
idle, made of self-love, which is the most inhibited sin in the
canon. Keep it not; you cannot choose but lose by't. Out with't.
Within ten year it will make itself ten, which is a goodly
increase; and the principal itself not much the worse. Away with't.

HELENA: How might one do, sir, to lose it to her own liking?

PAROLLES: Let me see. Marry, ill to like him that ne'er it likes.
'Tis a commodity will lose the gloss with lying; the longer kept,
the less worth. Off with't while 'tis vendible; answer the time
of request. Virginity, like an old courtier, wears her cap out of
fashion, richly suited but unsuitable; just like the brooch and
the toothpick, which wear not now. Your date is better in your
pie and your porridge than in your cheek. And your virginity,
your old virginity, is like one of our French wither'd pears: it
looks ill, it eats drily; marry, 'tis a wither'd pear; it was
formerly better; marry, yet 'tis a wither'd pear. Will you
anything with it?

HELENA: Not my virginity yet.
There shall your master have a thousand loves,
A mother, and a mistress, and a friend,
A phoenix, captain, and an enemy,
A guide, a goddess, and a sovereign,
A counsellor, a traitress, and a dear;
His humble ambition, proud humility,
His jarring concord, and his discord dulcet,
His faith, his sweet disaster; with a world
Of pretty, fond, adoptious christendoms
That blinking Cupid gossips. Now shall he-
I know not what he shall. God send him well!
The court's a learning-place, and he is one-

PAROLLES: What one, i' faith?

HELENA: That I wish well. 'Tis pity—

PAROLLES: What's pity?

HELENA: That wishing well had not a body in't
Which might be felt; that we, the poorer born,
Whose baser stars do shut us up in wishes,
Might with effects of them follow our friends
And show what we alone must think, which never
Returns us thanks.
  Enter Page

PAGE: Monsieur Parolles, my lord calls for you.
  Exit Page

PAROLLES: Little Helen, farewell; if I can remember thee, I will
think of thee at court.

HELENA: Monsieur Parolles, you were born under a charitable star.

PAROLLES: Under Mars, I.

HELENA: I especially think, under Mars.

PAROLLES: Why under Man?

HELENA: The wars hath so kept you under that you must needs be born
under Mars.

PAROLLES: When he was predominant.

HELENA: When he was retrograde, I think, rather.

PAROLLES: Why think you so?

LAFEU: You go so much backward when you fight.

PAROLLES: That's for advantage.

HELENA: So is running away, when fear proposes the safety: but the composition that your valour and fear makes in you is a virtue of a good wing, and I like the wear well.

PAROLLES: I am so full of business I cannot answer thee acutely. I will return perfect courtier; in the which my instruction shall serve to naturalize thee, so thou wilt be capable of a courtier's counsel, and understand what advice shall thrust upon thee; else thou diest in thine unthankfulness, and thine ignorance makes thee away. Farewell. When thou hast leisure, say thy prayers; when thou hast none, remember thy friends. Get thee a good husband and use him as he uses thee. So, farewell.
    Exit

HELENA: Our remedies oft in ourselves do lie,
Which we ascribe to heaven. The fated sky
Gives us free scope; only doth backward pull
Our slow designs when we ourselves are dull.
What power is it which mounts my love so high,
That makes me see, and cannot feed mine eye?
The mightiest space in fortune nature brings
To join like likes, and kiss like native things.
Impossible be strange attempts to those
That weigh their pains in sense, and do suppose
What hath been cannot be. Who ever strove
To show her merit that did miss her love?
The King's disease-my project may deceive me,
But my intents are fix'd, and will not leave me.
    Exit

ACT I. SCENE II. Paris. The King's Palace

Flourish of Cornets. Enter the King of France, with Letters, and Divers Attendants

KING: The Florentines and Senoys are by th' ears;
Have fought with equal fortune, and continue
A braving war.

FIRST LORD: So 'tis reported, sir.

KING: Nay, 'tis most credible. We here receive it,
A certainty, vouch'd from our cousin Austria,
With caution, that the Florentine will move us
For speedy aid; wherein our dearest friend
Prejudicates the business, and would seem
To have us make denial.

FIRST LORD: His love and wisdom,
Approv'd so to your Majesty, may plead
For amplest credence.

KING: He hath arm'd our answer,
And Florence is denied before he comes;
Yet, for our gentlemen that mean to see
The Tuscan service, freely have they leave
To stand on either part.

SECOND LORD: It well may serve
A nursery to our gentry, who are sick
For breathing and exploit.

KING: What's he comes here?
Enter Bertram, Lafeu, and Parolles

FIRST LORD: It is the Count Rousillon, my good lord,
Young Bertram.

KING: Youth, thou bear'st thy father's face;
Frank nature, rather curious than in haste,
Hath well compos'd thee. Thy father's moral parts
Mayst thou inherit too! Welcome to Paris.

BERTRAM: My thanks and duty are your Majesty's.

KING: I would I had that corporal soundness now,
As when thy father and myself in friendship
First tried our soldiership. He did look far
Into the service of the time, and was
Discipled of the bravest. He lasted long;
But on us both did haggish age steal on,
And wore us out of act. It much repairs me
To talk of your good father. In his youth
He had the wit which I can well observe
To-day in our young lords; but they may jest
Till their own scorn return to them unnoted
Ere they can hide their levity in honour.
So like a courtier, contempt nor bitterness
Were in his pride or sharpness; if they were,
His equal had awak'd them; and his honour,
Clock to itself, knew the true minute when
Exception bid him speak, and at this time
His tongue obey'd his hand. Who were below him
He us'd as creatures of another place;
And bow'd his eminent top to their low ranks,
Making them proud of his humility
In their poor praise he humbled. Such a man
Might be a copy to these younger times;
Which, followed well, would demonstrate them now
But goers backward.

BERTRAM: His good remembrance, sir,
Lies richer in your thoughts than on his tomb;
So in approof lives not his epitaph
As in your royal speech.

KING: Would I were with him! He would always say-
Methinks I hear him now; his plausive words
He scatter'd not in ears, but grafted them
To grow there, and to bear- 'Let me not live'-
This his good melancholy oft began,
On the catastrophe and heel of pastime,
When it was out-'Let me not live' quoth he
'After my flame lacks oil, to be the snuff
Of younger spirits, whose apprehensive senses
All but new things disdain; whose judgments are
Mere fathers of their garments; whose constancies
Expire before their fashions.' This he wish'd.
I, after him, do after him wish too,
Since I nor wax nor honey can bring home,
I quickly were dissolved from my hive,
To give some labourers room.

SECOND LORD: You're loved, sir;
They that least lend it you shall lack you first.

KING: I fill a place, I know't. How long is't, Count,
Since the physician at your father's died?
He was much fam'd.

BERTRAM: Some six months since, my lord.

KING: If he were living, I would try him yet-
Lend me an arm-the rest have worn me out
With several applications. Nature and sickness
Debate it at their leisure. Welcome, Count;
My son's no dearer.

BERTRAM: Thank your Majesty.
  Exeunt Flourish

ACT I. SCENE III. Rousillon. The Count's Palace

Enter Countess, Steward, and Clown

COUNTESS: I will now hear; what say you of this gentlewoman?

STEWARD: Madam, the care I have had to even your content I wish might be found in the calendar of my past endeavours; for then we wound our modesty, and make foul the clearness of our deservings, when of ourselves we publish them.

COUNTESS: What does this knave here? Get you gone, sirrah. The complaints I have heard of you I do not all believe; 'tis my slowness that I do not, for I know you lack not folly to commit them and have ability enough to make such knaveries yours.

CLOWN: 'Tis not unknown to you, madam, I am a poor fellow.

COUNTESS: Well, sir.

CLOWN: No, madam, 'tis not so well that I am poor, though many of the rich are damn'd; but if I may have your ladyship's good will to go to the world, Isbel the woman and I will do as we may.

COUNTESS: Wilt thou needs be a beggar?

CLOWN: I do beg your good will in this case.

COUNTESS: In what case?

CLOWN: In Isbel's case and mine own. Service is no heritage; and I think I shall never have the blessing of God till I have issue o' my body; for they say bames are blessings.

COUNTESS: Tell me thy reason why thou wilt marry.

CLOWN: My poor body, madam, requires it. I am driven on by the flesh; and he must needs go that the devil drives.

COUNTESS: Is this all your worship's reason?

CLOWN: Faith, madam, I have other holy reasons, such as they are.

COUNTESS: May the world know them?

CLOWN: I have been, madam, a wicked creature, as you and all flesh and blood are; and, indeed, I do marry that I may repent.

COUNTESS: Thy marriage, sooner than thy wickedness.

CLOWN: I am out o' friends, madam, and I hope to have friends for my wife's sake.

COUNTESS: Such friends are thine enemies, knave.

CLOWN: Y'are shallow, madam-in great friends; for the knaves come to do that for me which I am aweary of. He that ears my land spares my team, and gives me leave to in the crop. If I be his cuckold, he's my drudge. He that comforts my wife is the cherisher of my flesh and blood; he that cherishes my flesh and blood loves my flesh and blood; he that loves my flesh and blood is my friend; ergo, he that kisses my wife is my friend. If men could be contented to be what they are, there were no fear in marriage; for young Charbon the puritan and old Poysam the papist, howsome'er their hearts are sever'd in religion, their heads are both one; they may jowl horns together like any deer i' th' herd.

COUNTESS: Wilt thou ever be a foul-mouth'd and calumnious knave?

CLOWN: A prophet I, madam; and I speak the truth the next way:
    For I the ballad will repeat,
      Which men full true shall find:
    Your marriage comes by destiny,
      Your cuckoo sings by kind.

COUNTESS: Get you gone, sir; I'll talk with you more anon.

STEWARD: May it please you, madam, that he bid Helen come to you.
Of her I am to speak.

COUNTESS: Sirrah, tell my gentlewoman I would speak with her; Helen
I mean.

CLOWN: *Sings*

>'Was this fair face the cause' quoth she
> 'Why the Grecians sacked Troy?
>Fond done, done fond,
> Was this King Priam's joy?'
>With that she sighed as she stood,
>With that she sighed as she stood,
> And gave this sentence then:
>'Among nine bad if one be good,
>Among nine bad if one be good,
> There's yet one good in ten.'

COUNTESS: What, one good in ten? You corrupt the song, sirrah.

CLOWN: One good woman in ten, madam, which is a purifying o' th'
song. Would God would serve the world so all the year! We'd find
no fault with the tithe-woman, if I were the parson. One in ten,
quoth 'a! An we might have a good woman born before every blazing
star, or at an earthquake, 'twould mend the lottery well: a man
may draw his heart out ere 'a pluck one.

COUNTESS: You'll be gone, sir knave, and do as I command you.

CLOWN: That man should be at woman's command, and yet no hurt done!
Though honesty be no puritan, yet it will do no hurt; it will
wear the surplice of humility over the black gown of a big heart.
I am going, forsooth. The business is for Helen to come hither.
  Exit

COUNTESS: Well, now.

STEWARD: I know, madam, you love your gentlewoman entirely.

COUNTESS: Faith I do. Her father bequeath'd her to me; and she herself, without other advantage, may lawfully make title to as much love as she finds. There is more owing her than is paid; and more shall be paid her than she'll demand.

STEWARD: Madam, I was very late more near her than I think she wish'd me. Alone she was, and did communicate to herself her own words to her own ears; she thought, I dare vow for her, they touch'd not any stranger sense. Her matter was, she loved your son. Fortune, she said, was no goddess, that had put such difference betwixt their two estates; Love no god, that would not extend his might only where qualities were level; Diana no queen of virgins, that would suffer her poor knight surpris'd without rescue in the first assault, or ransom afterward. This she deliver'd in the most bitter touch of sorrow that e'er I heard virgin exclaim in; which I held my duty speedily to acquaint you withal; sithence, in the loss that may happen, it concerns you something to know it.

COUNTESS: YOU have discharg'd this honestly; keep it to yourself. Many likelihoods inform'd me of this before, which hung so tott'ring in the balance that I could neither believe nor misdoubt. Pray you leave me. Stall this in your bosom; and I thank you for your honest care. I will speak with you further anon.

    Exit Steward
    Enter Helena

Even so it was with me when I was young.
If ever we are nature's, these are ours; this thorn
Doth to our rose of youth rightly belong;
Our blood to us, this to our blood is born.
It is the show and seal of nature's truth,
Where love's strong passion is impress'd in youth.

By our remembrances of days foregone,
Such were our faults, or then we thought them none.
Her eye is sick on't; I observe her now.

HELENA: What is your pleasure, madam?

COUNTESS: You know, Helen,
I am a mother to you.

HELENA: Mine honourable mistress.

COUNTESS: Nay, a mother.
Why not a mother? When I said 'a mother,'
Methought you saw a serpent. What's in 'mother'
That you start at it? I say I am your mother,
And put you in the catalogue of those
That were enwombed mine. 'Tis often seen
Adoption strives with nature, and choice breeds
A native slip to us from foreign seeds.
You ne'er oppress'd me with a mother's groan,
Yet I express to you a mother's care.
God's mercy, maiden! does it curd thy blood
To say I am thy mother? What's the matter,
That this distempered messenger of wet,
The many-colour'd Iris, rounds thine eye?
Why, that you are my daughter?

HELENA: That I am not.

COUNTESS: I say I am your mother.

HELENA: Pardon, madam.
The Count Rousillon cannot be my brother:
I am from humble, he from honoured name;
No note upon my parents, his all noble.
My master, my dear lord he is; and I
His servant live, and will his vassal die.

He must not be my brother.

COUNTESS: Nor I your mother?

HELENA: You are my mother, madam; would you were-
So that my lord your son were not my brother-
Indeed my mother! Or were you both our mothers,
I care no more for than I do for heaven,
So I were not his sister. Can't no other,
But, I your daughter, he must be my brother?

COUNTESS: Yes, Helen, you might be my daughter-in-law.
God shield you mean it not! 'daughter' and 'mother'
So strive upon your pulse. What! pale again?
My fear hath catch'd your fondness. Now I see
The myst'ry of your loneliness, and find
Your salt tears' head. Now to all sense 'tis gross
You love my son; invention is asham'd,
Against the proclamation of thy passion,
To say thou dost not. Therefore tell me true;
But tell me then, 'tis so; for, look, thy cheeks
Confess it, th' one to th' other; and thine eyes
See it so grossly shown in thy behaviours
That in their kind they speak it; only sin
And hellish obstinacy tie thy tongue,
That truth should be suspected. Speak, is't so?
If it be so, you have wound a goodly clew;
If it be not, forswear't; howe'er, I charge thee,
As heaven shall work in me for thine avail,
To tell me truly.

HELENA: Good madam, pardon me.

COUNTESS: Do you love my son?

HELENA: Your pardon, noble mistress.

COUNTESS: Love you my son?

HELENA: Do not you love him, madam?

COUNTESS: Go not about; my love hath in't a bond
Whereof the world takes note. Come, come, disclose
The state of your affection; for your passions
Have to the full appeach'd.

HELENA: Then I confess,
Here on my knee, before high heaven and you,
That before you, and next unto high heaven,
I love your son.
My friends were poor, but honest; so's my love.
Be not offended, for it hurts not him
That he is lov'd of me; I follow him not
By any token of presumptuous suit,
Nor would I have him till I do deserve him;
Yet never know how that desert should be.
I know I love in vain, strive against hope;
Yet in this captious and intenible sieve
I still pour in the waters of my love,
And lack not to lose still. Thus, Indian-like,
Religious in mine error, I adore
The sun that looks upon his worshipper
But knows of him no more. My dearest madam,
Let not your hate encounter with my love,
For loving where you do; but if yourself,
Whose aged honour cites a virtuous youth,
Did ever in so true a flame of liking
Wish chastely and love dearly that your Dian
Was both herself and Love; O, then, give pity
To her whose state is such that cannot choose
But lend and give where she is sure to lose;
That seeks not to find that her search implies,
But, riddle-like, lives sweetly where she dies!

COUNTESS: Had you not lately an intent-speak truly-
To go to Paris?

HELENA: Madam, I had.

COUNTESS: Wherefore? Tell true.

HELENA: I will tell truth; by grace itself I swear.
You know my father left me some prescriptions
Of rare and prov'd effects, such as his reading
And manifest experience had collected
For general sovereignty; and that he will'd me
In heedfull'st reservation to bestow them,
As notes whose faculties inclusive were
More than they were in note. Amongst the rest
There is a remedy, approv'd, set down,
To cure the desperate languishings whereof
The King is render'd lost.

COUNTESS: This was your motive
For Paris, was it? Speak.

HELENA: My lord your son made me to think of this,
Else Paris, and the medicine, and the King,
Had from the conversation of my thoughts
Haply been absent then.

COUNTESS: But think you, Helen,
If you should tender your supposed aid,
He would receive it? He and his physicians
Are of a mind: he, that they cannot help him;
They, that they cannot help. How shall they credit
A poor unlearned virgin, when the schools,
Embowell'd of their doctrine, have let off
The danger to itself?

HELENA: There's something in't

More than my father's skill, which was the great'st
Of his profession, that his good receipt
Shall for my legacy be sanctified
By th' luckiest stars in heaven; and, would your honour
But give me leave to try success, I'd venture
The well-lost life of mine on his Grace's cure.
By such a day and hour.

COUNTESS: Dost thou believe't?

HELENA: Ay, madam, knowingly.

COUNTESS: Why, Helen, thou shalt have my leave and love,
Means and attendants, and my loving greetings
To those of mine in court. I'll stay at home,
And pray God's blessing into thy attempt.
Be gone to-morrow; and be sure of this,
What I can help thee to thou shalt not miss.
　　Exeunt

ACT II. SCENE I. Paris. The King's Palace

Flourish of Cornets. Enter the King with Divers Young Lords Taking Leave for the Florentine War; Bertram and Parolles; Attendants

KING: Farewell, young lords; these war-like principles
Do not throw from you. And you, my lords, farewell;
Share the advice betwixt you; if both gain all,
The gift doth stretch itself as 'tis receiv'd,
And is enough for both.

FIRST LORD: 'Tis our hope, sir,
After well-ent'red soldiers, to return
And find your Grace in health.

KING: No, no, it cannot be; and yet my heart
Will not confess he owes the malady
That doth my life besiege. Farewell, young lords;

Whether I live or die, be you the sons
Of worthy Frenchmen; let higher Italy-
Those bated that inherit but the fall
Of the last monarchy-see that you come
Not to woo honour, but to wed it; when
The bravest questant shrinks, find what you seek,
That fame may cry you aloud. I say farewell.

SECOND LORD: Health, at your bidding, serve your Majesty!

KING: Those girls of Italy, take heed of them;
They say our French lack language to deny,
If they demand; beware of being captives
Before you serve.

BOTH: Our hearts receive your warnings.

KING: Farewell. *To Attendants* Come hither to me.
  The King Retires Attended

FIRST LORD: O my sweet lord, that you will stay behind us!

PAROLLES: 'Tis not his fault, the spark.

SECOND LORD: O, 'tis brave wars!

PAROLLES: Most admirable! I have seen those wars.

BERTRAM: I am commanded here and kept a coil with
'Too young' and next year' and "Tis too early.'

PAROLLES: An thy mind stand to 't, boy, steal away bravely.

BERTRAM: I shall stay here the forehorse to a smock,
Creaking my shoes on the plain masonry,
Till honour be bought up, and no sword worn
But one to dance with. By heaven, I'll steal away.

FIRST LORD: There's honour in the theft.

PAROLLES: Commit it, Count.

SECOND LORD: I am your accessary; and so farewell.

BERTRAM: I grow to you, and our parting is a tortur'd body.

FIRST LORD: Farewell, Captain.

SECOND LORD: Sweet Monsieur Parolles!

PAROLLES: Noble heroes, my sword and yours are kin. Good sparks and
lustrous, a word, good metals: you shall find in the regiment of
the Spinii one Captain Spurio, with his cicatrice, an emblem of
war, here on his sinister cheek; it was this very sword
entrench'd it. Say to him I live; and observe his reports for me.

FIRST LORD: We shall, noble Captain.

PAROLLES: Mars dote on you for his novices!
    Exeunt Lords
What will ye do?
    Re-enter the King

BERTRAM: Stay; the King!

PAROLLES: Use a more spacious ceremony to the noble lords; you have
restrain'd yourself within the list of too cold an adieu. Be more
expressive to them; for they wear themselves in the cap of the
time; there do muster true gait; eat, speak, and move, under the
influence of the most receiv'd star; and though the devil lead
the measure, such are to be followed. After them, and take a more
dilated farewell.

BERTRAM: And I will do so.

PAROLLES: Worthy fellows; and like to prove most sinewy sword-men.
  Exeunt Bertram and Parolles
  Enter Lafeu

LAFEU: *Kneeling* Pardon, my lord, for me and for my tidings.

KING: I'll fee thee to stand up.

LAFEU: Then here's a man stands that has brought his pardon.
I would you had kneel'd, my lord, to ask me mercy;
And that at my bidding you could so stand up.

KING: I would I had; so I had broke thy pate,
And ask'd thee mercy for't.

LAFEU: Good faith, across!
But, my good lord, 'tis thus: will you be cur'd
Of your infirmity?

KING: No.

LAFEU: O, will you eat
No grapes, my royal fox? Yes, but you will
My noble grapes, an if my royal fox
Could reach them: I have seen a medicine
That's able to breathe life into a stone,
Quicken a rock, and make you dance canary
With spritely fire and motion; whose simple touch
Is powerful to araise King Pepin, nay,
To give great Charlemain a pen in's hand
And write to her a love-line.

KING: What her is this?

LAFEU: Why, Doctor She! My lord, there's one arriv'd,
If you will see her. Now, by my faith and honour,
If seriously I may convey my thoughts

In this my light deliverance, I have spoke
With one that in her sex, her years, profession,
Wisdom, and constancy, hath amaz'd me more
Than I dare blame my weakness. Will you see her,
For that is her demand, and know her business?
That done, laugh well at me.

KING: Now, good Lafeu,
Bring in the admiration, that we with the
May spend our wonder too, or take off thine
By wond'ring how thou took'st it.

LAFEU: Nay, I'll fit you,
And not be all day neither.
    Exit Lafeu

KING: Thus he his special nothing ever prologues.
    Re-enter Lafeu with Helena

LAFEU: Nay, come your ways.

KING: This haste hath wings indeed.

LAFEU: Nay, come your ways;
This is his Majesty; say your mind to him.
A traitor you do look like; but such traitors
His Majesty seldom fears. I am Cressid's uncle,
That dare leave two together. Fare you well.
    Exit

KING: Now, fair one, does your business follow us?

HELENA: Ay, my good lord.
Gerard de Narbon was my father,
In what he did profess, well found.

KING: I knew him.

HELENA: The rather will I spare my praises towards him;
Knowing him is enough. On's bed of death
Many receipts he gave me; chiefly one,
Which, as the dearest issue of his practice,
And of his old experience th' only darling,
He bade me store up as a triple eye,
Safer than mine own two, more dear. I have so:
And, hearing your high Majesty is touch'd
With that malignant cause wherein the honour
Of my dear father's gift stands chief in power,
I come to tender it, and my appliance,
With all bound humbleness.

KING: We thank you, maiden;
But may not be so credulous of cure,
When our most learned doctors leave us, and
The congregated college have concluded
That labouring art can never ransom nature
From her inaidable estate-I say we must not
So stain our judgment, or corrupt our hope,
To prostitute our past-cure malady
To empirics; or to dissever so
Our great self and our credit to esteem
A senseless help, when help past sense we deem.

HELENA: My duty then shall pay me for my pains.
I will no more enforce mine office on you;
Humbly entreating from your royal thoughts
A modest one to bear me back again.

KING: I cannot give thee less, to be call'd grateful.
Thou thought'st to help me; and such thanks I give
As one near death to those that wish him live.
But what at full I know, thou know'st no part;
I knowing all my peril, thou no art.

HELENA: What I can do can do no hurt to try,

Since you set up your rest 'gainst remedy.
He that of greatest works is finisher
Oft does them by the weakest minister.
So holy writ in babes hath judgment shown,
When judges have been babes. Great floods have flown
From simple sources, and great seas have dried
When miracles have by the greatest been denied.
Oft expectation fails, and most oft there
Where most it promises; and oft it hits
Where hope is coldest, and despair most fits.

KING: I must not hear thee. Fare thee well, kind maid;
Thy pains, not us'd, must by thyself be paid;
Proffers not took reap thanks for their reward.

HELENA: Inspired merit so by breath is barr'd.
It is not so with Him that all things knows,
As 'tis with us that square our guess by shows;
But most it is presumption in us when
The help of heaven we count the act of men.
Dear sir, to my endeavours give consent;
Of heaven, not me, make an experiment.
I am not an impostor, that proclaim
Myself against the level of mine aim;
But know I think, and think I know most sure,
My art is not past power nor you past cure.

KING: Art thou so confident? Within what space
Hop'st thou my cure?

HELENA: The greatest Grace lending grace.
Ere twice the horses of the sun shall bring
Their fiery torcher his diurnal ring,
Ere twice in murk and occidental damp
Moist Hesperus hath quench'd his sleepy lamp,
Or four and twenty times the pilot's glass
Hath told the thievish minutes how they pass,

What is infirm from your sound parts shall fly,
Health shall live free, and sickness freely die.

KING: Upon thy certainty and confidence
What dar'st thou venture?

HELENA: Tax of impudence,
A strumpet's boldness, a divulged shame,
Traduc'd by odious ballads; my maiden's name
Sear'd otherwise; ne worse of worst-extended
With vilest torture let my life be ended.

KING: Methinks in thee some blessed spirit doth speak
His powerful sound within an organ weak;
And what impossibility would slay
In common sense, sense saves another way.
Thy life is dear; for all that life can rate
Worth name of life in thee hath estimate:
Youth, beauty, wisdom, courage, all
That happiness and prime can happy call.
Thou this to hazard needs must intimate
Skill infinite or monstrous desperate.
Sweet practiser, thy physic I will try,
That ministers thine own death if I die.

HELENA: If I break time, or flinch in property
Of what I spoke, unpitied let me die;
And well deserv'd. Not helping, death's my fee;
But, if I help, what do you promise me?

KING: Make thy demand.

HELENA: But will you make it even?

KING: Ay, by my sceptre and my hopes of heaven.

HELENA: Then shalt thou give me with thy kingly hand

What husband in thy power I will command.
Exempted be from me the arrogance
To choose from forth the royal blood of France,
My low and humble name to propagate
With any branch or image of thy state;
But such a one, thy vassal, whom I know
Is free for me to ask, thee to bestow.

KING: Here is my hand; the premises observ'd,
Thy will by my performance shall be serv'd.
So make the choice of thy own time, for I,
Thy resolv'd patient, on thee still rely.
More should I question thee, and more I must,
Though more to know could not be more to trust,
From whence thou cam'st, how tended on. But rest
Unquestion'd welcome and undoubted blest.
Give me some help here, ho! If thou proceed
As high as word, my deed shall match thy deed.
   Flourish. Exeunt

ACT II. SCENE II. Rousillon. The Count's Palace
Enter Countess and Clown

COUNTESS: Come on, sir; I shall now put you to the height of your
breeding.

CLOWN: I will show myself highly fed and lowly taught. I know my
business is but to the court.

COUNTESS: To the court! Why, what place make you special, when you
put off that with such contempt? But to the court!

CLOWN: Truly, madam, if God have lent a man any manners, he may
easily put it off at court. He that cannot make a leg, put off's
cap, kiss his hand, and say nothing, has neither leg, hands, lip,
nor cap; and indeed such a fellow, to say precisely, were not for
the court; but for me, I have an answer will serve all men.

COUNTESS: Marry, that's a bountiful answer that fits all questions.

CLOWN: It is like a barber's chair, that fits all buttocks-the pin buttock, the quatch buttock, the brawn buttock, or any buttock.

COUNTESS: Will your answer serve fit to all questions?

CLOWN: As fit as ten groats is for the hand of an attorney, as your French crown for your taffety punk, as Tib's rush for Tom's forefinger, as a pancake for Shrove Tuesday, a morris for Mayday, as the nail to his hole, the cuckold to his horn, as a scolding quean to a wrangling knave, as the nun's lip to the friar's mouth; nay, as the pudding to his skin.

COUNTESS: Have you, I, say, an answer of such fitness for all questions?

CLOWN: From below your duke to beneath your constable, it will fit any question.

COUNTESS: It must be an answer of most monstrous size that must fit all demands.

CLOWN: But a trifle neither, in good faith, if the learned should speak truth of it. Here it is, and all that belongs to't. Ask me if I am a courtier: it shall do you no harm to learn.

COUNTESS: To be young again, if we could, I will be a fool in question, hoping to be the wiser by your answer. I pray you, sir, are you a courtier?

CLOWN: O Lord, sir!-There's a simple putting off. More, more, a hundred of them.

COUNTESS: Sir, I am a poor friend of yours, that loves you.

CLOWN: O Lord, sir!-Thick, thick; spare not me.

COUNTESS: I think, sir, you can eat none of this homely meat.

CLOWN: O Lord, sir!-Nay, put me to't, I warrant you.

COUNTESS: You were lately whipp'd, sir, as I think.

CLOWN: O Lord, sir!-Spare not me.

COUNTESS: Do you cry 'O Lord, sir!' at your whipping, and 'spare not me'? Indeed your 'O Lord, sir!' is very sequent to your whipping. You would answer very well to a whipping, if you were but bound to't.

CLOWN: I ne'er had worse luck in my life in my 'O Lord, sir!' I see thing's may serve long, but not serve ever.

COUNTESS: I play the noble housewife with the time,
To entertain it so merrily with a fool.

CLOWN: O Lord, sir!-Why, there't serves well again.

COUNTESS: An end, sir! To your business: give Helen this,
And urge her to a present answer back;
Commend me to my kinsmen and my son. This is not much.

CLOWN: Not much commendation to them?

COUNTESS: Not much employment for you. You understand me?

CLOWN: Most fruitfully; I am there before my legs.

COUNTESS: Haste you again.
  Exeunt

ACT II. SCENE III. Paris. The King's Palace

Enter Bertram, Lafeu, and Parolles

LAFEU: They say miracles are past; and we have our philosophical persons to make modern and familiar things supernatural and causeless. Hence is it that we make trifles of terrors, ensconcing ourselves into seeming knowledge when we should submit ourselves to an unknown fear.

PAROLLES: Why, 'tis the rarest argument of wonder that hath shot out in our latter times.

BERTRAM: And so 'tis.

LAFEU: To be relinquish'd of the artists-

PAROLLES: So I say-both of Galen and Paracelsus.

LAFEU: Of all the learned and authentic fellows-

PAROLLES: Right; so I say.

LAFEU: That gave him out incurable-

PAROLLES: Why, there 'tis; so say I too.

LAFEU: Not to be help'd-

PAROLLES: Right; as 'twere a man assur'd of a-

LAFEU: Uncertain life and sure death.

PAROLLES: Just; you say well; so would I have said.

LAFEU: I may truly say it is a novelty to the world.

PAROLLES: It is indeed. If you will have it in showing, you shall read it in what-do-ye-call't here.

LAFEU: *Reading the Ballad Title* 'A Showing of a Heavenly Effect in an Earthly Actor.'

PAROLLES: That's it; I would have said the very same.

LAFEU: Why, your dolphin is not lustier. 'Fore me, I speak in respect-

PAROLLES: Nay, 'tis strange, 'tis very strange; that is the brief and the tedious of it; and he's of a most facinerious spirit that will not acknowledge it to be the-

LAFEU: Very hand of heaven.

PAROLLES: Ay; so I say.

LAFEU: In a most weak-

PAROLLES: And debile minister, great power, great transcendence; which should, indeed, give us a further use to be made than alone the recov'ry of the King, as to be-

LAFEU: Generally thankful.
  Enter King, Helena, and Attendants

PAROLLES: I would have said it; you say well. Here comes the King.

LAFEU: Lustig, as the Dutchman says. I'll like a maid the better, whilst I have a tooth in my head. Why, he's able to lead her a coranto.

PAROLLES: Mort du vinaigre! Is not this Helen?

LAFEU: 'Fore God, I think so.

KING: Go, call before me all the lords in court.
Exit an Attendant
Sit, my preserver, by thy patient's side;
And with this healthful hand, whose banish'd sense
Thou has repeal'd, a second time receive
The confirmation of my promis'd gift,
Which but attends thy naming.
Enter Three or Four Lords
Fair maid, send forth thine eye. This youthful parcel
Of noble bachelors stand at my bestowing,
O'er whom both sovereign power and father's voice
I have to use. Thy frank election make;
Thou hast power to choose, and they none to forsake.

HELENA: To each of you one fair and virtuous mistress
Fall, when love please. Marry, to each but one!

LAFEU: I'd give bay Curtal and his furniture
My mouth no more were broken than these boys',
And writ as little beard.

KING: Peruse them well.
Not one of those but had a noble father.

HELENA: Gentlemen,
Heaven hath through me restor'd the King to health.

ALL: We understand it, and thank heaven for you.

HELENA: I am a simple maid, and therein wealthiest
That I protest I simply am a maid.
Please it your Majesty, I have done already.
The blushes in my cheeks thus whisper me:
'We blush that thou shouldst choose; but, be refused,
Let the white death sit on thy cheek for ever,
We'll ne'er come there again.'

KING: Make choice and see:
Who shuns thy love shuns all his love in me.

HELENA: Now, Dian, from thy altar do I fly,
And to imperial Love, that god most high,
Do my sighs stream. Sir, will you hear my suit?

FIRST LORD: And grant it.

HELENA: Thank you, sir; all the rest is mute.

LAFEU: I had rather be in this choice than throw ames-ace for my life.

HELENA: The honour, sir, that flames in your fair eyes,
Before I speak, too threat'ningly replies.
Love make your fortunes twenty times above
Her that so wishes, and her humble love!

SECOND LORD: No better, if you please.

HELENA: My wish receive,
Which great Love grant; and so I take my leave.

LAFEU: Do all they deny her? An they were sons of mine I'd have
them whipt; or I would send them to th' Turk to make eunuchs of.

HELENA: Be not afraid that I your hand should take;
I'll never do you wrong for your own sake.
Blessing upon your vows; and in your bed
Find fairer fortune, if you ever wed!

LAFEU: These boys are boys of ice; they'll none have her.
Sure, they are bastards to the English; the French ne'er got 'em.

HELENA: You are too young, too happy, and too good,
To make yourself a son out of my blood.

FOURTH LORD: Fair one, I think not so.

LAFEU: There's one grape yet; I am sure thy father drunk wine-but
if thou be'st not an ass, I am a youth of fourteen; I have known
thee already.

HELENA: *To Bertram* I dare not say I take you; but I give
Me and my service, ever whilst I live,
Into your guiding power. This is the man.

KING: Why, then, young Bertram, take her; she's thy wife.

BERTRAM: My wife, my liege! I shall beseech your Highness,
In such a business give me leave to use
The help of mine own eyes.

KING: Know'st thou not, Bertram,
What she has done for me?

BERTRAM: Yes, my good lord;
But never hope to know why I should marry her.

KING: Thou know'st she has rais'd me from my sickly bed.

BERTRAM: But follows it, my lord, to bring me down
Must answer for your raising? I know her well:
She had her breeding at my father's charge.
A poor physician's daughter my wife! Disdain
Rather corrupt me ever!

KING: 'Tis only title thou disdain'st in her, the which
I can build up. Strange is it that our bloods,
Of colour, weight, and heat, pour'd all together,
Would quite confound distinction, yet stand off
In differences so mighty. If she be
All that is virtuous-save what thou dislik'st,
A poor physician's daughter-thou dislik'st

Of virtue for the name; but do not so.
From lowest place when virtuous things proceed,
The place is dignified by the doer's deed;
Where great additions swell's, and virtue none,
It is a dropsied honour. Good alone
Is good without a name. Vileness is so:
The property by what it is should go,
Not by the title. She is young, wise, fair;
In these to nature she's immediate heir;
And these breed honour. That is honour's scorn
Which challenges itself as honour's born
And is not like the sire. Honours thrive
When rather from our acts we them derive
Than our fore-goers. The mere word's a slave,
Debauch'd on every tomb, on every grave
A lying trophy; and as oft is dumb
Where dust and damn'd oblivion is the tomb
Of honour'd bones indeed. What should be said?
If thou canst like this creature as a maid,
I can create the rest. Virtue and she
Is her own dower; honour and wealth from me.

BERTRAM: I cannot love her, nor will strive to do 't.

KING: Thou wrong'st thyself, if thou shouldst strive to choose.

HELENA: That you are well restor'd, my lord, I'm glad.
Let the rest go.

KING: My honour's at the stake; which to defeat,
I must produce my power. Here, take her hand,
Proud scornful boy, unworthy this good gift,
That dost in vile misprision shackle up
My love and her desert; that canst not dream
We, poising us in her defective scale,
Shall weigh thee to the beam; that wilt not know
It is in us to plant thine honour where

We please to have it grow. Check thy contempt;
Obey our will, which travails in thy good;
Believe not thy disdain, but presently
Do thine own fortunes that obedient right
Which both thy duty owes and our power claims;
Or I will throw thee from my care for ever
Into the staggers and the careless lapse
Of youth and ignorance; both my revenge and hate
Loosing upon thee in the name of justice,
Without all terms of pity. Speak; thine answer.

BERTRAM: Pardon, my gracious lord; for I submit
My fancy to your eyes. When I consider
What great creation and what dole of honour
Flies where you bid it, I find that she which late
Was in my nobler thoughts most base is now
The praised of the King; who, so ennobled,
Is as 'twere born so.

KING: Take her by the hand,
And tell her she is thine; to whom I promise
A counterpoise, if not to thy estate
A balance more replete.

BERTRAM: I take her hand.

KING: Good fortune and the favour of the King
Smile upon this contract; whose ceremony
Shall seem expedient on the now-born brief,
And be perform'd to-night. The solemn feast
Shall more attend upon the coming space,
Expecting absent friends. As thou lov'st her,
Thy love's to me religious; else, does err.
  *Exeunt All but Lafeu and Parolles Who Stay Behind, Commenting of this
Wedding*

LAFEU: Do you hear, monsieur? A word with you.

PAROLLES: Your pleasure, sir?

LAFEU: Your lord and master did well to make his recantation.

PAROLLES: Recantation! My Lord! my master!

LAFEU: Ay; is it not a language I speak?

PAROLLES: A most harsh one, and not to be understood without bloody succeeding. My master!

LAFEU: Are you companion to the Count Rousillon?

PAROLLES: To any count; to all counts; to what is man.

LAFEU: To what is count's man: count's master is of another style.

PAROLLES: You are too old, sir; let it satisfy you, you are too old.

LAFEU: I must tell thee, sirrah, I write man; to which title age cannot bring thee.

PAROLLES: What I dare too well do, I dare not do.

LAFEU: I did think thee, for two ordinaries, to be a pretty wise fellow; thou didst make tolerable vent of thy travel; it might pass. Yet the scarfs and the bannerets about thee did manifoldly dissuade me from believing thee a vessel of too great a burden. I have now found thee; when I lose thee again I care not; yet art thou good for nothing but taking up; and that thou'rt scarce worth.

PAROLLES: Hadst thou not the privilege of antiquity upon thee-

LAFEU: Do not plunge thyself too far in anger, lest thou hasten thy trial; which if-Lord have mercy on thee for a hen! So, my good window of lattice, fare thee well; thy casement I need not open, for I look through thee. Give me thy hand.

PAROLLES: My lord, you give me most egregious indignity.

LAFEU: Ay, with all my heart; and thou art worthy of it.

PAROLLES: I have not, my lord, deserv'd it.

LAFEU: Yes, good faith, ev'ry dram of it; and I will not bate thee a scruple.

PAROLLES: Well, I shall be wiser.

LAFEU: Ev'n as soon as thou canst, for thou hast to pull at a smack o' th' contrary. If ever thou be'st bound in thy scarf and beaten, thou shalt find what it is to be proud of thy bondage. I have a desire to hold my acquaintance with thee, or rather my knowledge, that I may say in the default 'He is a man I know.'

PAROLLES: My lord, you do me most insupportable vexation.

LAFEU: I would it were hell pains for thy sake, and my poor doing eternal; for doing I am past, as I will by thee, in what motion age will give me leave.
   Exit

PAROLLES: Well, thou hast a son shall take this disgrace off me: scurvy, old, filthy, scurvy lord! Well, I must be patient; there is no fettering of authority. I'll beat him, by my life, if I can meet him with any convenience, an he were double and double a lord. I'll have no more pity of his age than I would have of- I'll beat him, and if I could but meet him again.
   Re-enter Lafeu

LAFEU: Sirrah, your lord and master's married; there's news for you; you have a new mistress.

PAROLLES: I most unfeignedly beseech your lordship to make some reservation of your wrongs. He is my good lord: whom I serve above is my master.

LAFEU: Who? God?

PAROLLES: Ay, sir.

LAFEU: The devil it is that's thy master. Why dost thou garter up thy arms o' this fashion? Dost make hose of thy sleeves? Do other servants so? Thou wert best set thy lower part where thy nose stands. By mine honour, if I were but two hours younger, I'd beat thee. Methink'st thou art a general offence, and every man should beat thee. I think thou wast created for men to breathe themselves upon thee.

PAROLLES: This is hard and undeserved measure, my lord.

LAFEU: Go to, sir; you were beaten in Italy for picking a kernel out of a pomegranate; you are a vagabond, and no true traveller; you are more saucy with lords and honourable personages than the commission of your birth and virtue gives you heraldry. You are not worth another word, else I'd call you knave. I leave you.
  Exit
  Enter Bertram

PAROLLES: Good, very, good, it is so then. Good, very good; let it be conceal'd awhile.

BERTRAM: Undone, and forfeited to cares for ever!

PAROLLES: What's the matter, sweetheart?

BERTRAM: Although before the solemn priest I have sworn, I will not bed her.

PAROLLES: What, what, sweetheart?

BERTRAM: O my Parolles, they have married me!
I'll to the Tuscan wars, and never bed her.

PAROLLES: France is a dog-hole, and it no more merits
The tread of a man's foot. To th' wars!

BERTRAM: There's letters from my mother; what th' import is I know
not yet.

PAROLLES: Ay, that would be known. To th' wars, my boy, to th' wars!
He wears his honour in a box unseen
That hugs his kicky-wicky here at home,
Spending his manly marrow in her arms,
Which should sustain the bound and high curvet
Of Mars's fiery steed. To other regions!
France is a stable; we that dwell in't jades;
Therefore, to th' war!

BERTRAM: It shall be so; I'll send her to my house,
Acquaint my mother with my hate to her,
And wherefore I am fled; write to the King
That which I durst not speak. His present gift
Shall furnish me to those Italian fields
Where noble fellows strike. War is no strife
To the dark house and the detested wife.

PAROLLES: Will this capriccio hold in thee, art sure?

BERTRAM: Go with me to my chamber and advise me.
I'll send her straight away. To-morrow
I'll to the wars, she to her single sorrow.

PAROLLES: Why, these balls bound; there's noise in it. 'Tis hard:
A young man married is a man that's marr'd.
Therefore away, and leave her bravely; go.
The King has done you wrong; but, hush, 'tis so.
  Exeunt

ACT II. SCENE IV. Paris. The King's Palace

Enter Helena and Clown

HELENA: My mother greets me kindly; is she well?

CLOWN: She is not well, but yet she has her health; she's very merry, but yet she is not well. But thanks be given, she's very well, and wants nothing i' th' world; but yet she is not well.

HELENA: If she be very well, what does she ail that she's not very well?

CLOWN: Truly, she's very well indeed, but for two things.

HELENA: What two things?

CLOWN: One, that she's not in heaven, whither God send her quickly! The other, that she's in earth, from whence God send her quickly!
Enter Parolles

PAROLLES: Bless you, my fortunate lady!

HELENA: I hope, sir, I have your good will to have mine own good fortunes.

PAROLLES: You had my prayers to lead them on; and to keep them on, have them still. O, my knave, how does my old lady?

CLOWN: So that you had her wrinkles and I her money, I would she did as you say.

PAROLLES: Why, I say nothing.

CLOWN: Marry, you are the wiser man; for many a man's tongue shakes out his master's undoing. To say nothing, to do nothing, to know nothing, and to have nothing, is to be a great part of your title, which is within a very little of nothing.

PAROLLES: Away! th'art a knave.

CLOWN: You should have said, sir, 'Before a knave th'art a knave'; that's 'Before me th'art a knave.' This had been truth, sir.

PAROLLES: Go to, thou art a witty fool; I have found thee.

CLOWN: Did you find me in yourself, sir, or were you taught to find me? The search, sir, was profitable; and much fool may you find in you, even to the world's pleasure and the increase of laughter.

PAROLLES: A good knave, i' faith, and well fed.
Madam, my lord will go away to-night:
A very serious business calls on him.
The great prerogative and rite of love,
Which, as your due, time claims, he does acknowledge;
But puts it off to a compell'd restraint;
Whose want, and whose delay, is strew'd with sweets,
Which they distil now in the curbed time,
To make the coming hour o'erflow with joy
And pleasure drown the brim.

HELENA: What's his else?

PAROLLES: That you will take your instant leave o' th' King,
And make this haste as your own good proceeding,
Strength'ned with what apology you think
May make it probable need.

HELENA: What more commands he?

PAROLLES: That, having this obtain'd, you presently
Attend his further pleasure.

HELENA: In everything I wait upon his will.

PAROLLES: I shall report it so.

HELENA: I pray you.
  Exit Parolles
Come, sirrah. *Exeunt*

ACT II. SCENE V. Paris. The King's Palace
Enter Lafeu and Bertram

LAFEU: But I hope your lordship thinks not him a soldier.

BERTRAM: Yes, my lord, and of very valiant approof.

LAFEU: You have it from his own deliverance.

BERTRAM: And by other warranted testimony.

LAFEU: Then my dial goes not true; I took this lark for a bunting.

BERTRAM: I do assure you, my lord, he is very great in knowledge, and accordingly valiant.

LAFEU: I have then sinn'd against his experience and transgress'd against his valour; and my state that way is dangerous, since I cannot yet find in my heart to repent. Here he comes; I pray you make us friends; I will pursue the amity
  Enter Parolles

PAROLLES: *To Bertram* These things shall be done, sir.

LAFEU: Pray you, sir, who's his tailor?

PAROLLES: Sir!

LAFEU: O, I know him well. Ay, sir; he, sir, 's a good workman, a very good tailor.

BERTRAM: *Aside to Parolles* Is she gone to the King?

PAROLLES: She is.

BERTRAM: Will she away to-night?

PAROLLES: As you'll have her.

BERTRAM: I have writ my letters, casketed my treasure,
Given order for our horses; and to-night,
When I should take possession of the bride,
End ere I do begin.

LAFEU: A good traveller is something at the latter end of a dinner;
but one that lies three-thirds and uses a known truth to pass a
thousand nothings with, should be once heard and thrice beaten.
God save you, Captain.

BERTRAM: Is there any unkindness between my lord and you, monsieur?

PAROLLES: I know not how I have deserved to run into my lord's
displeasure.

LAFEU: You have made shift to run into 't, boots and spurs and all,
like him that leapt into the custard; and out of it you'll run
again, rather than suffer question for your residence.

BERTRAM: It may be you have mistaken him, my lord.

LAFEU: And shall do so ever, though I took him at's prayers.
Fare you well, my lord; and believe this of me: there can be no
kernal in this light nut; the soul of this man is his clothes;
trust him not in matter of heavy consequence; I have kept of them
tame, and know their natures. Farewell, monsieur; I have spoken
better of you than you have or will to deserve at my hand; but we
must do good against evil.
   Exit

PAROLLES: An idle lord, I swear.

BERTRAM: I think so.

PAROLLES: Why, do you not know him?

BERTRAM: Yes, I do know him well; and common speech
Gives him a worthy pass. Here comes my clog.
  Enter Helena

HELENA: I have, sir, as I was commanded from you,
Spoke with the King, and have procur'd his leave
For present parting; only he desires
Some private speech with you.

BERTRAM: I shall obey his will.
You must not marvel, Helen, at my course,
Which holds not colour with the time, nor does
The ministration and required office
On my particular. Prepar'd I was not
For such a business; therefore am I found
So much unsettled. This drives me to entreat you
That presently you take your way for home,
And rather muse than ask why I entreat you;
For my respects are better than they seem,
And my appointments have in them a need
Greater than shows itself at the first view
To you that know them not. This to my mother.
  Giving a Letter
'Twill be two days ere I shall see you; so
I leave you to your wisdom.

HELENA: Sir, I can nothing say
But that I am your most obedient servant.

BERTRAM: Come, come, no more of that.

HELENA: And ever shall
With true observance seek to eke out that
Wherein toward me my homely stars have fail'd
To equal my great fortune.

BERTRAM: Let that go.
My haste is very great. Farewell; hie home.

HELENA: Pray, sir, your pardon.

BERTRAM: Well, what would you say?

HELENA: I am not worthy of the wealth I owe,
Nor dare I say 'tis mine, and yet it is;
But, like a timorous thief, most fain would steal
What law does vouch mine own.

BERTRAM: What would you have?

HELENA: Something; and scarce so much; nothing, indeed.
I would not tell you what I would, my lord.
Faith, yes:
Strangers and foes do sunder and not kiss.

BERTRAM: I pray you, stay not, but in haste to horse.

HELENA: I shall not break your bidding, good my lord.

BERTRAM: Where are my other men, monsieur? Farewell!
  Exit Helena
Go thou toward home, where I will never come
Whilst I can shake my sword or hear the drum.
Away, and for our flight.

PAROLLES: Bravely, coragio!
  Exeunt

ACT III. SCENE I. Florence. The Duke's palace

Flourish. Enter the Duke of Florence, Attended; Two French Lords, with a Troop of Soldiers

DUKE: So that, from point to point, now have you hear
The fundamental reasons of this war;
Whose great decision hath much blood let forth
And more thirsts after.

FIRST LORD: Holy seems the quarrel
Upon your Grace's part; black and fearful
On the opposer.

DUKE: Therefore we marvel much our cousin France
Would in so just a business shut his bosom
Against our borrowing prayers.

SECOND LORD: Good my lord,
The reasons of our state I cannot yield,
But like a common and an outward man
That the great figure of a council frames
By self-unable motion; therefore dare not
Say what I think of it, since I have found
Myself in my incertain grounds to fail
As often as I guess'd.

DUKE: Be it his pleasure.

FIRST LORD: But I am sure the younger of our nature,
That surfeit on their ease, will day by day come here for physic.

DUKE: Welcome shall they be
And all the honours that can fly from us
Shall on them settle. You know your places well;
When better fall, for your avails they fell.
To-morrow to th' field. Flourish.
    Exeunt

ACT III. SCENE II. Rousillon. The Count's Palace
Enter Countess and Clown

COUNTESS: It hath happen'd all as I would have had it, save that he comes not along with her.

CLOWN: By my troth, I take my young lord to be a very melancholy man.

COUNTESS: By what observance, I pray you?

CLOWN: Why, he will look upon his boot and sing; mend the ruff and sing; ask questions and sing; pick his teeth and sing. I know a man that had this trick of melancholy sold a goodly manor for a song.

COUNTESS: Let me see what he writes, and when he means to come.
Opening a Letter

CLOWN: I have no mind to Isbel since I was at court. Our old ling and our Isbels o' th' country are nothing like your old ling and your Isbels o' th' court. The brains of my Cupid's knock'd out; and I begin to love, as an old man loves money, with no stomach.

COUNTESS: What have we here?

CLOWN: E'en that you have there.
Exit

COUNTESS: *Reads* 'I have sent you a daughter-in-law; she hath recovered the King and undone me. I have wedded her, not bedded her; and sworn to make the "not" eternal. You shall hear I am run away; know it before the report come. If there be breadth enough in the world, I will hold a long distance. My duty to you.
                         Your unfortunate son,
                              Bertram'
This is not well, rash and unbridled boy,

To fly the favours of so good a king,
To pluck his indignation on thy head
By the misprizing of a maid too virtuous
For the contempt of empire.
    Re-enter Clown

CLOWN: O madam, yonder is heavy news within between two soldiers
and my young lady.

COUNTESS: What is the -matter?

CLOWN: Nay, there is some comfort in the news, some comfort; your
son will not be kill'd so soon as I thought he would.

COUNTESS: Why should he be kill'd?

CLOWN: So say I, madam, if he run away, as I hear he does the
danger is in standing to 't; that's the loss of men, though it be
the getting of children. Here they come will tell you more. For my
part, I only hear your son was run away.
    Exit
    Enter Helena and the Two French Gentlemen

SECOND GENTLEMAN: Save you, good madam.

HELENA: Madam, my lord is gone, for ever gone.

FIRST GENTLEMAN: Do not say so.

COUNTESS: Think upon patience. Pray you, gentlemen-
I have felt so many quirks of joy and grief
That the first face of neither, on the start,
Can woman me unto 't. Where is my son, I pray you?

FIRST GENTLEMAN: Madam, he's gone to serve the Duke of Florence.
We met him thitherward; for thence we came,
And, after some dispatch in hand at court,

Thither we bend again.

HELENA: Look on this letter, madam; here's my passport.
Reads 'When thou canst get the ring upon my finger, which
never shall come off, and show me a child begotten of thy body
that I am father to, then call me husband; but in such a "then" I
write a "never."
This is a dreadful sentence.

COUNTESS: Brought you this letter, gentlemen?

FIRST GENTLEMAN: Ay, madam;
And for the contents' sake are sorry for our pains.

COUNTESS: I prithee, lady, have a better cheer;
If thou engrossest all the griefs are thine,
Thou robb'st me of a moiety. He was my son;
But I do wash his name out of my blood,
And thou art all my child. Towards Florence is he?

FIRST GENTLEMAN: Ay, madam.

COUNTESS: And to be a soldier?

FIRST GENTLEMAN: Such is his noble purpose; and, believe 't,
The Duke will lay upon him all the honour
That good convenience claims.

COUNTESS: Return you thither?

SECOND GENTLEMAN: Ay, madam, with the swiftest wing of speed.

HELENA: *Reads* 'Till I have no wife, I have nothing in France.'
'Tis bitter.

COUNTESS: Find you that there?

LAFEU: Ay, madam.

SECOND GENTLEMAN: 'Tis but the boldness of his hand haply, which his heart was not consenting to.

COUNTESS: Nothing in France until he have no wife!
There's nothing here that is too good for him
But only she; and she deserves a lord
That twenty such rude boys might tend upon,
And call her hourly mistress. Who was with him?

SECOND GENTLEMAN: A servant only, and a gentleman
Which I have sometime known.

COUNTESS: Parolles, was it not?

SECOND GENTLEMAN: Ay, my good lady, he.

COUNTESS: A very tainted fellow, and full of wickedness.
My son corrupts a well-derived nature
With his inducement.

SECOND GENTLEMAN: Indeed, good lady,
The fellow has a deal of that too much
Which holds him much to have.

COUNTESS: Y'are welcome, gentlemen.
I will entreat you, when you see my son,
To tell him that his sword can never win
The honour that he loses. More I'll entreat you
Written to bear along.

FIRST GENTLEMAN: We serve you, madam,
In that and all your worthiest affairs.

COUNTESS: Not so, but as we change our courtesies.
Will you draw near?

Exeunt Countess and Gentlemen

HELENA: 'Till I have no wife, I have nothing in France.'
Nothing in France until he has no wife!
Thou shalt have none, Rousillon, none in France
Then hast thou all again. Poor lord! is't
That chase thee from thy country, and expose
Those tender limbs of thine to the event
Of the non-sparing war? And is it I
That drive thee from the sportive court, where thou
Wast shot at with fair eyes, to be the mark
Of smoky muskets? O you leaden messengers,
That ride upon the violent speed of fire,
Fly with false aim; move the still-piecing air,
That sings with piercing; do not touch my lord.
Whoever shoots at him, I set him there;
Whoever charges on his forward breast,
I am the caitiff that do hold him to't;
And though I kill him not, I am the cause
His death was so effected. Better 'twere
I met the ravin lion when he roar'd
With sharp constraint of hunger; better 'twere
That all the miseries which nature owes
Were mine at once. No; come thou home, Rousillon,
Whence honour but of danger wins a scar,
As oft it loses all. I will be gone.
My being here it is that holds thee hence.
Shall I stay here to do 't? No, no, although
The air of paradise did fan the house,
And angels offic'd all. I will be gone,
That pitiful rumour may report my flight
To consolate thine ear. Come, night; end, day.
For with the dark, poor thief, I'll steal away.
　　Exit

ACT III. SCENE III. Florence. Before the Duke's Palace

Flourish. Enter the Duke of Florence, Bertram, Parolles, Soldiers, Drum and Trumpets

DUKE: The General of our Horse thou art; and we,
Great in our hope, lay our best love and credence
Upon thy promising fortune.

BERTRAM: Sir, it is
A charge too heavy for my strength; but yet
We'll strive to bear it for your worthy sake
To th' extreme edge of hazard.

DUKE: Then go thou forth;
And Fortune play upon thy prosperous helm,
As thy auspicious mistress!

BERTRAM: This very day,
Great Mars, I put myself into thy file;
Make me but like my thoughts, and I shall prove
A lover of thy drum, hater of love.
  Exeunt

ACT III. SCENE IV. Rousillon. The Count's Palace

Enter Countess and Steward

COUNTESS: Alas! and would you take the letter of her?
Might you not know she would do as she has done
By sending me a letter? Read it again.

STEWARD: *Reads* 'I am Saint Jaques' pilgrim, thither gone.
Ambitious love hath so in me offended
That barefoot plod I the cold ground upon,
With sainted vow my faults to have amended.
Write, write, that from the bloody course of war
My dearest master, your dear son, may hie.
Bless him at home in peace, whilst I from far

His name with zealous fervour sanctify.
His taken labours bid him me forgive;
I, his despiteful Juno, sent him forth
From courtly friends, with camping foes to live,
Where death and danger dogs the heels of worth.
He is too good and fair for death and me;
Whom I myself embrace to set him free.'

COUNTESS: Ah, what sharp stings are in her mildest words!
Rinaldo, you did never lack advice so much
As letting her pass so; had I spoke with her,
I could have well diverted her intents,
Which thus she hath prevented.

STEWARD: Pardon me, madam;
If I had given you this at over-night,
She might have been o'er ta'en; and yet she writes
Pursuit would be but vain.

COUNTESS: What angel shall
Bless this unworthy husband? He cannot thrive,
Unless her prayers, whom heaven delights to hear
And loves to grant, reprieve him from the wrath
Of greatest justice. Write, write, Rinaldo,
To this unworthy husband of his wife;
Let every word weigh heavy of her worth
That he does weigh too light. My greatest grief,
Though little he do feel it, set down sharply.
Dispatch the most convenient messenger.
When haply he shall hear that she is gone
He will return; and hope I may that she,
Hearing so much, will speed her foot again,
Led hither by pure love. Which of them both
Is dearest to me I have no skill in sense
To make distinction. Provide this messenger.
My heart is heavy, and mine age is weak;
Grief would have tears, and sorrow bids me speak.

Exeunt

ACT III. SCENE V. Without the Walls of Florence
A Tucket Afar Off. Enter an Old Widow of Florence, Her Daughter Diana, Violenta, and Mariana, with Other Citizens

WIDOW: Nay, come; for if they do approach the city we shall lose all the sight.

DIANA: They say the French count has done most honourable service.

WIDOW: It is reported that he has taken their great'st commander; and that with his own hand he slew the Duke's brother. *Tucket* We have lost our labour; they are gone a contrary way. Hark! you may know by their trumpets.

MARIANA: Come, let's return again, and suffice ourselves with the report of it. Well, Diana, take heed of this French earl; the honour of a maid is her name, and no legacy is so rich as honesty.

WIDOW: I have told my neighbour how you have been solicited by a gentleman his companion.

MARIANA: I know that knave, hang him! one Parolles; a filthy officer he is in those suggestions for the young earl. Beware of them, Diana: their promises, enticements, oaths, tokens, and all these engines of lust, are not the things they go under; many a maid hath been seduced by them; and the misery is, example, that so terrible shows in the wreck of maidenhood, cannot for all that dissuade succession, but that they are limed with the twigs that threatens them. I hope I need not to advise you further; but I hope your own grace will keep you where you are, though there were no further danger known but the modesty which is so lost.

DIANA: You shall not need to fear me.
Enter Helena in the Dress of a Pilgrim

WIDOW: I hope so. Look, here comes a pilgrim. I know she will lie at my house: thither they send one another. I'll question her. God save you, pilgrim! Whither are bound?

HELENA: To Saint Jaques le Grand.
Where do the palmers lodge, I do beseech you?

WIDOW: At the Saint Francis here, beside the port.

HELENA: Is this the way?
  A March Afar

WIDOW: Ay, marry, is't. Hark you! They come this way.
If you will tarry, holy pilgrim,
But till the troops come by,
I will conduct you where you shall be lodg'd;
The rather for I think I know your hostess
As ample as myself.

HELENA: Is it yourself?

WIDOW: If you shall please so, pilgrim.

HELENA: I thank you, and will stay upon your leisure.

WIDOW: You came, I think, from France?

HELENA: I did so.

WIDOW: Here you shall see a countryman of yours
That has done worthy service.

HELENA: His name, I pray you.

DIANA: The Count Rousillon. Know you such a one?

HELENA: But by the ear, that hears most nobly of him;
His face I know not.

DIANA: What some'er he is,
He's bravely taken here. He stole from France,
As 'tis reported, for the King had married him
Against his liking. Think you it is so?

HELENA: Ay, surely, mere the truth; I know his lady.

DIANA: There is a gentleman that serves the Count
Reports but coarsely of her.

HELENA: What's his name?

DIANA: Monsieur Parolles.

HELENA: O, I believe with him,
In argument of praise, or to the worth
Of the great Count himself, she is too mean
To have her name repeated; all her deserving
Is a reserved honesty, and that
I have not heard examin'd.

DIANA: Alas, poor lady!
'Tis a hard bondage to become the wife
Of a detesting lord.

WIDOW: I sweet, good creature, wheresoe'er she is
Her heart weighs sadly. This young maid might do her
A shrewd turn, if she pleas'd.

HELENA: How do you mean?
May be the amorous Count solicits her
In the unlawful purpose.

WIDOW: He does, indeed;

And brokes with all that can in such a suit
Corrupt the tender honour of a maid;
But she is arm'd for him, and keeps her guard
In honestest defence.
Enter, with Drum and Colours, Bertram, Parolles, and the Whole Army

MARIANA: The gods forbid else!

WIDOW: So, now they come.
That is Antonio, the Duke's eldest son;
That, Escalus.

HELENA: Which is the Frenchman?

DIANA: He-
That with the plume; 'tis a most gallant fellow.
I would he lov'd his wife; if he were honester
He were much goodlier. Is't not a handsome gentleman?

HELENA: I like him well.

DIANA: 'Tis pity he is not honest. Yond's that same knave
That leads him to these places; were I his lady
I would poison that vile rascal.

HELENA: Which is he?

DIANA: That jack-an-apes with scarfs. Why is he melancholy?

HELENA: Perchance he's hurt i' th' battle.

PAROLLES: Lose our drum! well.

MARIANA: He's shrewdly vex'd at something.
Look, he has spied us.

WIDOW: Marry, hang you!

MARIANA: And your courtesy, for a ring-carrier!
Exeunt Bertram, Parolles, and Army

WIDOW: The troop is past. Come, pilgrim, I will bring you
Where you shall host. Of enjoin'd penitents
There's four or five, to great Saint Jaques bound,
Already at my house.

HELENA: I humbly thank you.
Please it this matron and this gentle maid
To eat with us to-night; the charge and thanking
Shall be for me, and, to requite you further,
I will bestow some precepts of this virgin,
Worthy the note.

BOTH: We'll take your offer kindly.
Exeunt

ACT III. SCENE VI. Camp Before Florence
Enter Bertram, and the Two French Lords

SECOND LORD: Nay, good my lord, put him to't; let him have his way.

FIRST LORD: If your lordship find him not a hiding, hold me no more
in your respect.

SECOND LORD: On my life, my lord, a bubble.

BERTRAM: Do you think I am so far deceived in him?

SECOND LORD: Believe it, my lord, in mine own direct knowledge,
without any malice, but to speak of him as my kinsman, he's a
most notable coward, an infinite and endless liar, an hourly
promise-breaker, the owner of no one good quality worthy your
lordship's entertainment.

FIRST LORD: It were fit you knew him; lest, reposing too far in his

virtue, which he hath not, he might at some great and trusty
business in a main danger fail you.

BERTRAM: I would I knew in what particular action to try him.

FIRST LORD: None better than to let him fetch off his drum, which
you hear him so confidently undertake to do.

SECOND LORD: I with a troop of Florentines will suddenly surprise
him; such I will have whom I am sure he knows not from the enemy.
We will bind and hoodwink him so that he shall suppose no other
but that he is carried into the leaguer of the adversaries when
we bring him to our own tents. Be but your lordship present at
his examination; if he do not, for the promise of his life and in
the highest compulsion of base fear, offer to betray you and
deliver all the intelligence in his power against you, and that
with the divine forfeit of his soul upon oath, never trust my
judgment in anything.

FIRST LORD: O, for the love of laughter, let him fetch his drum; he
says he has a stratagem for't. When your lordship sees the bottom
of his success in't, and to what metal this counterfeit lump of
ore will be melted, if you give him not John Drum's
entertainment, your inclining cannot be removed. Here he comes.
   Enter Parolles

SECOND LORD: O, for the love of laughter, hinder not the honour of
his design; let him fetch off his drum in any hand.

BERTRAM: How now, monsieur! This drum sticks sorely in your
disposition.

FIRST LORD: A pox on 't; let it go; 'tis but a drum.

PAROLLES: But a drum! Is't but a drum? A drum so lost! There was
excellent command: to charge in with our horse upon our own
wings, and to rend our own soldiers!

FIRST LORD: That was not to be blam'd in the command of the service; it was a disaster of war that Caesar himself could not have prevented, if he had been there to command.

BERTRAM: Well, we cannot greatly condemn our success. Some dishonour we had in the loss of that drum; but it is not to be recovered.

PAROLLES: It might have been recovered.

BERTRAM: It might, but it is not now.

PAROLLES: It is to be recovered. But that the merit of service is seldom attributed to the true and exact performer, I would have that drum or another, or 'hic jacet.'

BERTRAM: Why, if you have a stomach, to't, monsieur. If you think your mystery in stratagem can bring this instrument of honour again into his native quarter, be magnanimous in the enterprise, and go on; I will grace the attempt for a worthy exploit. If you speed well in it, the Duke shall both speak of it and extend to you what further becomes his greatness, even to the utmost syllable of our worthiness.

PAROLLES: By the hand of a soldier, I will undertake it.

BERTRAM: But you must not now slumber in it.

PAROLLES: I'll about it this evening; and I will presently pen down my dilemmas, encourage myself in my certainty, put myself into my mortal preparation; and by midnight look to hear further from me.

BERTRAM: May I be bold to acquaint his Grace you are gone about it?

PAROLLES: I know not what the success will be, my lord, but the attempt I vow.

BERTRAM: I know th' art valiant; and, to the of thy soldiership,
will subscribe for thee. Farewell.

PAROLLES: I love not many words.
  Exit

SECOND LORD: No more than a fish loves water. Is not this a strange
fellow, my lord, that so confidently seems to undertake this
business, which he knows is not to be done; damns himself to do,
and dares better be damn'd than to do 't.

FIRST LORD: You do not know him, my lord, as we do. Certain it is
that he will steal himself into a man's favour, and for a week
escape a great deal of discoveries; but when you find him out,
you have him ever after.

BERTRAM: Why, do you think he will make no deed at all of this that
so seriously he does address himself unto?

SECOND LORD: None in the world; but return with an invention, and
clap upon you two or three probable lies. But we have almost
emboss'd him. You shall see his fall to-night; for indeed he is
not for your lordship's respect.

FIRST LORD: We'll make you some sport with the fox ere we case him.
He was first smok'd by the old Lord Lafeu. When his disguise and
he is parted, tell me what a sprat you shall find him; which you
shall see this very night.

SECOND LORD: I must go look my twigs; he shall be caught.

BERTRAM: Your brother, he shall go along with me.

SECOND LORD: As't please your lordship. I'll leave you.
  Exit

BERTRAM: Now will I lead you to the house, and show you

The lass I spoke of.

FIRST LORD: But you say she's honest.

BERTRAM: That's all the fault. I spoke with her but once,
And found her wondrous cold; but I sent to her,
By this same coxcomb that we have i' th' wind,
Tokens and letters which she did re-send;
And this is all I have done. She's a fair creature;
Will you go see her?

FIRST LORD: With all my heart, my lord.
  Exeunt

ACT III. SCENE VII. Florence. The Widow's House
Enter Helena and Widow

HELENA: If you misdoubt me that I am not she,
I know not how I shall assure you further
But I shall lose the grounds I work upon.

WIDOW: Though my estate be fall'n, I was well born,
Nothing acquainted with these businesses;
And would not put my reputation now
In any staining act.

HELENA: Nor would I wish you.
FIRST give me trust the Count he is my husband,
And what to your sworn counsel I have spoken
Is so from word to word; and then you cannot,
By the good aid that I of you shall borrow,
Err in bestowing it.

WIDOW: I should believe you;
For you have show'd me that which well approves
Y'are great in fortune.

HELENA: Take this purse of gold,
And let me buy your friendly help thus far,
Which I will over-pay and pay again
When I have found it. The Count he woos your daughter
Lays down his wanton siege before her beauty,
Resolv'd to carry her. Let her in fine consent,
As we'll direct her how 'tis best to bear it.
Now his important blood will nought deny
That she'll demand. A ring the County wears
That downward hath succeeded in his house
From son to son some four or five descents
Since the first father wore it. This ring he holds
In most rich choice; yet, in his idle fire,
To buy his will, it would not seem too dear,
Howe'er repented after.

WIDOW: Now I see
The bottom of your purpose.

HELENA: You see it lawful then. It is no more
But that your daughter, ere she seems as won,
Desires this ring; appoints him an encounter;
In fine, delivers me to fill the time,
Herself most chastely absent. After this,
To marry her, I'll add three thousand crowns
To what is pass'd already.

WIDOW: I have yielded.
Instruct my daughter how she shall persever,
That time and place with this deceit so lawful
May prove coherent. Every night he comes
With musics of all sorts, and songs compos'd
To her unworthiness. It nothing steads us
To chide him from our eaves, for he persists
As if his life lay on 't.

HELENA: Why then to-night

Let us assay our plot; which, if it speed,
Is wicked meaning in a lawful deed,
And lawful meaning in a lawful act;
Where both not sin, and yet a sinful fact.
But let's about it.
Exeunt

ACT IV. SCENE I. Without the Florentine Camp
Enter Second French Lord with Five or Six Other Soldiers in Ambush

SECOND LORD: He can come no other way but by this hedge-corner. When you sally upon him, speak what terrible language you will; though you understand it not yourselves, no matter; for we must not seem to understand him, unless some one among us, whom we must produce for an interpreter.

FIRST SOLDIER: Good captain, let me be th' interpreter.

SECOND LORD: Art not acquainted with him? Knows he not thy voice?

FIRST SOLDIER: No, sir, I warrant you.

SECOND LORD: But what linsey-woolsey has thou to speak to us again?

FIRST SOLDIER: E'en such as you speak to me.

SECOND LORD: He must think us some band of strangers i' th' adversary's entertainment. Now he hath a smack of all neighbouring languages, therefore we must every one be a man of his own fancy; not to know what we speak one to another, so we seem to know, is to know straight our purpose: choughs' language, gabble enough, and good enough. As for you, interpreter, you must seem very politic. But couch, ho! here he comes; to beguile two hours in a sleep, and then to return and swear the lies he forges.
Enter Parolles

PAROLLES: Ten o'clock. Within these three hours 'twill be time

enough to go home. What shall I say I have done? It must be a
very plausive invention that carries it. They begin to smoke me;
and disgraces have of late knock'd to often at my door. I find my
tongue is too foolhardy; but my heart hath the fear of Mars
before it, and of his creatures, not daring the reports of my
tongue.

SECOND LORD: This is the first truth that e'er thine own tongue was
guilty of.

PAROLLES: What the devil should move me to undertake the recovery
of this drum, being not ignorant of the impossibility, and
knowing I had no such purpose? I must give myself some hurts, and
say I got them in exploit. Yet slight ones will not carry it.
They will say 'Came you off with so little?' And great ones I
dare not give. Wherefore, what's the instance? Tongue, I must put
you into a butterwoman's mouth, and buy myself another of
Bajazet's mule, if you prattle me into these perils.

SECOND LORD: Is it possible he should know what he is, and be that he
is?

PAROLLES: I would the cutting of my garments would serve the turn,
or the breaking of my Spanish sword.

SECOND LORD: We cannot afford you so.

PAROLLES: Or the baring of my beard; and to say it was in stratagem.

SECOND LORD: 'Twould not do.

PAROLLES: Or to drown my clothes, and say I was stripp'd.

SECOND LORD: Hardly serve.

PAROLLES: Though I swore I leap'd from the window of the citadel-

SECOND LORD: How deep?

PAROLLES: Thirty fathom.

SECOND LORD: Three great oaths would scarce make that be believed.

PAROLLES: I would I had any drum of the enemy's; I would swear I recover'd it.

SECOND LORD: You shall hear one anon.
  Alarum Within

PAROLLES: A drum now of the enemy's!

SECOND LORD: Throca movousus, cargo, cargo, cargo.

ALL: Cargo, cargo, cargo, villianda par corbo, cargo.

PAROLLES: O, ransom, ransom! Do not hide mine eyes.
  They Blindfold Him

FIRST SOLDIER: Boskos thromuldo boskos.

PAROLLES: I know you are the Muskos' regiment,
And I shall lose my life for want of language.
If there be here German, or Dane, Low Dutch,
Italian, or French, let him speak to me;
I'll discover that which shall undo the Florentine.

FIRST SOLDIER: Boskos vauvado. I understand thee, and can speak thy tongue. Kerely-bonto, sir, betake thee to thy faith, for seventeen poniards are at thy bosom.

PAROLLES: O!

FIRST SOLDIER: O, pray, pray, pray! Manka revania dulche.

SECOND LORD: Oscorbidulchos volivorco.

FIRST SOLDIER: The General is content to spare thee yet;
And, hoodwink'd as thou art, will lead thee on
To gather from thee. Haply thou mayst inform
Something to save thy life.

PAROLLES: O, let me live,
And all the secrets of our camp I'll show,
Their force, their purposes. Nay, I'll speak that
Which you will wonder at.

FIRST SOLDIER: But wilt thou faithfully?

PAROLLES: If I do not, damn me.

FIRST SOLDIER: Acordo linta.
Come on; thou art granted space.
   Exit, Parolles Guarded. A Short Alarum Within

SECOND LORD: Go, tell the Count Rousillon and my brother
We have caught the woodcock, and will keep him muffled
Till we do hear from them.

SECOND SOLDIER. Captain, I will.

SECOND LORD: 'A will betray us all unto ourselves-
Inform on that.

SECOND SOLDIER:. So I will, sir.

SECOND LORD: Till then I'll keep him dark and safely lock'd.
   Exeunt

ACT IV. SCENE II. Florence. The Widow's House

Enter Bertram and Diana

BERTRAM: They told me that your name was Fontibell.

DIANA: No, my good lord, Diana.

BERTRAM: Titled goddess;
And worth it, with addition! But, fair soul,
In your fine frame hath love no quality?
If the quick fire of youth light not your mind,
You are no maiden, but a monument;
When you are dead, you should be such a one
As you are now, for you are cold and stern;
And now you should be as your mother was
When your sweet self was got.

DIANA: She then was honest.

BERTRAM: So should you be.

DIANA: No.
My mother did but duty; such, my lord,
As you owe to your wife.

BERTRAM: No more o'that!
I prithee do not strive against my vows.
I was compell'd to her; but I love the
By love's own sweet constraint, and will for ever
Do thee all rights of service.

DIANA: Ay, so you serve us
Till we serve you; but when you have our roses
You barely leave our thorns to prick ourselves,
And mock us with our bareness.

BERTRAM: How have I sworn!

DIANA: 'Tis not the many oaths that makes the truth,
But the plain single vow that is vow'd true.
What is not holy, that we swear not by,
But take the High'st to witness. Then, pray you, tell me:
If I should swear by Jove's great attributes
I lov'd you dearly, would you believe my oaths
When I did love you ill? This has no holding,
To swear by him whom I protest to love
That I will work against him. Therefore your oaths
Are words and poor conditions, but unseal'd-
At least in my opinion.

BERTRAM: Change it, change it;
Be not so holy-cruel. Love is holy;
And my integrity ne'er knew the crafts
That you do charge men with. Stand no more off,
But give thyself unto my sick desires,
Who then recovers. Say thou art mine, and ever
My love as it begins shall so persever.

DIANA: I see that men make ropes in such a scarre
That we'll forsake ourselves. Give me that ring.

BERTRAM: I'll lend it thee, my dear, but have no power
To give it from me.

DIANA: Will you not, my lord?

BERTRAM: It is an honour 'longing to our house,
Bequeathed down from many ancestors;
Which were the greatest obloquy i' th' world
In me to lose.

DIANA: Mine honour's such a ring:
My chastity's the jewel of our house,
Bequeathed down from many ancestors;
Which were the greatest obloquy i' th' world

In me to lose. Thus your own proper wisdom
Brings in the champion Honour on my part
Against your vain assault.

BERTRAM: Here, take my ring;
My house, mine honour, yea, my life, be thine,
And I'll be bid by thee.

DIANA: When midnight comes, knock at my chamber window;
I'll order take my mother shall not hear.
Now will I charge you in the band of truth,
When you have conquer'd my yet maiden bed,
Remain there but an hour, nor speak to me:
My reasons are most strong; and you shall know them
When back again this ring shall be deliver'd.
And on your finger in the night I'll put
Another ring, that what in time proceeds
May token to the future our past deeds.
Adieu till then; then fail not. You have won
A wife of me, though there my hope be done.

BERTRAM: A heaven on earth I have won by wooing thee.
   Exit

DIANA: For which live long to thank both heaven and me!
You may so in the end.
My mother told me just how he would woo,
As if she sat in's heart; she says all men
Have the like oaths. He had sworn to marry me
When his wife's dead; therefore I'll lie with him
When I am buried. Since Frenchmen are so braid,
Marry that will, I live and die a maid.
Only, in this disguise, I think't no sin
To cozen him that would unjustly win.
   Exit

ACT IV. SCENE III. The Florentine Camp

Enter the Two French Lords, and Two or Three Soldiers

SECOND LORD: You have not given him his mother's letter?

FIRST LORD: I have deliv'red it an hour since. There is something in't that stings his nature; for on the reading it he chang'd almost into another man.

SECOND LORD: He has much worthy blame laid upon him for shaking off so good a wife and so sweet a lady.

FIRST LORD: Especially he hath incurred the everlasting displeasure of the King, who had even tun'd his bounty to sing happiness to him. I will tell you a thing, but you shall let it dwell darkly with you.

SECOND LORD: When you have spoken it, 'tis dead, and I am the grave of it.

FIRST LORD: He hath perverted a young gentlewoman here in Florence, of a most chaste renown; and this night he fleshes his will in the spoil of her honour. He hath given her his monumental ring, and thinks himself made in the unchaste composition.

SECOND LORD: Now, God delay our rebellion! As we are ourselves, what things are we!

FIRST LORD: Merely our own traitors. And as in the common course of all treasons we still see them reveal themselves till they attain to their abhorr'd ends; so he that in this action contrives against his own nobility, in his proper stream, o'erflows himself.

SECOND LORD: Is it not meant damnable in us to be trumpeters of our unlawful intents? We shall not then have his company to-night?

FIRST LORD: Not till after midnight; for he is dieted to his hour.

SECOND LORD: That approaches apace. I would gladly have him see his company anatomiz'd, that he might take a measure of his own judgments, wherein so curiously he had set this counterfeit.

FIRST LORD: We will not meddle with him till he come; for his presence must be the whip of the other.

SECOND LORD: In the meantime, what hear you of these wars?

FIRST LORD: I hear there is an overture of peace.

SECOND LORD: Nay, I assure you, a peace concluded.

FIRST LORD: What will Count Rousillon do then? Will he travel higher, or return again into France?

SECOND LORD: I perceive, by this demand, you are not altogether of his counsel.

FIRST LORD: Let it be forbid, sir! So should I be a great deal of his act.

SECOND LORD: Sir, his wife, some two months since, fled from his house. Her pretence is a pilgrimage to Saint Jaques le Grand; which holy undertaking with most austere sanctimony she accomplish'd; and, there residing, the tenderness of her nature became as a prey to her grief; in fine, made a groan of her last breath, and now she sings in heaven.

FIRST LORD: How is this justified?

SECOND LORD: The stronger part of it by her own letters, which makes her story true even to the point of her death. Her death itself, which could not be her office to say is come, was faithfully confirm'd by the rector of the place.

FIRST LORD: Hath the Count all this intelligence?

SECOND LORD: Ay, and the particular confirmations, point from point, to the full arming of the verity.

FIRST LORD: I am heartily sorry that he'll be glad of this.

SECOND LORD: How mightily sometimes we make us comforts of our losses!

FIRST LORD: And how mightily some other times we drown our gain in tears! The great dignity that his valour hath here acquir'd for him shall at home be encount'red with a shame as ample.

SECOND LORD: The web of our life is of a mingled yarn, good and ill together. Our virtues would be proud if our faults whipt them not; and our crimes would despair if they were not cherish'd by our virtues.
Enter a Messenger
How now? Where's your master?

SERVANT: He met the Duke in the street, sir; of whom he hath taken a solemn leave. His lordship will next morning for France. The Duke hath offered him letters of commendations to the King.

SECOND LORD: They shall be no more than needful there, if they were more than they can commend.

FIRST LORD: They cannot be too sweet for the King's tartness. Here's his lordship now.
Enter Bertram
How now, my lord, is't not after midnight?

BERTRAM: I have to-night dispatch'd sixteen businesses, a month's length apiece; by an abstract of success: I have congied with the Duke, done my adieu with his nearest; buried a wife, mourn'd for her; writ to my lady mother I am returning; entertain'd my convoy; and between these main parcels of dispatch effected many nicer needs. The last was the greatest, but that I have not ended yet.

SECOND LORD: If the business be of any difficulty and this morning your departure hence, it requires haste of your lordship.

BERTRAM: I mean the business is not ended, as fearing to hear of it hereafter. But shall we have this dialogue between the Fool and the Soldier? Come, bring forth this counterfeit module has deceiv'd me like a double-meaning prophesier.

SECOND LORD: Bring him forth. *Exeunt Soldiers* Has sat i' th' stocks all night, poor gallant knave.

BERTRAM: No matter; his heels have deserv'd it, in usurping his spurs so long. How does he carry himself?

SECOND LORD: I have told your lordship already the stocks carry him. But to answer you as you would be understood: he weeps like a wench that had shed her milk; he hath confess'd himself to Morgan, whom he supposes to be a friar, from the time of his remembrance to this very instant disaster of his setting i' th' stocks. And what think you he hath confess'd?

BERTRAM: Nothing of me, has 'a?

SECOND LORD: His confession is taken, and it shall be read to his face; if your lordship be in't, as I believe you are, you must have the patience to hear it.
  Enter Parolles Guarded, and First Soldier as Interpreter

BERTRAM: A plague upon him! muffled! He can say nothing of me.

SECOND LORD: Hush, hush! Hoodman comes. Portotartarossa.

FIRST SOLDIER: He calls for the tortures. What will you say without 'em?

PAROLLES: I will confess what I know without constraint; if ye pinch me like a pasty, I can say no more.

FIRST SOLDIER: Bosko chimurcho.

SECOND LORD: Boblibindo chicurmurco.

FIRST SOLDIER: YOU are a merciful general. Our General bids you answer to what I shall ask you out of a note.

PAROLLES: And truly, as I hope to live.

FIRST SOLDIER: 'First demand of him how many horse the Duke is strong.' What say you to that?

PAROLLES: Five or six thousand; but very weak and unserviceable. The troops are all scattered, and the commanders very poor rogues, upon my reputation and credit, and as I hope to live.

FIRST SOLDIER: Shall I set down your answer so?

PAROLLES: Do; I'll take the sacrament on 't, how and which way you will.

BERTRAM: All's one to him. What a past-saving slave is this!

SECOND LORD: Y'are deceiv'd, my lord; this is Monsieur Parolles, the gallant militarist-that was his own phrase-that had the whole theoric of war in the knot of his scarf, and the practice in the chape of his dagger.

FIRST LORD: I will never trust a man again for keeping his sword clean; nor believe he can have everything in him by wearing his apparel neatly.

FIRST SOLDIER: Well, that's set down.

PAROLLES: 'Five or six thousand horse' I said-I will say true- 'or thereabouts' set down, for I'll speak truth.

SECOND LORD: He's very near the truth in this.

BERTRAM: But I con him no thanks for't in the nature he delivers it.

PAROLLES: 'Poor rogues' I pray you say.

FIRST SOLDIER: Well, that's set down.

PAROLLES: I humbly thank you, sir. A truth's a truth-the rogues are marvellous poor.

FIRST SOLDIER: 'Demand of him of what strength they are a-foot.' What say you to that?

PAROLLES: By my troth, sir, if I were to live this present hour, I will tell true. Let me see: Spurio, a hundred and fifty; Sebastian, so many; Corambus, so many; Jaques, so many; Guiltian, Cosmo, Lodowick, and Gratii, two hundred fifty each; mine own company, Chitopher, Vaumond, Bentii, two hundred fifty each; so that the muster-file, rotten and sound, upon my life, amounts not to fifteen thousand poll; half of the which dare not shake the snow from off their cassocks lest they shake themselves to pieces.

BERTRAM: What shall be done to him?

SECOND LORD: Nothing, but let him have thanks. Demand of him my condition, and what credit I have with the Duke.

FIRST SOLDIER: Well, that's set down. 'You shall demand of him whether one Captain Dumain be i' th' camp, a Frenchman; what his reputation is with the Duke, what his valour, honesty, expertness in wars; or whether he thinks it were not possible, with well-weighing sums of gold, to corrupt him to a revolt.' What say you to this? What do you know of it?

PAROLLES: I beseech you, let me answer to the particular of the inter'gatories. Demand them singly.

FIRST SOLDIER: Do you know this Captain Dumain?

PAROLLES: I know him: 'a was a botcher's prentice in Paris, from whence he was whipt for getting the shrieve's fool with child-a dumb innocent that could not say him nay.

BERTRAM: Nay, by your leave, hold your hands; though I know his brains are forfeit to the next tile that falls.

FIRST SOLDIER: Well, is this captain in the Duke of Florence's camp?

PAROLLES: Upon my knowledge, he is, and lousy.

SECOND LORD: Nay, look not so upon me; we shall hear of your lordship anon.

FIRST SOLDIER: What is his reputation with the Duke?

PAROLLES: The Duke knows him for no other but a poor officer of mine; and writ to me this other day to turn him out o' th' band. I think I have his letter in my pocket.

FIRST SOLDIER: Marry, we'll search.

PAROLLES: In good sadness, I do not know; either it is there or it is upon a file with the Duke's other letters in my tent.

FIRST SOLDIER: Here 'tis; here's a paper. Shall I read it to you?

PAROLLES: I do not know if it be it or no.

BERTRAM: Our interpreter does it well.

SECOND LORD: Excellently.

FIRST SOLDIER: *Reads* 'Dian, the Count's a fool, and full of gold.'

PAROLLES: That is not the Duke's letter, sir; that is an advertisement to a proper maid in Florence, one Diana, to take heed of the allurement of one Count Rousillon, a foolish idle boy, but for all that very ruttish. I pray you, sir, put it up again.

FIRST SOLDIER: Nay, I'll read it first by your favour.

PAROLLES: My meaning in't, I protest, was very honest in the behalf of the maid; for I knew the young Count to be a dangerous and lascivious boy, who is a whale to virginity, and devours up all the fry it finds.

BERTRAM: Damnable both-sides rogue!

FIRST SOLDIER: *Reads*
'When he swears oaths, bid him drop gold, and take it;
After he scores, he never pays the score.
Half won is match well made; match, and well make it;
He ne'er pays after-debts, take it before.
And say a soldier, Dian, told thee this:
Men are to mell with, boys are not to kiss;
For count of this, the Count's a fool, I know it,
Who pays before, but not when he does owe it.
Thine, as he vow'd to thee in thine ear, Parolles.'

BERTRAM: He shall be whipt through the army with this rhyme in's forehead.

FIRST LORD: This is your devoted friend, sir, the manifold linguist, and the amnipotent soldier.

BERTRAM: I could endure anything before but a cat, and now he's a cat to me.

FIRST SOLDIER: I perceive, sir, by our General's looks we shall be fain to hang you.

PAROLLES: My life, sir, in any case! Not that I am afraid to die, but that, my offences being many, I would repent out the remainder of nature. Let me live, sir, in a dungeon, i' th' stocks, or anywhere, so I may live.

FIRST SOLDIER: We'll see what may be done, so you confess freely; therefore, once more to this Captain Dumain: you have answer'd to his reputation with the Duke, and to his valour; what is his honesty?

PAROLLES: He will steal, sir, an egg out of a cloister; for rapes and ravishments he parallels Nessus. He professes not keeping of oaths; in breaking 'em he is stronger than Hercules. He will lie, sir, with such volubility that you would think truth were a fool. Drunkenness is his best virtue, for he will be swine-drunk; and in his sleep he does little harm, save to his bedclothes about him; but they know his conditions and lay him in straw. I have but little more to say, sir, of his honesty. He has everything that an honest man should not have; what an honest man should have he has nothing.

SECOND LORD: I begin to love him for this.

BERTRAM: For this description of thine honesty? A pox upon him! For me, he's more and more a cat.

FIRST SOLDIER: What say you to his expertness in war?

PAROLLES: Faith, sir, has led the drum before the English tragedians-to belie him I will not-and more of his soldier-ship I know not, except in that country he had the honour to be the officer at a place there called Mile-end to instruct for the doubling of files-I would do the man what honour I can-but of this I am not certain.

SECOND LORD: He hath out-villain'd villainy so far that the rarity redeems him.

BERTRAM: A pox on him! he's a cat still.

FIRST SOLDIER: His qualities being at this poor price, I need not to ask you if gold will corrupt him to revolt.

PAROLLES: Sir, for a cardecue he will sell the fee-simple of his salvation, the inheritance of it; and cut th' entail from all remainders and a perpetual succession for it perpetually.

FIRST SOLDIER: What's his brother, the other Captain Dumain?

FIRST LORD: Why does he ask him of me?

FIRST SOLDIER: What's he?

PAROLLES: E'en a crow o' th' same nest; not altogether so great as the first in goodness, but greater a great deal in evil. He excels his brother for a coward; yet his brother is reputed one of the best that is. In a retreat he outruns any lackey: marry, in coming on he has the cramp.

FIRST SOLDIER: If your life be saved, will you undertake to betray the Florentine?

PAROLLES: Ay, and the Captain of his Horse, Count Rousillon.

FIRST SOLDIER: I'll whisper with the General, and know his pleasure.

PAROLLES: *Aside* I'll no more drumming. A plague of all drums! Only to seem to deserve well, and to beguile the supposition of that lascivious young boy the Count, have I run into this danger. Yet who would have suspected an ambush where I was taken?

FIRST SOLDIER: There is no remedy, sir, but you must die.
The General says you that have so traitorously discover'd the
secrets of your army, and made such pestiferous reports of men
very nobly held, can serve the world for no honest use; therefore
you must die. Come, headsman, of with his head.

PAROLLES: O Lord, sir, let me live, or let me see my death!

FIRST SOLDIER: That shall you, and take your leave of all your
friends. *Unmuffling Him* So look about you; know you any here?

BERTRAM: Good morrow, noble Captain.

FIRST LORD: God bless you, Captain Parolles.

SECOND LORD: God save you, noble Captain.

FIRST LORD: Captain, what greeting will you to my Lord Lafeu? I am
for France.

SECOND LORD: Good Captain, will you give me a copy of the sonnet
you writ to Diana in behalf of the Count Rousillon? An I were not
a very coward I'd compel it of you; but fare you well.
    Exeunt Bertram and Lords

FIRST SOLDIER: You are undone, Captain, all but your scarf; that
has a knot on 't yet.

PAROLLES: Who cannot be crush'd with a plot?

FIRST SOLDIER: If you could find out a country where but women were
that had received so much shame, you might begin an impudent
nation. Fare ye well, sir; I am for France too; we shall speak of you there.
    Exit with Soldiers

PAROLLES: Yet am I thankful. If my heart were great,
'Twould burst at this. Captain I'll be no more;

But I will eat, and drink, and sleep as soft
As captain shall. Simply the thing I am
Shall make me live. Who knows himself a braggart,
Let him fear this; for it will come to pass
That every braggart shall be found an ass.
Rust, sword; cool, blushes; and, Parolles, live
Safest in shame. Being fool'd, by fool'ry thrive.
There's place and means for every man alive.
I'll after them.

> *Exit*

ACT IV SCENE IV. The Widow's House

Enter Helena, Widow, and Diana

HELENA: That you may well perceive I have not wrong'd you!
One of the greatest in the Christian world
Shall be my surety; fore whose throne 'tis needful,
Ere I can perfect mine intents, to kneel.
Time was I did him a desired office,
Dear almost as his life; which gratitude
Through flinty Tartar's bosom would peep forth,
And answer 'Thanks.' I duly am inform'd
His Grace is at Marseilles, to which place
We have convenient convoy. You must know
I am supposed dead. The army breaking,
My husband hies him home; where, heaven aiding,
And by the leave of my good lord the King,
We'll be before our welcome.

WIDOW: Gentle madam,
You never had a servant to whose trust
Your business was more welcome.

HELENA: Nor you, mistress,
Ever a friend whose thoughts more truly labour
To recompense your love. Doubt not but heaven
Hath brought me up to be your daughter's dower,

As it hath fated her to be my motive
And helper to a husband. But, O strange men!
That can such sweet use make of what they hate,
When saucy trusting of the cozen'd thoughts
Defiles the pitchy night. So lust doth play
With what it loathes, for that which is away.
But more of this hereafter. You, Diana,
Under my poor instructions yet must suffer
Something in my behalf.

DIANA: Let death and honesty
Go with your impositions, I am yours
Upon your will to suffer.

HELENA: Yet, I pray you:
But with the word the time will bring on summer,
When briers shall have leaves as well as thorns
And be as sweet as sharp. We must away;
Our waggon is prepar'd, and time revives us.
All's Well that Ends Well. Still the fine's the crown.
Whate'er the course, the end is the renown.
 Exeunt

ACT IV SCENE V. Rousillon. The Count's Palace
Enter Countess, Lafeu, and Clown

LAFEU: No, no, no, son was misled with a snipt-taffeta fellow
there, whose villainous saffron would have made all the unbak'd
and doughy youth of a nation in his colour. Your daughter-in-law
had been alive at this hour, and your son here at home, more
advanc'd by the King than by that red-tail'd humble-bee I speak
of.

COUNTESS: I would I had not known him. It was the death of the most
virtuous gentlewoman that ever nature had praise for creating. If
she had partaken of my flesh, and cost me the dearest groans of a
mother. I could not have owed her a more rooted love.

LAFEU: 'Twas a good lady, 'twas a good lady. We may pick a thousand sallets ere we light on such another herb.

CLOWN: Indeed, sir, she was the sweet-marjoram of the sallet, or, rather, the herb of grace.

LAFEU: They are not sallet-herbs, you knave; they are nose-herbs.

CLOWN: I am no great Nebuchadnezzar, sir; I have not much skill in grass.

LAFEU: Whether dost thou profess thyself-a knave or a fool?

CLOWN: A fool, sir, at a woman's service, and a knave at a man's.

LAFEU: Your distinction?

CLOWN: I would cozen the man of his wife, and do his service.

LAFEU: So you were a knave at his service, indeed.

CLOWN: And I would give his wife my bauble, sir, to do her service.

LAFEU: I will subscribe for thee; thou art both knave and fool.

CLOWN: At your service.

LAFEU: No, no, no.

CLOWN: Why, sir, if I cannot serve you, I can serve as great a prince as you are.

LAFEU: Who's that? A Frenchman?

CLOWN: Faith, sir, 'a has an English name; but his fisnomy is more hotter in France than there.

LAFEU: What prince is that?

CLOWN: The Black Prince, sir; alias, the Prince of Darkness; alias, the devil.

LAFEU: Hold thee, there's my purse. I give thee not this to suggest thee from thy master thou talk'st of; serve him still.

CLOWN: I am a woodland fellow, sir, that always loved a great fire; and the master I speak of ever keeps a good fire. But, sure, he is the prince of the world; let his nobility remain in's court. I am for the house with the narrow gate, which I take to be too little for pomp to enter. Some that humble themselves may; but the many will be too chill and tender: and they'll be for the flow'ry way that leads to the broad gate and the great fire.

LAFEU: Go thy ways, I begin to be aweary of thee; and I tell thee so before, because I would not fall out with thee. Go thy ways; let my horses be well look'd to, without any tricks.

CLOWN: If I put any tricks upon 'em, sir, they shall be jades' tricks, which are their own right by the law of nature.
    Exit

LAFEU: A shrewd knave, and an unhappy.

COUNTESS: So 'a is. My lord that's gone made himself much sport out of him. By his authority he remains here, which he thinks is a patent for his sauciness; and indeed he has no pace, but runs where he will.

LAFEU: I like him well; 'tis not amiss. And I was about to tell you, since I heard of the good lady's death, and that my lord your son was upon his return home, I moved the King my master to speak in the behalf of my daughter; which, in the minority of them both, his Majesty out of a self-gracious remembrance did first propose. His Highness hath promis'd me to do it; and, to stop up the displeasure he hath conceived against your son, there is no fitter matter. How does your ladyship like it?

COUNTESS: With very much content, my lord; and I wish it happily effected.

LAFEU: His Highness comes post from Marseilles, of as able body as when he number'd thirty; 'a will be here to-morrow, or I am deceiv'd by him that in such intelligence hath seldom fail'd.

COUNTESS: It rejoices me that I hope I shall see him ere I die. I have letters that my son will be here to-night. I shall beseech your lordship to remain with me tal they meet together.

LAFEU: Madam, I was thinking with what manners I might safely be admitted.

COUNTESS: You need but plead your honourable privilege.

LAFEU: Lady, of that I have made a bold charter; but, I thank my God, it holds yet.
   Re-enter Clown

CLOWN: O madam, yonder's my lord your son with a patch of velvet on's face; whether there be a scar under 't or no, the velvet knows; but 'tis a goodly patch of velvet. His left cheek is a cheek of two pile and a half, but his right cheek is worn bare.

LAFEU: A scar nobly got, or a noble scar, is a good liv'ry of honour; so belike is that.

CLOWN: But it is your carbonado'd face.

LAFEU: Let us go see your son, I pray you; I long to talk with the young noble soldier.

CLOWN: Faith, there's a dozen of 'em, with delicate fine hats, and most courteous feathers, which bow the head and nod at every man.

Exeunt

ACT V. SCENE I. Marseilles. A Street
Enter Helena, Widow, and Diana, with Two Attendants

HELENA: But this exceeding posting day and night
Must wear your spirits low; we cannot help it.
But since you have made the days and nights as one,
To wear your gentle limbs in my affairs,
Be bold you do so grow in my requital
As nothing can unroot you.
   Enter a Gentleman
In happy time!
This man may help me to his Majesty's ear,
If he would spend his power. God save you, sir.

GENTLEMAN: And you.

HELENA: Sir, I have seen you in the court of France.

GENTLEMAN: I have been sometimes there.

HELENA: I do presume, sir, that you are not fall'n
From the report that goes upon your goodness;
And therefore, goaded with most sharp occasions,
Which lay nice manners by, I put you to
The use of your own virtues, for the which
I shall continue thankful.

GENTLEMAN: What's your will?

HELENA: That it will please you
To give this poor petition to the King;
And aid me with that store of power you have
To come into his presence.

GENTLEMAN: The King's not here.

HELENA: Not here, sir?

GENTLEMAN: Not indeed.
He hence remov'd last night, and with more haste
Than is his use.

WIDOW: Lord, how we lose our pains!

HELENA: All's Well That Ends Well yet,
Though time seem so adverse and means unfit.
I do beseech you, whither is he gone?

GENTLEMAN: Marry, as I take it, to Rousillon;
Whither I am going.

HELENA: I do beseech you, sir,
Since you are like to see the King before me,
Commend the paper to his gracious hand;
Which I presume shall render you no blame,
But rather make you thank your pains for it.
I will come after you with what good speed
Our means will make us means.

GENTLEMAN: This I'll do for you.

HELENA: And you shall find yourself to be well thank'd,
Whate'er falls more. We must to horse again; go, go, provide.
Exeunt

ACT V SCENE II. Rousillon. The Inner Court of the Count's Palace
Enter Clown and Parolles

PAROLLES: Good Monsieur Lavache, give my Lord Lafeu this letter. I
have ere now, sir, been better known to you, when I have held
familiarity with fresher clothes; but I am now, sir, muddied in
Fortune's mood, and smell somewhat strong of her strong displeasure.

CLOWN: Truly, Fortune's displeasure is but sluttish, if it smell
so strongly as thou speak'st of. I will henceforth eat no fish
of Fortune's butt'ring. Prithee, allow the wind.

PAROLLES: Nay, you need not to stop your nose, sir; I spake but by
a metaphor.

CLOWN: Indeed, sir, if your metaphor stink, I will stop my nose; or
against any man's metaphor. Prithee, get thee further.

PAROLLES: Pray you, sir, deliver me this paper.

CLOWN: Foh! prithee stand away. A paper from Fortune's close-stool
to give to a nobleman! Look here he comes himself.
  Enter Lafeu
Here is a pur of Fortune's, sir, or of Fortune's cat, but not
a musk-cat, that has fall'n into the unclean fishpond of her
displeasure, and, as he says, is muddied withal. Pray you, sir,
use the carp as you may; for he looks like a poor, decayed,
ingenious, foolish, rascally knave. I do pity his distress
in my similes of comfort, and leave him to your lordship.
  Exit

PAROLLES: My lord, I am a man whom Fortune hath cruelly scratch'd.

LAFEU: And what would you have me to do? 'Tis too late to pare her
nails now. Wherein have you played the knave with Fortune, that
she should scratch you, who of herself is a good lady and would
not have knaves thrive long under her? There's a cardecue for
you. Let the justices make you and Fortune friends; I am for other business.

PAROLLES: I beseech your honour to hear me one single word.

LAFEU: You beg a single penny more; come, you shall ha't; save your word.

PAROLLES: My name, my good lord, is Parolles.

LAFEU: You beg more than word then. Cox my passion! give me your hand. How does your drum?

PAROLLES: O my good lord, you were the first that found me.

LAFEU: Was I, in sooth? And I was the first that lost thee.

PAROLLES: It lies in you, my lord, to bring me in some grace, for you did bring me out.

LAFEU: Out upon thee, knave! Dost thou put upon me at once both the office of God and the devil? One brings the in grace, and the other brings thee out. *Trumpets Sound* The King's coming; I know by his trumpets. Sirrah, inquire further after me; I had talk of you last night. Though you are a fool and a knave, you shall eat. Go to; follow.

PAROLLES: I praise God for you.
   Exeunt

ACT V SCENE III. Rousillon. The Count's Palace
Flourish. Enter King, Countess, Lafeu, the Two French Lords, with Attendants

KING: We lost a jewel of her, and our esteem
Was made much poorer by it; but your son,
As mad in folly, lack'd the sense to know
Her estimation home.

COUNTESS: 'Tis past, my liege;
And I beseech your Majesty to make it
Natural rebellion, done i' th' blaze of youth,
When oil and fire, too strong for reason's force,
O'erbears it and burns on.

KING: My honour'd lady,
I have forgiven and forgotten all;
Though my revenges were high bent upon him

And watch'd the time to shoot.

LAFEU: This I must say-
But first, I beg my pardon: the young lord
Did to his Majesty, his mother, and his lady,
Offence of mighty note; but to himself
The greatest wrong of all. He lost a wife
Whose beauty did astonish the survey
Of richest eyes; whose words all ears took captive;
Whose dear perfection hearts that scorn'd to serve
Humbly call'd mistress.

KING: Praising what is lost
Makes the remembrance dear. Well, call him hither;
We are reconcil'd, and the first view shall kill
All repetition. Let him not ask our pardon;
The nature of his great offence is dead,
And deeper than oblivion do we bury
Th' incensing relics of it; let him approach,
A stranger, no offender; and inform him
So 'tis our will he should.

GENTLEMAN: I shall, my liege.
Exit Gentleman

KING: What says he to your daughter? Have you spoke?

LAFEU: All that he is hath reference to your Highness.

KING: Then shall we have a match. I have letters sent me
That sets him high in fame.
Enter Bertram

LAFEU: He looks well on 't.

KING: I am not a day of season,
For thou mayst see a sunshine and a hail

In me at once. But to the brightest beams
Distracted clouds give way; so stand thou forth;
The time is fair again.

BERTRAM: My high-repented blames,
Dear sovereign, pardon to me.

KING: All is whole;
Not one word more of the consumed time.
Let's take the instant by the forward top;
For we are old, and on our quick'st decrees
Th' inaudible and noiseless foot of Time
Steals ere we can effect them. You remember
The daughter of this lord?

BERTRAM: Admiringly, my liege. At first
I stuck my choice upon her, ere my heart
Durst make too bold herald of my tongue;
Where the impression of mine eye infixing,
Contempt his scornful perspective did lend me,
Which warp'd the line of every other favour,
Scorn'd a fair colour or express'd it stol'n,
Extended or contracted all proportions
To a most hideous object. Thence it came
That she whom all men prais'd, and whom myself,
Since I have lost, have lov'd, was in mine eye
The dust that did offend it.

KING: Well excus'd.
That thou didst love her, strikes some scores away
From the great compt; but love that comes too late,
Like a remorseful pardon slowly carried,
To the great sender turns a sour offence,
Crying 'That's good that's gone.' Our rash faults
Make trivial price of serious things we have,
Not knowing them until we know their grave.
Oft our displeasures, to ourselves unjust,

Destroy our friends, and after weep their dust;
Our own love waking cries to see what's done,
While shameful hate sleeps out the afternoon.
Be this sweet Helen's knell. And now forget her.
Send forth your amorous token for fair Maudlin.
The main consents are had; and here we'll stay
To see our widower's second marriage-day.

COUNTESS: Which better than the first, O dear heaven, bless!
Or, ere they meet, in me, O nature, cesse!

LAFEU: Come on, my son, in whom my house's name
Must be digested; give a favour from you,
To sparkle in the spirits of my daughter,
That she may quickly come.
   Bertram Gives a Ring
By my old beard,
And ev'ry hair that's on 't, Helen, that's dead,
Was a sweet creature; such a ring as this,
The last that e'er I took her leave at court,
I saw upon her finger.

BERTRAM: Hers it was not.

KING: Now, pray you, let me see it; for mine eye,
While I was speaking, oft was fasten'd to't.
This ring was mine; and when I gave it Helen
I bade her, if her fortunes ever stood
Necessitied to help, that by this token
I would relieve her. Had you that craft to reave her
Of what should stead her most?

BERTRAM: My gracious sovereign,
Howe'er it pleases you to take it so,
The ring was never hers.

COUNTESS: Son, on my life,

I have seen her wear it; and she reckon'd it
At her life's rate.

LAFEU: I am sure I saw her wear it.

BERTRAM: You are deceiv'd, my lord; she never saw it.
In Florence was it from a casement thrown me,
Wrapp'd in a paper, which contain'd the name
Of her that threw it. Noble she was, and thought
I stood engag'd; but when I had subscrib'd
To mine own fortune, and inform'd her fully
I could not answer in that course of honour
As she had made the overture, she ceas'd,
In heavy satisfaction, and would never
Receive the ring again.

KING: Plutus himself,
That knows the tinct and multiplying med'cine,
Hath not in nature's mystery more science
Than I have in this ring. 'Twas mine, 'twas Helen's,
Whoever gave it you. Then, if you know
That you are well acquainted with yourself,
Confess 'twas hers, and by what rough enforcement
You got it from her. She call'd the saints to surety
That she would never put it from her finger
Unless she gave it to yourself in bed-
Where you have never come- or sent it us
Upon her great disaster.

BERTRAM: She never saw it.

KING: Thou speak'st it falsely, as I love mine honour;
And mak'st conjectural fears to come into me
Which I would fain shut out. If it should prove
That thou art so inhuman- 'twill not prove so.
And yet I know not- thou didst hate her deadly,
And she is dead; which nothing, but to close

Her eyes myself, could win me to believe
More than to see this ring. Take him away.
   Guards Seize Bertram
My fore-past proofs, howe'er the matter fall,
Shall tax my fears of little vanity,
Having vainly fear'd too little. Away with him.
We'll sift this matter further.

BERTRAM: If you shall prove
This ring was ever hers, you shall as easy
Prove that I husbanded her bed in Florence,
Where she yet never was.
   Exit, Guarded

KING: I am wrapp'd in dismal thinkings.
   Enter a Gentleman

GENTLEMAN: Gracious sovereign,
Whether I have been to blame or no, I know not:
Here's a petition from a Florentine,
Who hath, for four or five removes, come short
To tender it herself. I undertook it,
Vanquish'd thereto by the fair grace and speech
Of the poor suppliant, who by this, I know,
Is here attending; her business looks in her
With an importing visage; and she told me
In a sweet verbal brief it did concern
Your Highness with herself.

KING: *Reads the Letter* 'Upon his many protestations to marry me
when his wife was dead, I blush to say it, he won me. Now is the
Count Rousillon a widower; his vows are forfeited to me, and my
honour's paid to him. He stole from Florence, taking no leave,
and I follow him to his country for justice. Grant it me, O King!
in you it best lies; otherwise a seducer flourishes, and a poor
maid is undone.

                     Diana Capilet.'

LAFEU: I will buy me a son-in-law in a fair, and toll for this.
I'll none of him.

KING: The heavens have thought well on thee, Lafeu,
To bring forth this discov'ry. Seek these suitors.
Go speedily, and bring again the Count.
Exeunt Attendants
I am afeard the life of Helen, lady,
Was foully snatch'd.

COUNTESS: Now, justice on the doers!
Enter Bertram, Guarded

KING: I wonder, sir, sith wives are monsters to you.
And that you fly them as you swear them lordship,
Yet you desire to marry.
Enter Widow and Diana
What woman's that?

DIANA: I am, my lord, a wretched Florentine,
Derived from the ancient Capilet.
My suit, as I do understand, you know,
And therefore know how far I may be pitied.

WIDOW: I am her mother, sir, whose age and honour
Both suffer under this complaint we bring,
And both shall cease, without your remedy.

KING: Come hither, Count; do you know these women?

BERTRAM: My lord, I neither can nor will deny
But that I know them. Do they charge me further?

DIANA: Why do you look so strange upon your wife?

BERTRAM: She's none of mine, my lord.

DIANA: If you shall marry,
You give away this hand, and that is mine;
You give away heaven's vows, and those are mine;
You give away myself, which is known mine;
For I by vow am so embodied yours
That she which marries you must marry me,
Either both or none.

LAFEU: *To Bertram* Your reputation comes too short for
my daughter; you are no husband for her.

BERTRAM: My lord, this is a fond and desp'rate creature
Whom sometime I have laugh'd with. Let your Highness
Lay a more noble thought upon mine honour
Than for to think that I would sink it here.

KING: Sir, for my thoughts, you have them ill to friend
Till your deeds gain them. Fairer prove your honour
Than in my thought it lies!

DIANA: Good my lord,
Ask him upon his oath if he does think
He had not my virginity.

KING: What say'st thou to her?

BERTRAM: She's impudent, my lord,
And was a common gamester to the camp.

DIANA: He does me wrong, my lord; if I were so
He might have bought me at a common price.
Do not believe him. o, behold this ring,
Whose high respect and rich validity
Did lack a parallel; yet, for all that,
He gave it to a commoner o' th' camp,
If I be one.

COUNTESS: He blushes, and 'tis it.
Of six preceding ancestors, that gem
Conferr'd by testament to th' sequent issue,
Hath it been ow'd and worn. This is his wife:
That ring's a thousand proofs.

KING: Methought you said
You saw one here in court could witness it.

DIANA: I did, my lord, but loath am to produce
So bad an instrument; his name's Parolles.

LAFEU: I saw the man to-day, if man he be.

KING: Find him, and bring him hither.
   Exit an Attendant

BERTRAM: What of him?
He's quoted for a most perfidious slave,
With all the spots o' th' world tax'd and debauch'd,
Whose nature sickens but to speak a truth.
Am I or that or this for what he'll utter
That will speak anything?

KING: She hath that ring of yours.

BERTRAM: I think she has. Certain it is I lik'd her,
And boarded her i' th' wanton way of youth.
She knew her distance, and did angle for me,
Madding my eagerness with her restraint,
As all impediments in fancy's course
Are motives of more fancy; and, in fine,
Her infinite cunning with her modern grace
Subdu'd me to her rate. She got the ring;
And I had that which any inferior might
At market-price have bought.

DIANA: I must be patient.
You that have turn'd off a first so noble wife
May justly diet me. I pray you yet-
Since you lack virtue, I will lose a husband-
Send for your ring, I will return it home,
And give me mine again.

BERTRAM: I have it not.

KING: What ring was yours, I pray you?

DIANA: Sir, much like
The same upon your finger.

KING: Know you this ring? This ring was his of late.

DIANA: And this was it I gave him, being abed.

KING: The story, then, goes false you threw it him
Out of a casement.

DIANA: I have spoke the truth.
  Enter Parolles

BERTRAM: My lord, I do confess the ring was hers.

KING: You boggle shrewdly; every feather starts you.
Is this the man you speak of?

DIANA: Ay, my lord.

KING: Tell me, sirrah-but tell me true I charge you,
Not fearing the displeasure of your master,
Which, on your just proceeding, I'll keep off-
By him and by this woman here what know you?

PAROLLES: So please your Majesty, my master hath been an honourable gentleman; tricks he hath had in him, which gentlemen have.

KING: Come, come, to th' purpose. Did he love this woman?

PAROLLES: Faith, sir, he did love her; but how?

KING: How, I pray you?

PAROLLES: He did love her, sir, as a gentleman loves a woman.

KING: How is that?

PAROLLES: He lov'd her, sir, and lov'd her not.

KING: As thou art a knave and no knave.
What an equivocal companion is this!

PAROLLES: I am a poor man, and at your Majesty's command.

LAFEU: He's a good drum, my lord, but a naughty orator.

DIANA: Do you know he promis'd me marriage?

PAROLLES: Faith, I know more than I'll speak.

KING: But wilt thou not speak all thou know'st?

PAROLLES: Yes, so please your Majesty. I did go between them, as I
said; but more than that, he loved her-for indeed he was mad for
her, and talk'd of Satan, and of Limbo, and of Furies, and I know
not what. Yet I was in that credit with them at that time that I
knew of their going to bed; and of other motions, as promising
her marriage, and things which would derive me ill will to speak
of; therefore I will not speak what I know.

KING: Thou hast spoken all already, unless thou canst say they are
married; but thou art too fine in thy evidence; therefore stand aside.

This ring, you say, was yours?

DIANA: Ay, my good lord.

KING: Where did you buy it? Or who gave it you?

DIANA: It was not given me, nor I did not buy it.

KING: Who lent it you?

DIANA: It was not lent me neither.

KING: Where did you find it then?

DIANA: I found it not.

KING: If it were yours by none of all these ways,
How could you give it him?

DIANA: I never gave it him.

LAFEU: This woman's an easy glove, my lord; she goes of and on at pleasure.

KING: This ring was mine, I gave it his first wife.

DIANA: It might be yours or hers, for aught I know.

KING: Take her away, I do not like her now;
To prison with her. And away with him.
Unless thou tell'st me where thou hadst this ring,
Thou diest within this hour.

DIANA: I'll never tell you.

KING: Take her away.

DIANA: I'll put in bail, my liege.

KING: I think thee now some common customer.

DIANA: By Jove, if ever I knew man, 'twas you.

KING: Wherefore hast thou accus'd him all this while?

DIANA: Because he's guilty, and he is not guilty.
He knows I am no maid, and he'll swear to't:
I'll swear I am a maid, and he knows not.
Great King, I am no strumpet, by my life;
I am either maid, or else this old man's wife.
    Pointing to Lafeu

KING: She does abuse our ears; to prison with her.

DIANA: Good mother, fetch my bail. Stay, royal sir;
    Exit Widow
The jeweller that owes the ring is sent for,
And he shall surety me. But for this lord
Who hath abus'd me as he knows himself,
Though yet he never harm'd me, here I quit him.
He knows himself my bed he hath defil'd;
And at that time he got his wife with child.
Dead though she be, she feels her young one kick;
So there's my riddle: one that's dead is quick-
And now behold the meaning.
    Re-enter Widow with Helena

KING: Is there no exorcist
Beguiles the truer office of mine eyes?
Is't real that I see?

HELENA: No, my good lord;
'Tis but the shadow of a wife you see,
The name and not the thing.

BERTRAM: Both, both; o, pardon!

LAFEU: O, my good lord, when I was like this maid,
I found you wondrous kind. There is your ring,
And, look you, here's your letter. This it says:
'When from my finger you can get this ring,
And are by me with child,' etc. This is done.
Will you be mine now you are doubly won?

BERTRAM: If she, my liege, can make me know this clearly,
I'll love her dearly, ever, ever dearly.

LAFEU: If it appear not plain, and prove untrue,
Deadly divorce step between me and you!
O my dear mother, do I see you living?

LAFEU: Mine eyes smell onions; I shall weep anon.
To Parolles Good Tom Drum, lend me a handkercher. So, I
thank thee. Wait on me home, I'll make sport with thee;
let thy curtsies alone, they are scurvy ones.

KING: Let us from point to point this story know,
To make the even truth in pleasure flow.
To Diana If thou beest yet a fresh uncropped flower,
Choose thou thy husband, and I'll pay thy dower;
For I can guess that by thy honest aid
Thou kept'st a wife herself, thyself a maid.-
Of that and all the progress, more and less,
Resolvedly more leisure shall express.
All yet seems well; and if it end so meet,
The bitter past, more welcome is the sweet.
   Flourish

EPILOGUE.

KING: The King's a beggar, now the play is done.
All is well ended if this suit be won,

That you express content; which we will pay
With strife to please you, day exceeding day.
Ours be your patience then, and yours our parts;
Your gentle hands lend us, and take our hearts.
  Exeunt Omnes

END

Measure for Measure

Dramatis Personae

VINCENTIO, the Duke
ANGELO, the Deputy
ESCALUS, an ancient Lord
CLAUDIO, a young gentleman
LUCIO, a fantastic
Two other like Gentlemen
VARRIUS, a gentleman, servant to the Duke
PROVOST
THOMAS, friar
PETER, friar
A JUSTICE
ELBOW, a simple constable
FROTH, a foolish gentleman
POMPEY, a clown and servant to Mistress Overdone
ABHORSON, an executioner
BARNARDINE, a dissolute prisoner
ISABELLA, sister to Claudio
MARIANA, betrothed to Angelo
JULIET, beloved of Claudio
FRANCISCA, a nun
MISTRESS OVERDONE, a bawd
Lords, Officers, Citizens, Boy, and Attendants

SCENE: Vienna

ACT I. SCENE I. The Duke's Palace

Enter Duke, Escalus, Lords, and Attendants

DUKE: Escalus!

ESCALUS: My lord.

DUKE: Of government the properties to unfold
Would seem in me t' affect speech and discourse,

Since I am put to know that your own science
Exceeds, in that, the lists of all advice
My strength can give you; then no more remains
But that to your sufficiency- as your worth is able-
And let them work. The nature of our people,
Our city's institutions, and the terms
For common justice, y'are as pregnant in
As art and practice hath enriched any
That we remember. There is our commission,
From which we would not have you warp. Call hither,
I say, bid come before us, Angelo.
    Exit an Attendant
What figure of us think you he will bear?
For you must know we have with special soul
Elected him our absence to supply;
Lent him our terror, dress'd him with our love,
And given his deputation all the organs
Of our own power. What think you of it?

ESCALUS: If any in Vienna be of worth
To undergo such ample grace and honour,
It is Lord Angelo.
    Enter Angelo

DUKE: Look where he comes.

ANGELO: Always obedient to your Grace's will,
I come to know your pleasure.

DUKE: Angelo,
There is a kind of character in thy life
That to th' observer doth thy history
Fully unfold. Thyself and thy belongings
Are not thine own so proper as to waste
Thyself upon thy virtues, they on thee.
Heaven doth with us as we with torches do,
Not light them for themselves; for if our virtues

Did not go forth of us, 'twere all alike
As if we had them not. Spirits are not finely touch'd
But to fine issues; nor Nature never lends
The smallest scruple of her excellence
But, like a thrifty goddess, she determines
Herself the glory of a creditor,
Both thanks and use. But I do bend my speech
To one that can my part in him advertise.
Hold, therefore, Angelo-
In our remove be thou at full ourself;
Mortality and mercy in Vienna
Live in thy tongue and heart. Old Escalus,
Though first in question, is thy secondary.
Take thy commission.

ANGELO: Now, good my lord,
Let there be some more test made of my metal,
Before so noble and so great a figure
Be stamp'd upon it.

DUKE: No more evasion!
We have with a leaven'd and prepared choice
Proceeded to you; therefore take your honours.
Our haste from hence is of so quick condition
That it prefers itself, and leaves unquestion'd
Matters of needful value. We shall write to you,
As time and our concernings shall importune,
How it goes with us, and do look to know
What doth befall you here. So, fare you well.
To th' hopeful execution do I leave you
Of your commissions.

ANGELO: Yet give leave, my lord,
That we may bring you something on the way.

DUKE: My haste may not admit it;
Nor need you, on mine honour, have to do

With any scruple: your scope is as mine own,
So to enforce or qualify the laws
As to your soul seems good. Give me your hand;
I'll privily away. I love the people,
But do not like to stage me to their eyes;
Though it do well, I do not relish well
Their loud applause and Aves vehement;
Nor do I think the man of safe discretion
That does affect it. Once more, fare you well.

ANGELO: The heavens give safety to your purposes!

ESCALUS: Lead forth and bring you back in happiness!

DUKE: I thank you. Fare you well.
  Exit

ESCALUS: I shall desire you, sir, to give me leave
To have free speech with you; and it concerns me
To look into the bottom of my place:
A pow'r I have, but of what strength and nature
I am not yet instructed.

ANGELO: 'Tis so with me. Let us withdraw together,
And we may soon our satisfaction have
Touching that point.

ESCALUS: I'll wait upon your honour.
  Exeunt

ACT I. SCENE II. A Street
Enter Lucio and Two Other Gentlemen

LUCIO: If the Duke, with the other dukes, come not to composition
with the King of Hungary, why then all the dukes fall upon the King.

FIRST GENTLEMAN: Heaven grant us its peace, but not the King of

Hungary's!

SECOND GENTLEMAN: Amen.

LUCIO: Thou conclud'st like the sanctimonious pirate that went to sea with the Ten Commandments, but scrap'd one out of the table.

SECOND GENTLEMAN: 'Thou shalt not steal'?

LUCIO: Ay, that he raz'd.

FIRST GENTLEMAN: Why, 'twas a commandment to command the captain and all the rest from their functions: they put forth to steal. There's not a soldier of us all that, in the thanksgiving before meat, do relish the petition well that prays for peace.

SECOND GENTLEMAN: I never heard any soldier dislike it.

LUCIO: I believe thee; for I think thou never wast where grace was said.

SECOND GENTLEMAN: No? A dozen times at least.

FIRST GENTLEMAN: What, in metre?

LUCIO: In any proportion or in any language.

FIRST GENTLEMAN: I think, or in any religion.

LUCIO: Ay, why not? Grace is grace, despite of all controversy; as, for example, thou thyself art a wicked villain, despite of all grace.

FIRST GENTLEMAN: Well, there went but a pair of shears between us.

LUCIO: I grant; as there may between the lists and the velvet. Thou art the list.

FIRST GENTLEMAN: And thou the velvet; thou art good

velvet; thou'rt a three-pil'd piece, I warrant thee. I had as lief
be a list of an English kersey as be pil'd, as thou art pil'd, f
or a French velvet. Do I speak feelingly now?

LUCIO: I think thou dost; and, indeed, with most painful feeling of
thy speech. I will, out of thine own confession, learn to begin
thy health; but, whilst I live, forget to drink after thee.

FIRST GENTLEMAN: I think I have done myself wrong, have I not?

SECOND GENTLEMAN: Yes, that thou hast, whether thou art tainted or
free.
    Enter Mistress Overdone

LUCIO: Behold, behold, where Madam Mitigation comes! I have
purchas'd as many diseases under her roof as come to-

SECOND GENTLEMAN: To what, I pray?

FIRST GENTLEMAN: Judge.

SECOND GENTLEMAN: To three thousand dolours a year.

FIRST GENTLEMAN: Ay, and more.

LUCIO: A French crown more.

FIRST GENTLEMAN: Thou art always figuring diseases in me, but thou
art full of error; I am sound.

LUCIO: Nay, not, as one would say, healthy; but so sound as things
that are hollow: thy bones are hollow; impiety has made a feast of thee.

FIRST GENTLEMAN: How now! which of your hips has the most
profound sciatica?

MRS. OVERDONE: Well, well! there's one yonder arrested and carried

to prison was worth five thousand of you all.

FIRST GENTLEMAN: Who's that, I pray thee?

MRS. OVERDONE: Marry, sir, that's Claudio, Signior Claudio.

FIRST GENTLEMAN: Claudio to prison? 'Tis not so.

MRS. OVERDONE: Nay, but I know 'tis so: I saw him arrested; saw him
carried away; and, which is more, within these three days his
head to be chopp'd off.

LUCIO: But, after all this fooling, I would not have it so. Art
thou sure of this?

MRS. OVERDONE: I am too sure of it; and it is for getting Madam
Julietta with child.

LUCIO: Believe me, this may be; he promis'd to meet me two hours
since, and he was ever precise in promise-keeping.

SECOND GENTLEMAN: Besides, you know, it draws something near to
the speech we had to such a purpose.

FIRST GENTLEMAN: But most of all agreeing with the proclamation.

LUCIO: Away; let's go learn the truth of it.
  Exeunt Lucio and Gentlemen

MRS. OVERDONE: Thus, what with the war, what with the sweat, what
with the gallows, and what with poverty, I am custom-shrunk.
  Enter Pompey
How now! what's the news with you?

POMPEY: Yonder man is carried to prison.

MRS. OVERDONE: Well, what has he done?

POMPEY: A woman.

MRS. OVERDONE: But what's his offence?

POMPEY: Groping for trouts in a peculiar river.

MRS. OVERDONE: What! is there a maid with child by him?

POMPEY: No; but there's a woman with maid by him. You have not heard of the proclamation, have you?

MRS. OVERDONE: What proclamation, man?

POMPEY: All houses in the suburbs of Vienna must be pluck'd down.

MRS. OVERDONE: And what shall become of those in the city?

POMPEY: They shall stand for seed; they had gone down too, but that a wise burgher put in for them.

MRS. OVERDONE: But shall all our houses of resort in the suburbs be pull'd down?

POMPEY: To the ground, mistress.

MRS. OVERDONE: Why, here's a change indeed in the commonwealth! What shall become of me?

POMPEY: Come, fear not you: good counsellors lack no clients. Though you change your place you need not change your trade; I'll be your tapster still. Courage, there will be pity taken on you; you that have worn your eyes almost out in the service, you will be considered.

MRS. OVERDONE: What's to do here, Thomas Tapster? Let's withdraw.

POMPEY: Here comes Signior Claudio, led by the provost to prison;

and there's Madam Juliet.
Exeunt
Enter Provost, Claudio, Juliet, and Officers; Lucio Following

CLAUDIO: Fellow, why dost thou show me thus to th' world?
Bear me to prison, where I am committed.

PROVOST: I do it not in evil disposition,
But from Lord Angelo by special charge.

CLAUDIO: Thus can the demigod Authority
Make us pay down for our offence by weight
The words of heaven: on whom it will, it will;
On whom it will not, so; yet still 'tis just.

LUCIO: Why, how now, Claudio, whence comes this restraint?

CLAUDIO: From too much liberty, my Lucio, liberty;
As surfeit is the father of much fast,
So every scope by the immoderate use
Turns to restraint. Our natures do pursue,
Like rats that ravin down their proper bane,
A thirsty evil; and when we drink we die.

LUCIO: If I could speak so wisely under an arrest, I would send for
certain of my creditors; and yet, to say the truth, I had as lief
have the foppery of freedom as the morality of imprisonment.
What's thy offence, Claudio?

CLAUDIO: What but to speak of would offend again.

LUCIO: What, is't murder?

CLAUDIO: No.

LUCIO: Lechery?

CLAUDIO: Call it so.

PROVOST: Away, sir; you must go.

CLAUDIO: One word, good friend. Lucio, a word with you.

LUCIO: A hundred, if they'll do you any good. Is lechery so look'd after?

CLAUDIO: Thus stands it with me: upon a true contract
I got possession of Julietta's bed.
You know the lady; she is fast my wife,
Save that we do the denunciation lack
Of outward order; this we came not to,
Only for propagation of a dow'r
Remaining in the coffer of her friends.
From whom we thought it meet to hide our love
Till time had made them for us. But it chances
The stealth of our most mutual entertainment,
With character too gross, is writ on Juliet.

LUCIO: With child, perhaps?

CLAUDIO: Unhappily, even so.
And the new deputy now for the Duke-
Whether it be the fault and glimpse of newness,
Or whether that the body public be
A horse whereon the governor doth ride,
Who, newly in the seat, that it may know
He can command, lets it straight feel the spur;
Whether the tyranny be in his place,
Or in his eminence that fills it up,
I stagger in. But this new governor
Awakes me all the enrolled penalties
Which have, like unscour'd armour, hung by th' wall
So long that nineteen zodiacs have gone round
And none of them been worn; and, for a name,
Now puts the drowsy and neglected act

Freshly on me. 'Tis surely for a name.

LUCIO: I warrant it is; and thy head stands so tickle on thy
shoulders that a milkmaid, if she be in love, may sigh it off.
Send after the Duke, and appeal to him.

CLAUDIO: I have done so, but he's not to be found.
I prithee, Lucio, do me this kind service:
This day my sister should the cloister enter,
And there receive her approbation;
Acquaint her with the danger of my state;
Implore her, in my voice, that she make friends
To the strict deputy; bid herself assay him.
I have great hope in that; for in her youth
There is a prone and speechless dialect
Such as move men; beside, she hath prosperous art
When she will play with reason and discourse,
And well she can persuade.

LUCIO: I pray she may; as well for the encouragement of the like,
which else would stand under grievous imposition, as for the
enjoying of thy life, who I would be sorry should be thus
foolishly lost at a game of tick-tack. I'll to her.

CLAUDIO: I thank you, good friend Lucio.

LUCIO: Within two hours.

CLAUDIO: Come, officer, away.
  Exeunt

ACT I. SCENE III. A Monastery
Enter Duke and Friar Thomas

DUKE: No, holy father; throw away that thought;
Believe not that the dribbling dart of love
Can pierce a complete bosom. Why I desire thee

To give me secret harbour hath a purpose
More grave and wrinkled than the aims and ends
Of burning youth.

FRIAR: May your Grace speak of it?

DUKE: My holy sir, none better knows than you
How I have ever lov'd the life removed,
And held in idle price to haunt assemblies
Where youth, and cost, a witless bravery keeps.
I have deliver'd to Lord Angelo,
A man of stricture and firm abstinence,
My absolute power and place here in Vienna,
And he supposes me travell'd to Poland;
For so I have strew'd it in the common ear,
And so it is received. Now, pious sir,
You will demand of me why I do this.

FRIAR: Gladly, my lord.

DUKE: We have strict statutes and most biting laws,
The needful bits and curbs to headstrong steeds,
Which for this fourteen years we have let slip;
Even like an o'ergrown lion in a cave,
That goes not out to prey. Now, as fond fathers,
Having bound up the threat'ning twigs of birch,
Only to stick it in their children's sight
For terror, not to use, in time the rod
Becomes more mock'd than fear'd; so our decrees,
Dead to infliction, to themselves are dead;
And liberty plucks justice by the nose;
The baby beats the nurse, and quite athwart
Goes all decorum.

FRIAR: It rested in your Grace
To unloose this tied-up justice when you pleas'd;
And it in you more dreadful would have seem'd

Than in Lord Angelo.

DUKE: I do fear, too dreadful.
Sith 'twas my fault to give the people scope,
'Twould be my tyranny to strike and gall them
For what I bid them do; for we bid this be done,
When evil deeds have their permissive pass
And not the punishment. Therefore, indeed, my father,
I have on Angelo impos'd the office;
Who may, in th' ambush of my name, strike home,
And yet my nature never in the fight
To do in slander. And to behold his sway,
I will, as 'twere a brother of your order,
Visit both prince and people. Therefore, I prithee,
Supply me with the habit, and instruct me
How I may formally in person bear me
Like a true friar. Moe reasons for this action
At our more leisure shall I render you.
Only, this one: Lord Angelo is precise;
Stands at a guard with envy; scarce confesses
That his blood flows, or that his appetite
Is more to bread than stone. Hence shall we see,
If power change purpose, what our seemers be.
Exeunt

ACT I. SCENE IV. A Nunnery
Enter Isabella and Francisca

ISABELLA: And have you nuns no farther privileges?

IFRANCISCA: Are not these large enough?

ISABELLA: Yes, truly; I speak not as desiring more,
But rather wishing a more strict restraint
Upon the sisterhood, the votarists of Saint Clare.

LUCIO: *Within* Ho! Peace be in this place!

ISABELLA: Who's that which calls?

IFRANCISCA: It is a man's voice. Gentle Isabella,
Turn you the key, and know his business of him:
You may, I may not; you are yet unsworn;
When you have vow'd, you must not speak with men
But in the presence of the prioress;
Then, if you speak, you must not show your face,
Or, if you show your face, you must not speak.
He calls again; I pray you answer him.
    Exit Francisca

ISABELLA: Peace and prosperity! Who is't that calls?
    Enter Lucio

LUCIO: Hail, virgin, if you be, as those cheek-roses
Proclaim you are no less. Can you so stead me
As bring me to the sight of Isabella,
A novice of this place, and the fair sister
To her unhappy brother Claudio?

ISABELLA: Why her 'unhappy brother'? Let me ask
The rather, for I now must make you know
I am that Isabella, and his sister.

LUCIO: Gentle and fair, your brother kindly greets you.
Not to be weary with you, he's in prison.

ISABELLA: Woe me! For what?

LUCIO: For that which, if myself might be his judge,
He should receive his punishment in thanks:
He hath got his friend with child.

ISABELLA: Sir, make me not your story.

LUCIO: It is true.

I would not- though 'tis my familiar sin
With maids to seem the lapwing, and to jest,
Tongue far from heart- play with all virgins so:
I hold you as a thing enskied and sainted,
By your renouncement an immortal spirit,
And to be talk'd with in sincerity,
As with a saint.

ISABELLA: You do blaspheme the good in mocking me.

LUCIO: Do not believe it. Fewness and truth, 'tis thus:
Your brother and his lover have embrac'd.
As those that feed grow full, as blossoming time
That from the seedness the bare fallow brings
To teeming foison, even so her plenteous womb
Expresseth his full tilth and husbandry.

ISABELLA: Some one with child by him? My cousin Juliet?

LUCIO: Is she your cousin?

ISABELLA: Adoptedly, as school-maids change their names
By vain though apt affection.

LUCIO: She it is.

ISABELLA: O, let him marry her!

LUCIO: This is the point.
The Duke is very strangely gone from hence;
Bore many gentlemen, myself being one,
In hand, and hope of action; but we do learn,
By those that know the very nerves of state,
His givings-out were of an infinite distance
From his true-meant design. Upon his place,
And with full line of his authority,
Governs Lord Angelo, a man whose blood

Is very snow-broth, one who never feels
The wanton stings and motions of the sense,
But doth rebate and blunt his natural edge
With profits of the mind, study and fast.
He- to give fear to use and liberty,
Which have for long run by the hideous law,
As mice by lions- hath pick'd out an act
Under whose heavy sense your brother's life
Falls into forfeit; he arrests him on it,
And follows close the rigour of the statute
To make him an example. All hope is gone,
Unless you have the grace by your fair prayer
To soften Angelo. And that's my pith of business
'Twixt you and your poor brother.

ISABELLA: Doth he so seek his life?

LUCIO: Has censur'd him
Already, and, as I hear, the Provost hath
A warrant for his execution.

ISABELLA: Alas! what poor ability's in me
To do him good?

LUCIO: Assay the pow'r you have.

ISABELLA: My power, alas, I doubt!

LUCIO: Our doubts are traitors,
And make us lose the good we oft might win
By fearing to attempt. Go to Lord Angelo,
And let him learn to know, when maidens sue,
Men give like gods; but when they weep and kneel,
All their petitions are as freely theirs
As they themselves would owe them.

ISABELLA: I'll see what I can do.

LUCIO: But speedily.

ISABELLA: I will about it straight;
No longer staying but to give the Mother
Notice of my affair. I humbly thank you.
Commend me to my brother; soon at night
I'll send him certain word of my success.

LUCIO: I take my leave of you.

ISABELLA: Good sir, adieu.
Exeunt

ACT II. SCENE I. A Hall in Angelo's House
Enter Angelo, Escalus, a Justice, Provost, Officers, and Other Attendants

ANGELO: We must not make a scarecrow of the law,
Setting it up to fear the birds of prey,
And let it keep one shape till custom make it
Their perch, and not their terror.

ESCALUS: Ay, but yet
Let us be keen, and rather cut a little
Than fall and bruise to death. Alas! this gentleman,
Whom I would save, had a most noble father.
Let but your honour know,
Whom I believe to be most strait in virtue,
That, in the working of your own affections,
Had time coher'd with place, or place with wishing,
Or that the resolute acting of our blood
Could have attain'd th' effect of your own purpose
Whether you had not sometime in your life
Err'd in this point which now you censure him,
And pull'd the law upon you.

ANGELO: 'Tis one thing to be tempted, Escalus,
Another thing to fall. I not deny

The jury, passing on the prisoner's life,
May in the sworn twelve have a thief or two
Guiltier than him they try. What's open made to justice,
That justice seizes. What knows the laws
That thieves do pass on thieves? 'Tis very pregnant,
The jewel that we find, we stoop and take't,
Because we see it; but what we do not see
We tread upon, and never think of it.
You may not so extenuate his offence
For I have had such faults; but rather tell me,
When I, that censure him, do so offend,
Let mine own judgment pattern out my death,
And nothing come in partial. Sir, he must die.

ESCALUS: Be it as your wisdom will.

ANGELO: Where is the Provost?

PROVOST: Here, if it like your honour.

ANGELO: See that Claudio
Be executed by nine to-morrow morning;
Bring him his confessor; let him be prepar'd;
For that's the utmost of his pilgrimage.
   Exit Provost

ESCALUS: *Aside* Well, heaven forgive him! and forgive us all!
Some rise by sin, and some by virtue fall;
Some run from breaks of ice, and answer none,
And some condemned for a fault alone.
   Enter Elbow and Officers with Froth and Pompey

ELBOW: Come, bring them away; if these be good people in a
commonweal that do nothing but use their abuses in common houses,
I know no law; bring them away.

ANGELO: How now, sir! What's your name, and what's the matter?

ELBOW: If it please your honour, I am the poor Duke's constable, and my name is Elbow; I do lean upon justice, sir, and do bring in here before your good honour two notorious benefactors.

ANGELO: Benefactors! Well- what benefactors are they? Are they not malefactors?

ELBOW: If it please your honour, I know not well what they are; but precise villains they are, that I am sure of, and void of all profanation in the world that good Christians ought to have.

ESCALUS: This comes off well; here's a wise officer.

ANGELO: Go to; what quality are they of? Elbow is your name? Why dost thou not speak, Elbow?

POMPEY: He cannot, sir; he's out at elbow.

ANGELO: What are you, sir?

ELBOW: He, sir? A tapster, sir; parcel-bawd; one that serves a bad woman; whose house, sir, was, as they say, pluck'd down in the suburbs; and now she professes a hot-house, which, I think, is a very ill house too.

ESCALUS: How know you that?

ELBOW: My Wife, sir, whom I detest before heaven and your honour-

ESCALUS: How! thy wife!

ELBOW: Ay, sir; whom I thank heaven, is an honest woman-

ESCALUS: Dost thou detest her therefore?

ELBOW: I say, sir, I will detest myself also, as well as she, that this house, if it be not a bawd's house, it is pity of her life, for it is a naughty house.

ESCALUS: How dost thou know that, constable?

ELBOW: Marry, sir, by my wife; who, if she had been a woman cardinally given, might have been accus'd in fornication, adultery, and all uncleanliness there.

ESCALUS: By the woman's means?

ELBOW: Ay, sir, by Mistress Overdone's means; but as she spit in his face, so she defied him.

POMPEY: Sir, if it please your honour, this is not so.

ELBOW: Prove it before these varlets here, thou honourable man, prove it.

ESCALUS: Do you hear how he misplaces?

POMPEY: Sir, she came in great with child; and longing, saving your honour's reverence, for stew'd prunes. Sir, we had but two in the house, which at that very distant time stood, as it were, in a fruit dish, a dish of some three pence; your honours have seen such dishes; they are not China dishes, but very good dishes.

ESCALUS: Go to, go to; no matter for the dish, sir.

POMPEY: No, indeed, sir, not of a pin; you are therein in the right; but to the point. As I say, this Mistress Elbow, being, as I say, with child, and being great-bellied, and longing, as I said, for prunes; and having but two in the dish, as I said, Master Froth here, this very man, having eaten the rest, as I said, and, as I say, paying for them very honestly; for, as you know, Master Froth, I could not give you three pence again-

FROTH: No, indeed.

POMPEY: Very well; you being then, if you be rememb'red, cracking the stones of the foresaid prunes-

FROTH: Ay, so I did indeed.

POMPEY: Why, very well; I telling you then, if you be rememb'red, that such a one and such a one were past cure of the thing you wot of, unless they kept very good diet, as I told you-

FROTH: All this is true.

POMPEY: Why, very well then-

ESCALUS: Come, you are a tedious fool. To the purpose: what was done to Elbow's wife that he hath cause to complain of? Come me to what was done to her.

POMPEY: Sir, your honour cannot come to that yet.

ESCALUS: No, sir, nor I mean it not.

POMPEY: Sir, but you shall come to it, by your honour's leave. And, I beseech you, look into Master Froth here, sir, a man of fourscore pound a year; whose father died at Hallowmas- was't not at Hallowmas, Master Froth?

FROTH: All-hallond eve.

POMPEY: Why, very well; I hope here be truths. He, sir, sitting, as I say, in a lower chair, sir; 'twas in the Bunch of Grapes, where, indeed, you have a delight to sit, have you not?
FROTH: I have so; because it is an open room, and good for winter.

POMPEY: Why, very well then; I hope here be truths.

ANGELO: This will last out a night in Russia,
When nights are longest there; I'll take my leave,

And leave you to the hearing of the cause,
Hoping you'll find good cause to whip them all.

ESCALUS: I think no less. Good morrow to your lordship.
   Exit Angelo
Now, sir, come on; what was done to Elbow's wife, once more?

POMPEY: Once?- sir. There was nothing done to her once.

ELBOW: I beseech you, sir, ask him what this man did to my wife.

POMPEY: I beseech your honour, ask me.

ESCALUS: Well, sir, what did this gentleman to her?

POMPEY: I beseech you, sir, look in this gentleman's face. Good Master Froth, look upon his honour; 'tis for a good purpose. Doth your honour mark his face?

ESCALUS: Ay, sir, very well.

POMPEY: Nay, I beseech you, mark it well.

ESCALUS: Well, I do so.

POMPEY: Doth your honour see any harm in his face?

ESCALUS: Why, no.

POMPEY: I'll be suppos'd upon a book his face is the worst thing about him. Good then; if his face be the worst thing about him, how could Master Froth do the constable's wife any harm? I would know that of your honour.

ESCALUS: He's in the right, constable; what say you to it?

ELBOW: First, an it like you, the house is a respected house; next, this is a respected fellow; and his mistress is a respected woman.

POMPEY: By this hand, sir, his wife is a more respected person than any of us all.

ELBOW: Varlet, thou liest; thou liest, wicket varlet; the time is yet to come that she was ever respected with man, woman, or child.

POMPEY: Sir, she was respected with him before he married with her.

ESCALUS: Which is the wiser here, Justice or Iniquity? Is this true?

ELBOW: O thou caitiff! O thou varlet! O thou wicked Hannibal! I respected with her before I was married to her! If ever I was respected with her, or she with me, let not your worship think me the poor Duke's officer. Prove this, thou wicked Hannibal, or I'll have mine action of batt'ry on thee.

ESCALUS: If he took you a box o' th' ear, you might have your action of slander too.

ELBOW: Marry, I thank your good worship for it. What is't your worship's pleasure I shall do with this wicked caitiff?

ESCALUS: Truly, officer, because he hath some offences in him that thou wouldst discover if thou couldst, let him continue in his courses till thou know'st what they are.

ELBOW: Marry, I thank your worship for it. Thou seest, thou wicked varlet, now, what's come upon thee: thou art to continue now, thou varlet; thou art to continue.

ESCALUS: Where were you born, friend?

FROTH: Here in Vienna, sir.

ESCALUS: Are you of fourscore pounds a year?

FROTH: Yes, an't please you, sir.

ESCALUS: So. What trade are you of, sir?

POMPEY: A tapster, a poor widow's tapster.

ESCALUS: Your mistress' name?

POMPEY: Mistress Overdone.

ESCALUS: Hath she had any more than one husband?

POMPEY: Nine, sir; Overdone by the last.

ESCALUS: Nine! Come hither to me, Master Froth. Master Froth, I would not have you acquainted with tapsters: they will draw you, Master Froth, and you will hang them. Get you gone, and let me hear no more of you.

FROTH: I thank your worship. For mine own part, I never come into any room in a taphouse but I am drawn in.

ESCALUS: Well, no more of it, Master Froth; farewell. *Exit Froth* Come you hither to me, Master Tapster; what's your name, Master Tapster?

POMPEY: Pompey.

ESCALUS: What else?

POMPEY: Bum, sir.

ESCALUS: Troth, and your bum is the greatest thing about you; so that, in the beastliest sense, you are Pompey the Great. Pompey, you are partly a bawd, Pompey, howsoever you colour it in being a tapster. Are you not? Come, tell me true; it shall be the better for you.

POMPEY: Truly, sir, I am a poor fellow that would live.

ESCALUS: How would you live, Pompey- by being a bawd? What do you think of the trade, Pompey? Is it a lawful trade?

POMPEY: If the law would allow it, sir.

ESCALUS: But the law will not allow it, Pompey; nor it shall not be allowed in Vienna.

POMPEY: Does your worship mean to geld and splay all the youth of the city?

ESCALUS: No, Pompey.

POMPEY: Truly, sir, in my poor opinion, they will to't then. If your worship will take order for the drabs and the knaves, you need not to fear the bawds.

ESCALUS: There is pretty orders beginning, I can tell you: but it is but heading and hanging.

POMPEY: If you head and hang all that offend that way but for ten year together, you'll be glad to give out a commission for more heads; if this law hold in Vienna ten year, I'll rent the fairest house in it, after threepence a bay. If you live to see this come to pass, say Pompey told you so.

ESCALUS: Thank you, good Pompey; and, in requital of your prophecy, hark you: I advise you, let me not find you before me again upon any complaint whatsoever- no, not for dwelling where you do; if I do, Pompey, I shall beat you to your tent, and prove a shrewd Caesar to you; in plain dealing, Pompey, I shall have you whipt. So for this time, Pompey, fare you well.

POMPEY: I thank your worship for your good counsel; *Aside* but I shall follow it as the flesh and fortune shall better determine. Whip me? No, no; let carman whip his jade; The valiant heart's not whipt out of his trade.

Exit

ESCALUS: Come hither to me, Master Elbow; come hither, Master

CONSTABLE: How long have you been in this place of constable?

ELBOW: Seven year and a half, sir.

ESCALUS: I thought, by the readiness in the office, you had continued in it some time. You say seven years together?

ELBOW: And a half, sir.

ESCALUS: Alas, it hath been great pains to you! They do you wrong to put you so oft upon't. Are there not men in your ward sufficient to serve it?

ELBOW: Faith, sir, few of any wit in such matters; as they are chosen, they are glad to choose me for them; I do it for some piece of money, and go through with all.

ESCALUS: Look you, bring me in the names of some six or seven, the most sufficient of your parish.

ELBOW: To your worship's house, sir?

ESCALUS: To my house. Fare you well.
   Exit Elbow
What's o'clock, think you?

JUSTICE: Eleven, sir.

ESCALUS: I pray you home to dinner with me.

JUSTICE: I humbly thank you.

ESCALUS: It grieves me for the death of Claudio;

But there's no remedy.

JUSTICE: Lord Angelo is severe.

ESCALUS: It is but needful:
Mercy is not itself that oft looks so;
Pardon is still the nurse of second woe.
But yet, poor Claudio! There is no remedy.
Come, sir.
Exeunt

ACT II. SCENE II. Another Room in Angelo's House
Enter Provost and a Servant

SERVANT: He's hearing of a cause; he will come straight.
I'll tell him of you.

PROVOST: Pray you do.
Exit Servant
I'll know his pleasure; may be he will relent. Alas,
He hath but as offended in a dream!
All sects, all ages, smack of this vice; and he
To die for 't!
Enter Angelo

ANGELO: Now, what's the matter, Provost?

PROVOST: Is it your will Claudio shall die to-morrow?

ANGELO: Did not I tell thee yea? Hadst thou not order?
Why dost thou ask again?

PROVOST: Lest I might be too rash;
Under your good correction, I have seen
When, after execution, judgment hath
Repented o'er his doom.

ANGELO: Go to; let that be mine.
Do you your office, or give up your place,
And you shall well be spar'd.

PROVOST: I crave your honour's pardon.
What shall be done, sir, with the groaning Juliet?
She's very near her hour.

ANGELO: Dispose of her
To some more fitter place, and that with speed.
   Re-enter Servant

SERVANT: Here is the sister of the man condemn'd
Desires access to you.

ANGELO: Hath he a sister?

PROVOST: Ay, my good lord; a very virtuous maid,
And to be shortly of a sisterhood,
If not already.

ANGELO: Well, let her be admitted.
   Exit Servant
See you the fornicatress be remov'd;
Let her have needful but not lavish means;
There shall be order for't.
   Enter Lucio and Isabella

PROVOST: *Going* Save your honour!

ANGELO: Stay a little while.
To Isabella Y'are welcome; what's your will?

ISABELLA: I am a woeful suitor to your honour,
Please but your honour hear me.

ANGELO: Well; what's your suit?

ISABELLA: There is a vice that most I do abhor,
And most desire should meet the blow of justice;
For which I would not plead, but that I must;
For which I must not plead, but that I am
At war 'twixt will and will not.

ANGELO: Well; the matter?

ISABELLA: I have a brother is condemn'd to die;
I do beseech you, let it be his fault,
And not my brother.

PROVOST: *Aside* Heaven give thee moving graces.

ANGELO: Condemn the fault and not the actor of it!
Why, every fault's condemn'd ere it be done;
Mine were the very cipher of a function,
To fine the faults whose fine stands in record,
And let go by the actor.

ISABELLA: O just but severe law!
I had a brother, then. Heaven keep your honour!

LUCIO: *To Isabella* Give't not o'er so; to him again, entreat him,
Kneel down before him, hang upon his gown;
You are too cold: if you should need a pin,
You could not with more tame a tongue desire it.
To him, I say.

ISABELLA: Must he needs die?

ANGELO: Maiden, no remedy.

ISABELLA: Yes; I do think that you might pardon him.
And neither heaven nor man grieve at the mercy.

ANGELO: I will not do't.

ISABELLA: But can you, if you would?

ANGELO: Look, what I will not, that I cannot do.

ISABELLA: But might you do't, and do the world no wrong,
If so your heart were touch'd with that remorse
As mine is to him?

ANGELO: He's sentenc'd; 'tis too late.

LUCIO: *To Isabella* You are too cold.

ISABELLA: Too late? Why, no; I, that do speak a word,
May call it back again. Well, believe this:
No ceremony that to great ones longs,
Not the king's crown nor the deputed sword,
The marshal's truncheon nor the judge's robe,
Become them with one half so good a grace
As mercy does.
If he had been as you, and you as he,
You would have slipp'd like him; but he, like you,
Would not have been so stern.

ANGELO: Pray you be gone.

ISABELLA: I would to heaven I had your potency,
And you were Isabel! Should it then be thus?
No; I would tell what 'twere to be a judge
And what a prisoner.

LUCIO: *To Isabella* Ay, touch him; there's the vein.

ANGELO: Your brother is a forfeit of the law,
And you but waste your words.

ISABELLA: Alas! Alas!
Why, all the souls that were were forfeit once;

And He that might the vantage best have took
Found out the remedy. How would you be
If He, which is the top of judgment, should
But judge you as you are? O, think on that;
And mercy then will breathe within your lips,
Like man new made.

ANGELO: Be you content, fair maid.
It is the law, not I condemn your brother.
Were he my kinsman, brother, or my son,
It should be thus with him. He must die to-morrow.

ISABELLA: To-morrow! O, that's sudden! Spare him, spare him.
He's not prepar'd for death. Even for our kitchens
We kill the fowl of season; shall we serve heaven
With less respect than we do minister
To our gross selves? Good, good my lord, bethink you.
Who is it that hath died for this offence?
There's many have committed it.

LUCIO: *Aside* Ay, well said.

ANGELO: The law hath not been dead, though it hath slept.
Those many had not dar'd to do that evil
If the first that did th' edict infringe
Had answer'd for his deed. Now 'tis awake,
Takes note of what is done, and, like a prophet,
Looks in a glass that shows what future evils-
Either now or by remissness new conceiv'd,
And so in progress to be hatch'd and born-
Are now to have no successive degrees,
But here they live to end.

ISABELLA: Yet show some pity.

ANGELO: I show it most of all when I show justice;
For then I pity those I do not know,

Which a dismiss'd offence would after gall,
And do him right that, answering one foul wrong,
Lives not to act another. Be satisfied;
Your brother dies to-morrow; be content.

ISABELLA: So you must be the first that gives this sentence,
And he that suffers. O, it is excellent
To have a giant's strength! But it is tyrannous
To use it like a giant.

LUCIO: *To Isabella* That's well said.

ISABELLA: Could great men thunder
As Jove himself does, Jove would never be quiet,
For every pelting petty officer
Would use his heaven for thunder,
Nothing but thunder. Merciful Heaven,
Thou rather, with thy sharp and sulphurous bolt,
Splits the unwedgeable and gnarled oak
Than the soft myrtle. But man, proud man,
Dress'd in a little brief authority,
Most ignorant of what he's most assur'd,
His glassy essence, like an angry ape,
Plays such fantastic tricks before high heaven
As makes the angels weep; who, with our speens,
Would all themselves laugh mortal.

LUCIO: *To Isabella* O, to him, to him, wench! He will relent;
He's coming; I perceive 't.

PROVOST: *Aside* Pray heaven she win him.

ISABELLA: We cannot weigh our brother with ourself.
Great men may jest with saints: 'tis wit in them;
But in the less foul profanation.

LUCIO: *To Isabella* Thou'rt i' th' right, girl; more o' that.

ISABELLA: That in the captain's but a choleric word
Which in the soldier is flat blasphemy.

LUCIO: *To Isabella* Art avis'd o' that? More on't.

ANGELO: Why do you put these sayings upon me?

ISABELLA: Because authority, though it err like others,
Hath yet a kind of medicine in itself
That skins the vice o' th' top. Go to your bosom,
Knock there, and ask your heart what it doth know
That's like my brother's fault. If it confess
A natural guiltiness such as is his,
Let it not sound a thought upon your tongue
Against my brother's life.

ANGELO: *Aside* She speaks, and 'tis
Such sense that my sense breeds with it.- Fare you well.

ISABELLA: Gentle my lord, turn back.

ANGELO: I will bethink me. Come again to-morrow.

ISABELLA: Hark how I'll bribe you; good my lord, turn back.

ANGELO: How, bribe me?

ISABELLA: Ay, with such gifts that heaven shall share with you.

LUCIO: *To Isabella)* You had marr'd all else.

ISABELLA: Not with fond sicles of the tested gold,
Or stones, whose rate are either rich or poor
As fancy values them; but with true prayers
That shall be up at heaven and enter there
Ere sun-rise, prayers from preserved souls,
From fasting maids, whose minds are dedicate

To nothing temporal.

ANGELO: Well; come to me to-morrow.

LUCIO: *To Isabella* Go to; 'tis well; away.

ISABELLA: Heaven keep your honour safe!

ANGELO: *Aside* Amen; for I
Am that way going to temptation
Where prayers cross.

ISABELLA: At what hour to-morrow
Shall I attend your lordship?

ANGELO: At any time 'fore noon.

ISABELLA: Save your honour!
   Exeunt All but Angelo

ANGELO: From thee; even from thy virtue!
What's this, what's this? Is this her fault or mine?
The tempter or the tempted, who sins most?
Ha! Not she; nor doth she tempt; but it is I
That, lying by the violet in the sun,
Do as the carrion does, not as the flow'r,
Corrupt with virtuous season. Can it be
That modesty may more betray our sense
Than woman's lightness? Having waste ground enough,
Shall we desire to raze the sanctuary,
And pitch our evils there? O, fie, fie, fie!
What dost thou, or what art thou, Angelo?
Dost thou desire her foully for those things
That make her good? O, let her brother live!
Thieves for their robbery have authority
When judges steal themselves. What, do I love her,
That I desire to hear her speak again,

And feast upon her eyes? What is't I dream on?
O cunning enemy, that, to catch a saint,
With saints dost bait thy hook! Most dangerous
Is that temptation that doth goad us on
To sin in loving virtue. Never could the strumpet,
With all her double vigour, art and nature,
Once stir my temper; but this virtuous maid
Subdues me quite. Ever till now,
When men were fond, I smil'd and wond'red how.
   Exit

ACT II. SCENE III. A Prison
Enter, Severally, Duke, Disguised as a Friar, and Provost

DUKE: Hail to you, Provost! so I think you are.

PROVOST: I am the Provost. What's your will, good friar?

DUKE: Bound by my charity and my blest order,
I come to visit the afflicted spirits
Here in the prison. Do me the common right
To let me see them, and to make me know
The nature of their crimes, that I may minister
To them accordingly.

PROVOST: I would do more than that, if more were needful.
   Enter Juliet
Look, here comes one; a gentlewoman of mine,
Who, falling in the flaws of her own youth,
Hath blister'd her report. She is with child;
And he that got it, sentenc'd- a young man
More fit to do another such offence
Than die for this.

DUKE: When must he die?

PROVOST: As I do think, to-morrow.

To Juliet I have provided for you; stay awhile
And you shall be conducted.

DUKE: Repent you, fair one, of the sin you carry?

JULIET: I do; and bear the shame most patiently.

DUKE: I'll teach you how you shall arraign your conscience,
And try your penitence, if it be sound
Or hollowly put on.

JULIET: I'll gladly learn.

DUKE: Love you the man that wrong'd you?

JULIET: Yes, as I love the woman that wrong'd him.

DUKE: So then, it seems, your most offenceful act
Was mutually committed.

JULIET: Mutually.

DUKE: Then was your sin of heavier kind than his.

JULIET: I do confess it, and repent it, father.

DUKE: 'Tis meet so, daughter; but lest you do repent
As that the sin hath brought you to this shame,
Which sorrow is always toward ourselves, not heaven,
Showing we would not spare heaven as we love it,
But as we stand in fear-

JULIET: I do repent me as it is an evil,
And take the shame with joy.

DUKE: There rest.
Your partner, as I hear, must die to-morrow,

And I am going with instruction to him.
Grace go with you! Benedicite!
Exit

JULIET: Must die to-morrow! O, injurious law,
That respites me a life whose very comfort
Is still a dying horror!

PROVOST: 'Tis pity of him.
Exeunt

ACT II. SCENE IV. Angelo's House

Enter Angelo

ANGELO: When I would pray and think, I think and pray
To several subjects. Heaven hath my empty words,
Whilst my invention, hearing not my tongue,
Anchors on Isabel. Heaven in my mouth,
As if I did but only chew his name,
And in my heart the strong and swelling evil
Of my conception. The state whereon I studied
Is, like a good thing being often read,
Grown sere and tedious; yea, my gravity,
Wherein- let no man hear me- I take pride,
Could I with boot change for an idle plume
Which the air beats for vain. O place, O form,
How often dost thou with thy case, thy habit,
Wrench awe from fools, and tie the wiser souls
To thy false seeming! Blood, thou art blood.
Let's write 'good angel' on the devil's horn;
'Tis not the devil's crest.
Enter Servant
How now, who's there?

SERVANT: One Isabel, a sister, desires access to you.

ANGELO: Teach her the way.

Exit Servant
O heavens! Why does my blood thus muster to my heart,
Making both it unable for itself
And dispossessing all my other parts
Of necessary fitness?
So play the foolish throngs with one that swoons;
Come all to help him, and so stop the air
By which he should revive; and even so
The general subject to a well-wish'd king
Quit their own part, and in obsequious fondness
Crowd to his presence, where their untaught love
Must needs appear offence.
   Enter Isabella
How now, fair maid?

ISABELLA: I am come to know your pleasure.

ANGELO: That you might know it would much better please me
Than to demand what 'tis. Your brother cannot live.

ISABELLA: Even so! Heaven keep your honour!

ANGELO: Yet may he live awhile, and, it may be,
As long as you or I; yet he must die.

ISABELLA: Under your sentence?

ANGELO: Yea.

ISABELLA: When? I beseech you; that in his reprieve,
Longer or shorter, he may be so fitted
That his soul sicken not.

ANGELO: Ha! Fie, these filthy vices! It were as good
To pardon him that hath from nature stol'n
A man already made, as to remit
Their saucy sweetness that do coin heaven's image

In stamps that are forbid; 'tis all as easy
Falsely to take away a life true made
As to put metal in restrained means
To make a false one.

ISABELLA: 'Tis set down so in heaven, but not in earth.

ANGELO: Say you so? Then I shall pose you quickly.
Which had you rather- that the most just law
Now took your brother's life; or, to redeem him,
Give up your body to such sweet uncleanness
As she that he hath stain'd?

ISABELLA: Sir, believe this:
I had rather give my body than my soul.

ANGELO: I talk not of your soul; our compell'd sins
Stand more for number than for accompt.

ISABELLA: How say you?

ANGELO: Nay, I'll not warrant that; for I can speak
Against the thing I say. Answer to this:
I, now the voice of the recorded law,
Pronounce a sentence on your brother's life;
Might there not be a charity in sin
To save this brother's life?

ISABELLA: Please you to do't,
I'll take it as a peril to my soul
It is no sin at all, but charity.

ANGELO: Pleas'd you to do't at peril of your soul,
Were equal poise of sin and charity.

ISABELLA: That I do beg his life, if it be sin,
Heaven let me bear it! You granting of my suit,

If that be sin, I'll make it my morn prayer
To have it added to the faults of mine,
And nothing of your answer.

ANGELO: Nay, but hear me;
Your sense pursues not mine; either you are ignorant
Or seem so, craftily; and that's not good.

ISABELLA: Let me be ignorant, and in nothing good
But graciously to know I am no better.

ANGELO: Thus wisdom wishes to appear most bright
When it doth tax itself; as these black masks
Proclaim an enshielded beauty ten times louder
Than beauty could, display'd. But mark me:
To be received plain, I'll speak more gross-
Your brother is to die.

ISABELLA: So.

ANGELO: And his offence is so, as it appears,
Accountant to the law upon that pain.

ISABELLA: True.

ANGELO: Admit no other way to save his life,
As I subscribe not that, nor any other,
But, in the loss of question, that you, his sister,
Finding yourself desir'd of such a person
Whose credit with the judge, or own great place,
Could fetch your brother from the manacles
Of the all-binding law; and that there were
No earthly mean to save him but that either
You must lay down the treasures of your body
To this supposed, or else to let him suffer-
What would you do?

ISABELLA: As much for my poor brother as myself;
That is, were I under the terms of death,
Th' impression of keen whips I'd wear as rubies,
And strip myself to death as to a bed
That longing have been sick for, ere I'd yield
My body up to shame.

ANGELO: Then must your brother die.

ISABELLA: And 'twere the cheaper way:
Better it were a brother died at once
Than that a sister, by redeeming him,
Should die for ever.

ANGELO: Were not you, then, as cruel as the sentence
That you have slander'd so?

ISABELLA: Ignominy in ransom and free pardon
Are of two houses: lawful mercy
Is nothing kin to foul redemption.

ANGELO: You seem'd of late to make the law a tyrant;
And rather prov'd the sliding of your brother
A merriment than a vice.

ISABELLA: O, pardon me, my lord! It oft falls out,
To have what we would have, we speak not what we mean:
I something do excuse the thing I hate
For his advantage that I dearly love.

ANGELO: We are all frail.

ISABELLA: Else let my brother die,
If not a fedary but only he
Owe and succeed thy weakness.

ANGELO: Nay, women are frail too.

ISABELLA: Ay, as the glasses where they view themselves,
Which are as easy broke as they make forms.
Women, help heaven! Men their creation mar
In profiting by them. Nay, call us ten times frail;
For we are soft as our complexions are,
And credulous to false prints.

ANGELO: I think it well;
And from this testimony of your own sex,
Since I suppose we are made to be no stronger
Than faults may shake our frames, let me be bold.
I do arrest your words. Be that you are,
That is, a woman; if you be more, you're none;
If you be one, as you are well express'd
By all external warrants, show it now
By putting on the destin'd livery.

ISABELLA: I have no tongue but one; gentle, my lord,
Let me intreat you speak the former language.

ANGELO: Plainly conceive, I love you.

ISABELLA: My brother did love Juliet,
And you tell me that he shall die for't.

ANGELO: He shall not, Isabel, if you give me love.

ISABELLA: I know your virtue hath a license in't,
Which seems a little fouler than it is,
To pluck on others.

ANGELO: Believe me, on mine honour,
My words express my purpose.

ISABELLA: Ha! little honour to be much believ'd,
And most pernicious purpose! Seeming, seeming!
I will proclaim thee, Angelo, look for't.

Sign me a present pardon for my brother
Or, with an outstretch'd throat, I'll tell the world aloud
What man thou art.

ANGELO: Who will believe thee, Isabel?
My unsoil'd name, th' austereness of my life,
My vouch against you, and my place i' th' state,
Will so your accusation overweigh
That you shall stifle in your own report,
And smell of calumny. I have begun,
And now I give my sensual race the rein:
Fit thy consent to my sharp appetite;
Lay by all nicety and prolixious blushes
That banish what they sue for; redeem thy brother
By yielding up thy body to my will;
Or else he must not only die the death,
But thy unkindness shall his death draw out
To ling'ring sufferance. Answer me to-morrow,
Or, by the affection that now guides me most,
I'll prove a tyrant to him. As for you,
Say what you can: my false o'erweighs your true.
  Exit

ISABELLA: To whom should I complain? Did I tell this,
Who would believe me? O perilous mouths
That bear in them one and the self-same tongue
Either of condemnation or approof,
Bidding the law make curtsy to their will;
Hooking both right and wrong to th' appetite,
To follow as it draws! I'll to my brother.
Though he hath fall'n by prompture of the blood,
Yet hath he in him such a mind of honour
That, had he twenty heads to tender down
On twenty bloody blocks, he'd yield them up
Before his sister should her body stoop
To such abhorr'd pollution.
Then, Isabel, live chaste, and, brother, die:

More than our brother is our chastity.
I'll tell him yet of Angelo's request,
And fit his mind to death, for his soul's rest.
  Exit

ACT III. SCENE I. The Prison
Enter Duke, Disguised as Before, Claudio, and Provost

DUKE: So, then you hope of pardon from Lord Angelo?

CLAUDIO: The miserable have no other medicine
But only hope: I have hope to Eve, and am prepar'd to die.

DUKE: Be absolute for death; either death or life
Shall thereby be the sweeter. Reason thus with life.
If I do lose thee, I do lose a thing
That none but fools would keep. A breath thou art,
Servile to all the skyey influences,
That dost this habitation where thou keep'st
Hourly afflict. Merely, thou art Death's fool;
For him thou labour'st by thy flight to shun
And yet run'st toward him still. Thou art not noble;
For all th' accommodations that thou bear'st
Are nurs'd by baseness. Thou 'rt by no means valiant;
For thou dost fear the soft and tender fork
Of a poor worm. Thy best of rest is sleep,
And that thou oft provok'st; yet grossly fear'st
Thy death, which is no more. Thou art not thyself;
For thou exists on many a thousand grains
That issue out of dust. Happy thou art not;
For what thou hast not, still thou striv'st to get,
And what thou hast, forget'st. Thou art not certain;
For thy complexion shifts to strange effects,
After the moon. If thou art rich, thou'rt poor;
For, like an ass whose back with ingots bows,
Thou bear'st thy heavy riches but a journey,
And Death unloads thee. Friend hast thou none;

For thine own bowels which do call thee sire,
The mere effusion of thy proper loins,
Do curse the gout, serpigo, and the rheum,
For ending thee no sooner. Thou hast nor youth nor age,
But, as it were, an after-dinner's sleep,
Dreaming on both; for all thy blessed youth
Becomes as aged, and doth beg the alms
Of palsied eld; and when thou art old and rich,
Thou hast neither heat, affection, limb, nor beauty,
To make thy riches pleasant. What's yet in this
That bears the name of life? Yet in this life
Lie hid moe thousand deaths; yet death we fear,
That makes these odds all even.

CLAUDIO: I humbly thank you.
To sue to live, I find I seek to die;
And, seeking death, find life. Let it come on.

ISABELLA: *Within* What, ho! Peace here; grace and good company!

PROVOST: Who's there? Come in; the wish deserves a welcome.

DUKE: Dear sir, ere long I'll visit you again.

CLAUDIO: Most holy sir, I thank you.
  Enter Isabella

ISABELLA: My business is a word or two with Claudio.

PROVOST: And very welcome. Look, signior, here's your sister.

DUKE: Provost, a word with you.

PROVOST: As many as you please.

DUKE: Bring me to hear them speak, where I may be conceal'd.
  Exeunt Duke and Provost

CLAUDIO: Now, sister, what's the comfort?

ISABELLA: Why,
As all comforts are; most good, most good, indeed.
Lord Angelo, having affairs to heaven,
Intends you for his swift ambassador,
Where you shall be an everlasting leiger.
Therefore, your best appointment make with speed;
To-morrow you set on.

CLAUDIO: Is there no remedy?

ISABELLA: None, but such remedy as, to save a head,
To cleave a heart in twain.

CLAUDIO: But is there any?

ISABELLA: Yes, brother, you may live:
There is a devilish mercy in the judge,
If you'll implore it, that will free your life,
But fetter you till death.

CLAUDIO: Perpetual durance?

ISABELLA: Ay, just; perpetual durance, a restraint,
Though all the world's vastidity you had,
To a determin'd scope.

CLAUDIO: But in what nature?

ISABELLA: In such a one as, you consenting to't,
Would bark your honour from that trunk you bear,
And leave you naked.

CLAUDIO: Let me know the point.

ISABELLA: O, I do fear thee, Claudio; and I quake,

Lest thou a feverous life shouldst entertain,
And six or seven winters more respect
Than a perpetual honour. Dar'st thou die?
The sense of death is most in apprehension;
And the poor beetle that we tread upon
In corporal sufferance finds a pang as great
As when a giant dies.

CLAUDIO: Why give you me this shame?
Think you I can a resolution fetch
From flow'ry tenderness? If I must die,
I will encounter darkness as a bride
And hug it in mine arms.

ISABELLA: There spake my brother; there my father's grave
Did utter forth a voice. Yes, thou must die:
Thou art too noble to conserve a life
In base appliances. This outward-sainted deputy,
Whose settled visage and deliberate word
Nips youth i' th' head, and follies doth enew
As falcon doth the fowl, is yet a devil;
His filth within being cast, he would appear
A pond as deep as hell.

CLAUDIO: The precise Angelo!

ISABELLA: O, 'tis the cunning livery of hell
The damned'st body to invest and cover
In precise guards! Dost thou think, Claudio,
If I would yield him my virginity
Thou mightst be freed?

CLAUDIO: O heavens! it cannot be.

ISABELLA: Yes, he would give't thee, from this rank offence,
So to offend him still. This night's the time
That I should do what I abhor to name,

Or else thou diest to-morrow.

CLAUDIO: Thou shalt not do't.

ISABELLA: O, were it but my life!
I'd throw it down for your deliverance
As frankly as a pin.

CLAUDIO: Thanks, dear Isabel.

ISABELLA: Be ready, Claudio, for your death to-morrow.

CLAUDIO: Yes. Has he affections in him
That thus can make him bite the law by th' nose
When he would force it? Sure it is no sin;
Or of the deadly seven it is the least.

ISABELLA: Which is the least?

CLAUDIO: If it were damnable, he being so wise,
Why would he for the momentary trick
Be perdurably fin'd?- O Isabel!

ISABELLA: What says my brother?

CLAUDIO: Death is a fearful thing.

ISABELLA: And shamed life a hateful.

CLAUDIO: Ay, but to die, and go we know not where;
To lie in cold obstruction, and to rot;
This sensible warm motion to become
A kneaded clod; and the delighted spirit
To bathe in fiery floods or to reside
In thrilling region of thick-ribbed ice;
To be imprison'd in the viewless winds,
And blown with restless violence round about

The pendent world; or to be worse than worst
Of those that lawless and incertain thought
Imagine howling- 'tis too horrible.
The weariest and most loathed worldly life
That age, ache, penury, and imprisonment,
Can lay on nature is a paradise
To what we fear of death.

ISABELLA: Alas, alas!

CLAUDIO: Sweet sister, let me live.
What sin you do to save a brother's life,
Nature dispenses with the deed so far
That it becomes a virtue.

ISABELLA: O you beast!
O faithless coward! O dishonest wretch!
Wilt thou be made a man out of my vice?
Is't not a kind of incest to take life
From thine own sister's shame? What should I think?
Heaven shield my mother play'd my father fair!
For such a warped slip of wilderness
Ne'er issu'd from his blood. Take my defiance;
Die; perish. Might but my bending down
Reprieve thee from thy fate, it should proceed.
I'll pray a thousand prayers for thy death,
No word to save thee.

CLAUDIO: Nay, hear me, Isabel.

ISABELLA: O fie, fie, fie!
Thy sin's not accidental, but a trade.
Mercy to thee would prove itself a bawd;
'Tis best that thou diest quickly.

CLAUDIO: O, hear me, Isabella.
    Re-enter Duke

DUKE: Vouchsafe a word, young sister, but one word.

ISABELLA: What is your will?

DUKE: Might you dispense with your leisure, I would by and by have some speech with you; the satisfaction I would require is likewise your own benefit.

ISABELLA: I have no superfluous leisure; my stay must be stolen out of other affairs; but I will attend you awhile.
    Walks Apart

DUKE: Son, I have overheard what hath pass'd between you and your sister. Angelo had never the purpose to corrupt her; only he hath made an assay of her virtue to practise his judgment with the disposition of natures. She, having the truth of honour in her, hath made him that gracious denial which he is most glad to receive. I am confessor to Angelo, and I know this to be true; therefore prepare yourself to death. Do not satisfy your resolution with hopes that are fallible; to-morrow you must die; go to your knees and make ready.

CLAUDIO: Let me ask my sister pardon. I am so out of love with life that I will sue to be rid of it.

DUKE: Hold you there. Farewell.
    Exit Claudio
Provost, a word with you.
    Re-enter Provost

PROVOST: What's your will, father?

DUKE: That, now you are come, you will be gone. Leave me a while with the maid; my mind promises with my habit no loss shall touch her by my company.

PROVOST: In good time.

Exit Provost

DUKE: The hand that hath made you fair hath made you good; the
goodness that is cheap in beauty makes beauty brief in goodness;
but grace, being the soul of your complexion, shall keep the body
of it ever fair. The assault that Angelo hath made to you,
fortune hath convey'd to my understanding; and, but that frailty
hath examples for his falling, I should wonder at Angelo. How
will you do to content this substitute, and to save your brother?

ISABELLA: I am now going to resolve him; I had rather my brother
die by the law than my son should be unlawfully born. But, O, how
much is the good Duke deceiv'd in Angelo! If ever he return, and
I can speak to him, I will open my lips in vain, or discover his government.

DUKE: That shall not be much amiss; yet, as the matter now stands,
he will avoid your accusation: he made trial of you only.
Therefore fasten your ear on my advisings; to the love I have in
doing good a remedy presents itself. I do make myself believe
that you may most uprighteously do a poor wronged lady a merited
benefit; redeem your brother from the angry law; do no stain to
your own gracious person; and much please the absent Duke, if
peradventure he shall ever return to have hearing of this business.

ISABELLA: Let me hear you speak farther; I have spirit to do
anything that appears not foul in the truth of my spirit.

DUKE: Virtue is bold, and goodness never fearful. Have you not
heard speak of Mariana, the sister of Frederick, the great
soldier who miscarried at sea?

ISABELLA: I have heard of the lady, and good words went with her name.

DUKE: She should this Angelo have married; was affianced to her by
oath, and the nuptial appointed; between which time of the
contract and limit of the solemnity her brother Frederick was
wreck'd at sea, having in that perished vessel the dowry of his

sister. But mark how heavily this befell to the poor gentlewoman: there she lost a noble and renowned brother, in his love toward her ever most kind and natural; with him the portion and sinew of her fortune, her marriage-dowry; with both, her combinate husband, this well-seeming Angelo.

ISABELLA: Can this be so? Did Angelo so leave her?

DUKE: Left her in her tears, and dried not one of them with his comfort; swallowed his vows whole, pretending in her discoveries of dishonour; in few, bestow'd her on her own lamentation, which she yet wears for his sake; and he, a marble to her tears, is washed with them, but relents not.

ISABELLA: What a merit were it in death to take this poor maid from the world! What corruption in this life that it will let this man live! But how out of this can she avail?

DUKE: It is a rupture that you may easily heal; and the cure of it not only saves your brother, but keeps you from dishonour in doing it.

ISABELLA: Show me how, good father.

DUKE: This forenamed maid hath yet in her the continuance of her first affection; his unjust unkindness, that in all reason should have quenched her love, hath, like an impediment in the current, made it more violent and unruly. Go you to Angelo; answer his requiring with a plausible obedience; agree with his demands to the point; only refer yourself to this advantage: first, that your stay with him may not be long; that the time may have all shadow and silence in it; and the place answer to convenience. This being granted in course- and now follows all: we shall advise this wronged maid to stead up your appointment, go in your place. If the encounter acknowledge itself hereafter, it may compel him to her recompense; and here, by this, is your brother saved, your honour untainted, the poor Mariana advantaged, and the corrupt deputy scaled. The maid will I frame and make fit for

his attempt. If you think well to carry this as you may, the
doubleness of the benefit defends the deceit from reproof. What
think you of it?

ISABELLA: The image of it gives me content already; and I trust it
will grow to a most prosperous perfection.

DUKE: It lies much in your holding up. Haste you speedily to
Angelo; if for this night he entreat you to his bed, give him
promise of satisfaction. I will presently to Saint Luke's; there,
at the moated grange, resides this dejected Mariana. At that
place call upon me; and dispatch with Angelo, that it may be
quickly.

ISABELLA: I thank you for this comfort. Fare you well, good father.
Exeunt Severally

ACT III. SCENE II. The Street Before the Prison
*Enter, on One Side, Duke Disguised as Before; on the Other, Elbow, and
Officers with Pompey*

ELBOW: Nay, if there be no remedy for it, but that you will needs
buy and sell men and women like beasts, we shall have all the
world drink brown and white bastard.

DUKE: O heavens! what stuff is here?

POMPEY: 'Twas never merry world since, of two usuries, the merriest
was put down, and the worser allow'd by order of law a furr'd
gown to keep him warm; and furr'd with fox on lamb-skins too, to
signify that craft, being richer than innocency, stands for the facing.

ELBOW: Come your way, sir. Bless you, good father friar.

DUKE: And you, good brother father. What offence hath this man made
you, sir?

ELBOW: Marry, sir, he hath offended the law; and, sir, we take him
to be a thief too, sir, for we have found upon him, sir, a
strange picklock, which we have sent to the deputy.

DUKE: Fie, sirrah, a bawd, a wicked bawd!
The evil that thou causest to be done,
That is thy means to live. Do thou but think
What 'tis to cram a maw or clothe a back
From such a filthy vice; say to thyself
'From their abominable and beastly touches
I drink, I eat, array myself, and live.'
Canst thou believe thy living is a life,
So stinkingly depending? Go mend, go mend.

POMPEY: Indeed, it does stink in some sort, sir; but yet, sir,
I would prove-

DUKE: Nay, if the devil have given thee proofs for sin,
Thou wilt prove his. Take him to prison, officer;
Correction and instruction must both work
Ere this rude beast will profit.

ELBOW: He must before the deputy, sir; he has given him warning.
The deputy cannot abide a whoremaster; if he be a whoremonger,
and comes before him, he were as good go a mile on his errand.

DUKE: That we were all, as some would seem to be,
From our faults, as his faults from seeming, free.

ELBOW: His neck will come to your waist- a cord, sir.
  Enter Lucio

POMPEY: I spy comfort; I cry bail. Here's a gentleman, and a friend of mine.

LUCIO: How now, noble Pompey! What, at the wheels of Caesar? Art
thou led in triumph? What, is there none of Pygmalion's images,
newly made woman, to be had now for putting the hand in the

pocket and extracting it clutch'd? What reply, ha? What say'st thou to this tune, matter, and method? Is't not drown'd i' th' last rain, ha? What say'st thou, trot? Is the world as it was, man? Which is the way? Is it sad, and few words? or how? The trick of it?

DUKE: Still thus, and thus; still worse!

LUCIO: How doth my dear morsel, thy mistress? Procures she still, ha?

POMPEY: Troth, sir, she hath eaten up all her beef, and she is herself in the tub.

LUCIO: Why, 'tis good; it is the right of it; it must be so; ever your fresh whore and your powder'd bawd- an unshunn'd consequence; it must be so. Art going to prison, Pompey?

POMPEY: Yes, faith, sir.

LUCIO: Why, 'tis not amiss, Pompey. Farewell; go, say I sent thee thither. For debt, Pompey- or how?

ELBOW: For being a bawd, for being a bawd.

LUCIO: Well, then, imprison him. If imprisonment be the due of a bawd, why, 'tis his right. Bawd is he doubtless, and of antiquity, too; bawd-born. Farewell, good Pompey. Commend me to the prison, Pompey. You will turn good husband now, Pompey; you will keep the house.

POMPEY: I hope, sir, your good worship will be my bail.

LUCIO: No, indeed, will I not, Pompey; it is not the wear. I will pray, Pompey, to increase your bondage. If you take it not patiently, why, your mettle is the more. Adieu trusty Pompey. Bless you, friar.

DUKE: And you.

LUCIO: Does Bridget paint still, Pompey, ha?

ELBOW: Come your ways, sir; come.

POMPEY: You will not bail me then, sir?

LUCIO: Then, Pompey, nor now. What news abroad, friar? what news?

ELBOW: Come your ways, sir; come.

LUCIO: Go to kennel, Pompey, go.
  Exeunt Elbow, Pompey and Officers
What news, friar, of the Duke?

DUKE: I know none. Can you tell me of any?

LUCIO: Some say he is with the Emperor of Russia; other some, he is
in Rome; but where is he, think you?

DUKE: I know not where; but wheresoever, I wish him well.

LUCIO: It was a mad fantastical trick of him to steal from the
state and usurp the beggary he was never born to. Lord Angelo
dukes it well in his absence; he puts transgression to't.

DUKE: He does well in't.

LUCIO: A little more lenity to lechery would do no harm in him;
something too crabbed that way, friar.

DUKE: It is too general a vice, and severity must cure it.

LUCIO: Yes, in good sooth, the vice is of a great kindred; it is
well allied; but it is impossible to extirp it quite, friar, till
eating and drinking be put down. They say this Angelo was not

made by man and woman after this downright way of creation. Is it true, think you?

DUKE: How should he be made, then?

LUCIO: Some report a sea-maid spawn'd him; some, that he was begot between two stock-fishes. But it is certain that when he makes water his urine is congeal'd ice; that I know to be true. And he is a motion generative; that's infallible.

DUKE: You are pleasant, sir, and speak apace.

LUCIO: Why, what a ruthless thing is this in him, for the rebellion of a codpiece to take away the life of a man! Would the Duke that is absent have done this? Ere he would have hang'd a man for the getting a hundred bastards, he would have paid for the nursing a thousand. He had some feeling of the sport; he knew the service, and that instructed him to mercy.

DUKE: I never heard the absent Duke much detected for women; he was not inclin'd that way.

LUCIO: O, sir, you are deceiv'd.

DUKE: 'Tis not possible.

LUCIO: Who- not the Duke? Yes, your beggar of fifty; and his use was to put a ducat in her clack-dish. The Duke had crotchets in him. He would be drunk too; that let me inform you.

DUKE: You do him wrong, surely.

LUCIO: Sir, I was an inward of his. A shy fellow was the Duke; and I believe I know the cause of his withdrawing.

DUKE: What, I prithee, might be the cause?

LUCIO: No, pardon; 'tis a secret must be lock'd within the teeth and the lips; but this I can let you understand: the greater file of the subject held the Duke to be wise.

DUKE: Wise? Why, no question but he was.

LUCIO: A very superficial, ignorant, unweighing fellow.

DUKE: Either this is envy in you, folly, or mistaking; the very stream of his life, and the business he hath helmed, must, upon a warranted need, give him a better proclamation. Let him be but testimonied in his own bringings-forth, and he shall appear to the envious a scholar, a statesman, and a soldier. Therefore you speak unskilfully; or, if your knowledge be more, it is much dark'ned in your malice.

LUCIO: Sir, I know him, and I love him.

DUKE: Love talks with better knowledge, and knowledge with dearer love.

LUCIO: Come, sir, I know what I know.

DUKE: I can hardly believe that, since you know not what you speak. But, if ever the Duke return, as our prayers are he may, let me desire you to make your answer before him. If it be honest you have spoke, you have courage to maintain it; I am bound to call upon you; and I pray you your name?

LUCIO: Sir, my name is Lucio, well known to the Duke.

DUKE: He shall know you better, sir, if I may live to report you.

LUCIO: I fear you not.

DUKE: O, you hope the Duke will return no more; or you imagine me too unhurtful an opposite. But, indeed, I can do you little harm: you'll forswear this again.

LUCIO: I'll be hang'd first. Thou art deceiv'd in me, friar. But no more of this. Canst thou tell if Claudio die to-morrow or no?

DUKE: Why should he die, sir?

LUCIO: Why? For filling a bottle with a tun-dish. I would the Duke we talk of were return'd again. This ungenitur'd agent will unpeople the province with continency; sparrows must not build in his house-eaves because they are lecherous. The Duke yet would have dark deeds darkly answered; he would never bring them to light. Would he were return'd! Marry, this Claudio is condemned for untrussing. Farewell, good friar; I prithee pray for me. The Duke, I say to thee again, would eat mutton on Fridays. He's not past it yet; and, I say to thee, he would mouth with a beggar though she smelt brown bread and garlic. Say that I said so. Farewell.
 Exit

DUKE: No might nor greatness in mortality
Can censure scape; back-wounding calumny
The whitest virtue strikes. What king so strong
Can tie the gall up in the slanderous tongue?
But who comes here?
 Enter Escalus, Provost, and Officers with Mistress Overdone

ESCALUS: Go, away with her to prison.

MRS. OVERDONE: Good my lord, be good to me; your honour is accounted a merciful man; good my lord.

ESCALUS: Double and treble admonition, and still forfeit in the same kind! This would make mercy swear and play the tyrant.

PROVOST: A bawd of eleven years' continuance, may it please your honour.

MRS. OVERDONE: My lord, this is one Lucio's information against me.

Mistress Kate Keepdown was with child by him in the Duke's time;
he promis'd her marriage. His child is a year and a quarter old
come Philip and Jacob; I have kept it myself; and see how he goes
about to abuse me.

ESCALUS: That fellow is a fellow of much license. Let him be call'd
before us. Away with her to prison. Go to; no more words.
  Exeunt Officers with Mistress Overdone
Provost, my brother Angelo will
not be alter'd: Claudio must die to-morrow. Let him be furnish'd
with divines, and have all charitable preparation. If my brother
wrought by my pity, it should not be so with him.

PROVOST: So please you, this friar hath been with him, and advis'd
him for th' entertainment of death.

ESCALUS: Good even, good father.

DUKE: Bliss and goodness on you!

ESCALUS: Of whence are you?

DUKE: Not of this country, though my chance is now
To use it for my time. I am a brother
Of gracious order, late come from the See
In special business from his Holiness.

ESCALUS: What news abroad i' th' world?

DUKE: None, but that there is so great a fever on goodness that the
dissolution of it must cure it. Novelty is only in request; and,
as it is, as dangerous to be aged in any kind of course as it is
virtuous to be constant in any undertaking. There is scarce
truth enough alive to make societies secure; but security enough
to make fellowships accurst. Much upon this riddle runs the
wisdom of the world. This news is old enough, yet it is every
day's news. I pray you, sir, of what disposition was the Duke?

ESCALUS: One that, above all other strifes, contended especially to know himself.

DUKE: What pleasure was he given to?

ESCALUS: Rather rejoicing to see another merry than merry at anything which profess'd to make him rejoice; a gentleman of all temperance. But leave we him to his events, with a prayer they may prove prosperous; and let me desire to know how you find Claudio prepar'd. I am made to understand that you have lent him visitation.

DUKE: He professes to have received no sinister measure from his judge, but most willingly humbles himself to the determination of justice. Yet had he framed to himself, by the instruction of his frailty, many deceiving promises of life; which I, by my good leisure, have discredited to him, and now he is resolv'd to die.

ESCALUS: You have paid the heavens your function, and the prisoner the very debt of your calling. I have labour'd for the poor gentleman to the extremest shore of my modesty; but my brother justice have I found so severe that he hath forc'd me to tell him he is indeed Justice.

DUKE: If his own life answer the straitness of his proceeding, it shall become him well; wherein if he chance to fail, he hath sentenc'd himself.

ESCALUS: I am going to visit the prisoner. Fare you well.

DUKE: Peace be with you!
Exeunt Escalus and Provost
   He who the sword of heaven will bear
   Should be as holy as severe;
   Pattern in himself to know,
   Grace to stand, and virtue go;
   More nor less to others paying

Than by self-offences weighing.
Shame to him whose cruel striking
Kills for faults of his own liking!
Twice treble shame on Angelo,
To weed my vice and let his grow!
O, what may man within him hide,
Though angel on the outward side!
How may likeness, made in crimes,
Make a practice on the times,
To draw with idle spiders' strings
Most ponderous and substantial things!
Craft against vice I must apply.
With Angelo to-night shall lie
His old betrothed but despised;
So disguise shall, by th' disguised,
Pay with falsehood false exacting,
And perform an old contracting. *Exit*

ACT IV. SCENE I. The Moated Grange at Saint Duke's

Enter Mariana; and Boy Singing
                    SONG
  Take, O, take those lips away,
    That so sweetly were forsworn;
  And those eyes, the break of day,
    Lights that do mislead the morn;
  But my kisses bring again, bring again;
  Seals of love, but seal'd in vain, seal'd in vain.
Enter Duke, Disguised as Before

MARIANA: Break off thy song, and haste thee quick away;
Here comes a man of comfort, whose advice
Hath often still'd my brawling discontent.
  Exit Boy
I cry you mercy, sir, and well could wish
You had not found me here so musical.
Let me excuse me, and believe me so,
My mirth it much displeas'd, but pleas'd my woe.

DUKE: 'Tis good; though music oft hath such a charm
To make bad good and good provoke to harm.
I pray you tell me hath anybody inquir'd for me here to-day. Much
upon this time have I promis'd here to meet.

MARIANA: You have not been inquir'd after; I have sat here all day.
Enter Isabella

DUKE: I do constantly believe you. The time is come even now. I
shall crave your forbearance a little. May be I will call upon
you anon, for some advantage to yourself.

MARIANA: I am always bound to you.
Exit

DUKE: Very well met, and well come.
What is the news from this good deputy?

ISABELLA: He hath a garden circummur'd with brick,
Whose western side is with a vineyard back'd;
And to that vineyard is a planched gate
That makes his opening with this bigger key;
This other doth command a little door
Which from the vineyard to the garden leads.
There have I made my promise
Upon the heavy middle of the night
To call upon him.

DUKE: But shall you on your knowledge find this way?

ISABELLA: I have ta'en a due and wary note upon't;
With whispering and most guilty diligence,
In action all of precept, he did show me
The way twice o'er.

DUKE: Are there no other tokens
Between you 'greed concerning her observance?

ISABELLA: No, none, but only a repair i' th' dark;
And that I have possess'd him my most stay
Can be but brief; for I have made him know
I have a servant comes with me along,
That stays upon me; whose persuasion is
I come about my brother.

DUKE: 'Tis well borne up.
I have not yet made known to Mariana
A word of this. What ho, within! come forth.
　　Re-enter Mariana
I pray you be acquainted with this maid;
She comes to do you good.

ISABELLA: I do desire the like.

DUKE: Do you persuade yourself that I respect you?

MARIANA: Good friar, I know you do, and have found it.

DUKE: Take, then, this your companion by the hand,
Who hath a story ready for your ear.
I shall attend your leisure; but make haste;
The vaporous night approaches.

MARIANA: Will't please you walk aside?
　　Exeunt Mariana and Isabella

DUKE: O place and greatness! Millions of false eyes
Are stuck upon thee. Volumes of report
Run with these false, and most contrarious quest
Upon thy doings. Thousand escapes of wit
Make thee the father of their idle dream,
And rack thee in their fancies.
　　Re-enter Mariana and Isabella
Welcome, how agreed?

ISABELLA: She'll take the enterprise upon her, father,
If you advise it.

DUKE: It is not my consent,
But my entreaty too.

ISABELLA: Little have you to say,
When you depart from him, but, soft and low,
'Remember now my brother.'

MARIANA: Fear me not.

DUKE: Nor, gentle daughter, fear you not at all.
He is your husband on a pre-contract.
To bring you thus together 'tis no sin,
Sith that the justice of your title to him
Doth flourish the deceit. Come, let us go;
Our corn's to reap, for yet our tithe's to sow.
   Exeunt

ACT IV. SCENE II. The Prison

Enter Provost and Pompey

PROVOST: Come hither, sirrah. Can you cut off a man's head?

POMPEY: If the man be a bachelor, sir, I can; but if he be a
married man, he's his wife's head, and I can never cut off a woman's head.

PROVOST: Come, sir, leave me your snatches and yield me a direct
answer. To-morrow morning are to die Claudio and Barnardine. Here
is in our prison a common executioner, who in his office lacks a
helper; if you will take it on you to assist him, it shall redeem
you from your gyves; if not, you shall have your full time of
imprisonment, and your deliverance with an unpitied whipping, for
you have been a notorious bawd.

POMPEY: Sir, I have been an unlawful bawd time out of mind; but yet

I will be content to be a lawful hangman. I would be glad to
receive some instructions from my fellow partner.

PROVOST: What ho, Abhorson! Where's Abhorson there?
Enter Abhorson

ABHORSON: Do you call, sir?

PROVOST: Sirrah, here's a fellow will help you to-morrow in your
execution. If you think it meet, compound with him by the year,
and let him abide here with you; if not, use him for the present,
and dismiss him. He cannot plead his estimation with you; he hath
been a bawd.

ABHORSON: A bawd, sir? Fie upon him! He will discredit our mystery.

PROVOST: Go to, sir; you weigh equally; a feather will turn the scale.
Exit

POMPEY: Pray, sir, by your good favour- for surely, sir, a good
favour you have but that you have a hanging look- do you call,
sir, your occupation a mystery?

ABHORSON: Ay, sir; a mystery.

POMPEY: Painting, sir, I have heard say, is a mystery; and your
whores, sir, being members of my occupation, using painting, do
prove my occupation a mystery; but what mystery there should be
in hanging, if I should be hang'd, I cannot imagine.

ABHORSON: Sir, it is a mystery.

POMPEY: Proof?

ABHORSON: Every true man's apparel fits your thief: if it be too
little for your thief, your true man thinks it big enough; if it
be too big for your thief, your thief thinks it little enough; so

every true man's apparel fits your thief.
Re-enter Provost

PROVOST: Are you agreed?

POMPEY: Sir, I will serve him; for I do find your hangman is a more
penitent trade than your bawd; he doth oftener ask forgiveness.

PROVOST: You, sirrah, provide your block and your axe to-morrow
four o'clock.

ABHORSON: Come on, bawd; I will instruct thee in my trade; follow.

POMPEY: I do desire to learn, sir; and I hope, if you have occasion
to use me for your own turn, you shall find me yare; for truly,
sir, for your kindness I owe you a good turn.

PROVOST: Call hither Barnardine and Claudio.
Exeunt Abhorson and Pompey
Th' one has my pity; not a jot the other,
Being a murderer, though he were my brother.
Enter Claudio
Look, here's the warrant, Claudio, for thy death;
'Tis now dead midnight, and by eight to-morrow
Thou must be made immortal. Where's Barnardine?

CLAUDIO: As fast lock'd up in sleep as guiltless labour
When it lies starkly in the traveller's bones.
He will not wake.

PROVOST: Who can do good on him?
Well, go, prepare yourself. *Knocking Within* But hark, what noise?
Heaven give your spirits comfort! *Exit Claudio*
Knocking Continues By and by.
I hope it is some pardon or reprieve
For the most gentle Claudio.
Enter Duke, Disguised as Before

Welcome, father.

DUKE: The best and wholesom'st spirits of the night
Envelop you, good Provost! Who call'd here of late?

PROVOST: None, since the curfew rung.

DUKE: Not Isabel?

PROVOST: No.

DUKE: They will then, ere't be long.

PROVOST: What comfort is for Claudio?

DUKE: There's some in hope.

PROVOST: It is a bitter deputy.

DUKE: Not so, not so; his life is parallel'd
Even with the stroke and line of his great justice;
He doth with holy abstinence subdue
That in himself which he spurs on his pow'r
To qualify in others. Were he meal'd with that
Which he corrects, then were he tyrannous;
But this being so, he's just. *Knocking Within* Now are they come.
    Exit Provost
This is a gentle provost; seldom when
The steeled gaoler is the friend of men. *Knocking Within*
How now, what noise! That spirit's possess'd with haste
That wounds th' unsisting postern with these strokes.
    Re-enter Provost

PROVOST: There he must stay until the officer
Arise to let him in; he is call'd up.

DUKE: Have you no countermand for Claudio yet

But he must die to-morrow?

PROVOST: None, sir, none.

DUKE: As near the dawning, Provost, as it is,
You shall hear more ere morning.

PROVOST: Happily
You something know; yet I believe there comes
No countermand; no such example have we.
Besides, upon the very siege of justice,
Lord Angelo hath to the public ear
Profess'd the contrary.
 Enter Messenger
This is his lordship's man.

DUKE: And here comes Claudio's pardon.

MESSENGER: My lord hath sent you this note; and by me this further
charge, that you swerve not from the smallest article of it,
neither in time, matter, or other circumstance. Good morrow; for
as I take it, it is almost day.

PROVOST: I shall obey him.
 Exit Messenger

DUKE: *Aside* This is his pardon, purchas'd by such sin
For which the pardoner himself is in;
Hence hath offence his quick celerity,
When it is borne in high authority.
When vice makes mercy, mercy's so extended
That for the fault's love is th' offender friended.
Now, sir, what news?

PROVOST: I told you: Lord Angelo, belike thinking me remiss in mine
office, awakens me with this unwonted putting-on; methinks
strangely, for he hath not us'd it before.

DUKE: Pray you, let's hear.

PROVOST: *Reads* 'Whatsoever you may hear to the contrary, let
Claudio be executed by four of the clock, and, in the afternoon,

BARNARDINE: For my better satisfaction, let me have Claudio's
head sent me by five. Let this be duly performed, with a thought
that more depends on it than we must yet deliver. Thus fail not
to do your office, as you will answer it at your peril.'
What say you to this, sir?

DUKE: What is that Barnardine who is to be executed in th'
afternoon?

PROVOST: A Bohemian born; but here nurs'd up and bred.
One that is a prisoner nine years old.

DUKE: How came it that the absent Duke had not either deliver'd him
to his liberty or executed him? I have heard it was ever his
manner to do so.

PROVOST: His friends still wrought reprieves for him; and, indeed,
his fact, till now in the government of Lord Angelo, came not to
an undoubted proof.

DUKE: It is now apparent?

PROVOST: Most manifest, and not denied by himself.

DUKE: Hath he borne himself penitently in prison? How seems he to
be touch'd?

PROVOST: A man that apprehends death no more dreadfully but as a
drunken sleep; careless, reckless, and fearless, of what's past,
present, or to come; insensible of mortality and desperately mortal.

DUKE: He wants advice.

PROVOST: He will hear none. He hath evermore had the liberty of the prison; give him leave to escape hence, he would not; drunk many times a day, if not many days entirely drunk. We have very oft awak'd him, as if to carry him to execution, and show'd him a seeming warrant for it; it hath not moved him at all.

DUKE: More of him anon. There is written in your brow, Provost, honesty and constancy. If I read it not truly, my ancient skill beguiles me; but in the boldness of my cunning I will lay myself in hazard. Claudio, whom here you have warrant to execute, is no greater forfeit to the law than Angelo who hath sentenc'd him. To make you understand this in a manifested effect, I crave but four days' respite; for the which you are to do me both a present and a dangerous courtesy.

PROVOST: Pray, sir, in what?

DUKE: In the delaying death.

PROVOST: Alack! How may I do it, having the hour limited, and an express command, under penalty, to deliver his head in the view of Angelo? I may make my case as Claudio's, to cross this in the smallest.

DUKE: By the vow of mine order, I warrant you, if my instructions may be your guide. Let this Barnardine be this morning executed, and his head borne to Angelo.

PROVOST: Angelo hath seen them both, and will discover the favour.

DUKE: O, death's a great disguiser; and you may add to it. Shave the head and tie the beard; and say it was the desire of the penitent to be so bar'd before his death. You know the course is common. If anything fall to you upon this more than thanks and good fortune, by the saint whom I profess, I will plead against it with my life.

PROVOST: Pardon me, good father; it is against my oath.

DUKE: Were you sworn to the Duke, or to the deputy?

PROVOST: To him and to his substitutes.

DUKE: You will think you have made no offence if the Duke avouch the justice of your dealing?

PROVOST: But what likelihood is in that?

DUKE: Not a resemblance, but a certainty. Yet since I see you fearful, that neither my coat, integrity, nor persuasion, can with ease attempt you, I will go further than I meant, to pluck all fears out of you. Look you, sir, here is the hand and seal of the Duke. You know the character, I doubt not; and the signet is not strange to you.

PROVOST: I know them both.

DUKE: The contents of this is the return of the Duke; you shall anon over-read it at your pleasure, where you shall find within these two days he will be here. This is a thing that Angelo knows not; for he this very day receives letters of strange tenour, perchance of the Duke's death, perchance entering into some monastery; but, by chance, nothing of what is writ. Look, th' unfolding star calls up the shepherd. Put not yourself into amazement how these things should be: all difficulties are but easy when they are known. Call your executioner, and off with Barnardine's head. I will give him a present shrift, and advise him for a better place. Yet you are amaz'd, but this shall absolutely resolve you. Come away; it is almost clear dawn.

Exeunt

ACT IV. SCENE III. The Prison

Enter Pompey

POMPEY: I am as well acquainted here as
I was in our house of profession; one would
think it were Mistress Overdone's own house,
for here be many of her old customers.
First, here's young Master Rash; he's in for a
commodity of brown paper and old ginger,
nine score and seventeen pounds, of which
he made five marks ready money. Marry,
then ginger was not much in request, for the
old women were all dead. Then is there here
one Master Caper, at the suit of Master
Threepile the mercer, for some four suits of
peach-colour'd satin, which now peaches
him a beggar. Then have we here young Dizy,
and young Master Deepvow, and Master
Copperspur, and Master Starvelackey,
the rapier and dagger man, and young
Dropheir that kill'd lusty Pudding, and
Master Forthlight the tilter, and brave
Master Shootie the great traveller, and
wild Halfcan that stabb'd Pots, and,
I think, forty more- all great doers
in our trade, and are now 'for the Lord's sake.'
  Enter Abhorson

ABHORSON: Sirrah, bring Barnardine hither.

POMPEY: Master Barnardine! You must rise and be hang'd, Master Barnardine!

ABHORSON: What ho, Barnardine!

BARNARDINE: *Within* A pox o' your throats! Who makes that noise there? What are you?

POMPEY: Your friends, sir; the hangman. You must be so good, sir, to rise and be put to death.

BARNARDINE: *Within* Away, you rogue, away; I am sleepy.

ABHORSON: Tell him he must awake, and that quickly too.

POMPEY: Pray, Master Barnardine, awake till you are executed, and sleep afterwards.

ABHORSON: Go in to him, and fetch him out.

POMPEY: He is coming, sir, he is coming; I hear his straw rustle.
  Enter Barnardine

ABHORSON: Is the axe upon the block, sirrah?

POMPEY: Very ready, sir.

BARNARDINE: How now, Abhorson, what's the news with you?

ABHORSON: Truly, sir, I would desire you to clap into your prayers; for, look you, the warrant's come.

BARNARDINE: You rogue, I have been drinking all night; I am not fitted for't.

POMPEY: O, the better, sir! For he that drinks all night and is hanged betimes in the morning may sleep the sounder all the next day.
  Enter Duke, Disguised as Before

ABHORSON: Look you, sir, here comes your ghostly father. Do we jest now, think you?

DUKE: Sir, induced by my charity, and hearing how hastily you are to depart, I am come to advise you, comfort you, and pray with you.

BARNARDINE: Friar, not I; I have been drinking hard all night, and I will have more time to prepare me, or they shall beat out my brains with billets. I will not consent to die this day, that's certain.

DUKE: O, Sir, you must; and therefore I beseech you
Look forward on the journey you shall go.

BARNARDINE: I swear I will not die to-day for any man's persuasion.

DUKE: But hear you—

BARNARDINE: Not a word; if you have anything to say to me, come to my ward; for thence will not I to-day.
    Exit

DUKE: Unfit to live or die. O gravel heart!
After him, fellows; bring him to the block.
    Exeunt Abhorson and Pompey
    Enter Provost

PROVOST: Now, sir, how do you find the prisoner?

DUKE: A creature unprepar'd, unmeet for death;
And to transport him in the mind he is were damnable.

PROVOST: Here in the prison, father,
There died this morning of a cruel fever
One Ragozine, a most notorious pirate,
A man of Claudio's years; his beard and head
Just of his colour. What if we do omit
This reprobate till he were well inclin'd,
And satisfy the deputy with the visage
Of Ragozine, more like to Claudio?

DUKE: O, 'tis an accident that heaven provides!
Dispatch it presently; the hour draws on
Prefix'd by Angelo. See this be done,

And sent according to command; whiles I
Persuade this rude wretch willingly to die.

PROVOST: This shall be done, good father, presently.
But Barnardine must die this afternoon;
And how shall we continue Claudio,
To save me from the danger that might come
If he were known alive?

DUKE: Let this be done:
Put them in secret holds, both Barnardine and Claudio.
Ere twice the sun hath made his journal greeting
To the under generation, you shall find
Your safety manifested.

PROVOST: I am your free dependant.

DUKE: Quick, dispatch, and send the head to Angelo.
    Exit Provost
Now will I write letters to Angelo-
The Provost, he shall bear them- whose contents
Shall witness to him I am near at home,
And that, by great injunctions, I am bound
To enter publicly. Him I'll desire
To meet me at the consecrated fount,
A league below the city; and from thence,
By cold gradation and well-balanc'd form.
We shall proceed with Angelo.
    Re-enter Provost

PROVOST: Here is the head; I'll carry it myself.

DUKE: Convenient is it. Make a swift return;
For I would commune with you of such things
That want no ear but yours.

PROVOST: I'll make all speed.

Exit

ISABELLA: *Within* Peace, ho, be here!

DUKE: The tongue of Isabel. She's come to know
If yet her brother's pardon be come hither;
But I will keep her ignorant of her good,
To make her heavenly comforts of despair
When it is least expected.
   Enter Isabella

ISABELLA: Ho, by your leave!

DUKE: Good morning to you, fair and gracious daughter.

ISABELLA: The better, given me by so holy a man.
Hath yet the deputy sent my brother's pardon?

DUKE: He hath releas'd him, Isabel, from the world.
His head is off and sent to Angelo.

ISABELLA: Nay, but it is not so.

DUKE: It is no other.
Show your wisdom, daughter, in your close patience,

ISABELLA: O, I will to him and pluck out his eyes!

DUKE: You shall not be admitted to his sight.

ISABELLA: Unhappy Claudio! Wretched Isabel!
Injurious world! Most damned Angelo!

DUKE: This nor hurts him nor profits you a jot;
Forbear it, therefore; give your cause to heaven.
Mark what I say, which you shall find
By every syllable a faithful verity.

The Duke comes home to-morrow. Nay, dry your eyes.
One of our covent, and his confessor,
Gives me this instance. Already he hath carried
Notice to Escalus and Angelo,
Who do prepare to meet him at the gates,
There to give up their pow'r. If you can, pace your wisdom
In that good path that I would wish it go,
And you shall have your bosom on this wretch,
Grace of the Duke, revenges to your heart,
And general honour.

ISABELLA: I am directed by you.

DUKE: This letter, then, to Friar Peter give;
'Tis that he sent me of the Duke's return.
Say, by this token, I desire his company
At Mariana's house to-night. Her cause and yours
I'll perfect him withal; and he shall bring you
Before the Duke; and to the head of Angelo
Accuse him home and home. For my poor self,
I am combined by a sacred vow,
And shall be absent. Wend you with this letter.
Command these fretting waters from your eyes
With a light heart; trust not my holy order,
If I pervert your course. Who's here?
    Enter Lucio

LUCIO: Good even. Friar, where's the Provost?

DUKE: Not within, sir.

LUCIO: O pretty Isabella, I am pale at mine heart to see thine eyes
so red. Thou must be patient. I am fain to dine and sup with
water and bran; I dare not for my head fill my belly; one
fruitful meal would set me to't. But they say the Duke will be
here to-morrow. By my troth, Isabel, I lov'd thy brother. If the
old fantastical Duke of dark corners had been at home, he had

lived.

Exit Isabella

DUKE: Sir, the Duke is marvellous little beholding to your reports; but the best is, he lives not in them.

LUCIO: Friar, thou knowest not the Duke so well as I do; he's a better woodman than thou tak'st him for.

DUKE: Well, you'll answer this one day. Fare ye well.

LUCIO: Nay, tarry; I'll go along with thee; I can tell thee pretty tales of the Duke.

DUKE: You have told me too many of him already, sir, if they be true; if not true, none were enough.

LUCIO: I was once before him for getting a wench with child.

DUKE: Did you such a thing?

LUCIO: Yes, marry, did I; but I was fain to forswear it: they would else have married me to the rotten medlar.

DUKE: Sir, your company is fairer than honest. Rest you well.

LUCIO: By my troth, I'll go with thee to the lane's end. If bawdy talk offend you, we'll have very little of it. Nay, friar, I am a kind of burr; I shall stick.

Exeunt

ACT IV. SCENE IV. Angelo's House

Enter Angelo and Escalus

ESCALUS: Every letter he hath writ hath disvouch'd other.

ANGELO: In most uneven and distracted manner. His actions show much

like to madness; pray heaven his wisdom be not tainted! And why
meet him at the gates, and redeliver our authorities there?

ESCALUS: I guess not.

ANGELO: And why should we proclaim it in an hour before his
ent'ring that, if any crave redress of injustice, they should
exhibit their petitions in the street?

ESCALUS: He shows his reason for that: to have a dispatch of
complaints; and to deliver us from devices hereafter, which
shall then have no power to stand against us.

ANGELO: Well, I beseech you, let it be proclaim'd;
Betimes i' th' morn I'll call you at your house;
Give notice to such men of sort and suit
As are to meet him.

ESCALUS: I shall, sir; fare you well.

ANGELO: Good night.
  Exit Escalus
This deed unshapes me quite, makes me unpregnant
And dull to all proceedings. A deflow'red maid!
And by an eminent body that enforc'd
The law against it! But that her tender shame
Will not proclaim against her maiden loss,
How might she tongue me! Yet reason dares her no;
For my authority bears a so credent bulk
That no particular scandal once can touch
But it confounds the breather. He should have liv'd,
Save that his riotous youth, with dangerous sense,
Might in the times to come have ta'en revenge,
By so receiving a dishonour'd life
With ransom of such shame. Would yet he had liv'd!
Alack, when once our grace we have forgot,
Nothing goes right; we would, and we would not.

Exit

ACT IV. SCENE V. Fields Without the Town
Enter Duke in His Own Habit, and Friar Peter

DUKE: These letters at fit time deliver me. *Giving Letters*
The Provost knows our purpose and our plot.
The matter being afoot, keep your instruction
And hold you ever to our special drift;
Though sometimes you do blench from this to that
As cause doth minister. Go, call at Flavius' house,
And tell him where I stay; give the like notice
To Valentinus, Rowland, and to Crassus,
And bid them bring the trumpets to the gate;
But send me Flavius first.

PETER: It shall be speeded well.
  Exit Friar
  Enter Varrius

DUKE: I thank thee, Varrius; thou hast made good haste.
Come, we will walk. There's other of our friends
Will greet us here anon. My gentle Varrius!
  Exeunt

ACT IV. SCENE VI. A Street near the City Gate
Enter Isabella and Mariana

ISABELLA: To speak so indirectly I am loath;
I would say the truth; but to accuse him so,
That is your part. Yet I am advis'd to do it;
He says, to veil full purpose.

MARIANA: Be rul'd by him.

ISABELLA: Besides, he tells me that, if peradventure
He speak against me on the adverse side,

I should not think it strange; for 'tis a physic
That's bitter to sweet end.

MARIANA: I would Friar Peter-
  Enter Friar Peter

ISABELLA: O, peace! the friar is come.

PETER: Come, I have found you out a stand most fit,
Where you may have such vantage on the Duke
He shall not pass you. Twice have the trumpets sounded;
The generous and gravest citizens
Have hent the gates, and very near upon
The Duke is ent'ring; therefore, hence, away.
  Exeunt

ACT V. SCENE I. the City Gate
  Enter at Several Doors Duke, Varrius, Lords; Angelo, Escalus, Lucio, Provost, Officers, and Citizens

DUKE: My very worthy cousin, fairly met!
Our old and faithful friend, we are glad to see you.

ANGELO, ESCALUS: Happy return be to your royal Grace!

DUKE: Many and hearty thankings to you both.
We have made inquiry of you, and we hear
Such goodness of your justice that our soul
Cannot but yield you forth to public thanks,
Forerunning more requital.

ANGELO: You make my bonds still greater.

DUKE: O, your desert speaks loud; and I should wrong it
To lock it in the wards of covert bosom,
When it deserves, with characters of brass,
A forted residence 'gainst the tooth of time

And razure of oblivion. Give me your hand.
And let the subject see, to make them know
That outward courtesies would fain proclaim
Favours that keep within. Come, Escalus,
You must walk by us on our other hand,
And good supporters are you.
  Enter Friar Peter and Isabella

PETER: Now is your time; speak loud, and kneel before him.

ISABELLA: Justice, O royal Duke! Vail your regard
Upon a wrong'd- I would fain have said a maid!
O worthy Prince, dishonour not your eye
By throwing it on any other object
Till you have heard me in my true complaint,
And given me justice, justice, justice, justice.

DUKE: Relate your wrongs. In what? By whom? Be brief.
Here is Lord Angelo shall give you justice;
Reveal yourself to him.

ISABELLA: O worthy Duke,
You bid me seek redemption of the devil!
Hear me yourself; for that which I must speak
Must either punish me, not being believ'd,
Or wring redress from you. Hear me, O, hear me, here!

ANGELO: My lord, her wits, I fear me, are not firm;
She hath been a suitor to me for her brother,
Cut off by course of justice-

ISABELLA: By course of justice!

ANGELO: And she will speak most bitterly and strange.

ISABELLA: Most strange, but yet most truly, will I speak.
That Angelo's forsworn, is it not strange?

That Angelo's a murderer, is't not strange?
That Angelo is an adulterous thief,
An hypocrite, a virgin-violator,
Is it not strange and strange?

DUKE: Nay, it is ten times strange.

ISABELLA: It is not truer he is Angelo
Than this is all as true as it is strange;
Nay, it is ten times true; for truth is truth
To th' end of reck'ning.

DUKE: Away with her. Poor soul,
She speaks this in th' infirmity of sense.

ISABELLA: O Prince! I conjure thee, as thou believ'st
There is another comfort than this world,
That thou neglect me not with that opinion
That I am touch'd with madness. Make not impossible
That which but seems unlike: 'tis not impossible
But one, the wicked'st caitiff on the ground,
May seem as shy, as grave, as just, as absolute,
As Angelo; even so may Angelo,
In all his dressings, characts, titles, forms,
Be an arch-villain. Believe it, royal Prince,
If he be less, he's nothing; but he's more,
Had I more name for badness.

DUKE: By mine honesty,
If she be mad, as I believe no other,
Her madness hath the oddest frame of sense,
Such a dependency of thing on thing,
As e'er I heard in madness.

ISABELLA: O gracious Duke,
Harp not on that; nor do not banish reason
For inequality; but let your reason serve

To make the truth appear where it seems hid,
And hide the false seems true.

DUKE: Many that are not mad
Have, sure, more lack of reason. What would you say?

ISABELLA: I am the sister of one Claudio,
Condemn'd upon the act of fornication
To lose his head; condemn'd by Angelo.
I, in probation of a sisterhood,
Was sent to by my brother; one Lucio
As then the messenger-

LUCIO: That's I, an't like your Grace.
I came to her from Claudio, and desir'd her
To try her gracious fortune with Lord Angelo
For her poor brother's pardon.

ISABELLA: That's he, indeed.

DUKE: You were not bid to speak.

LUCIO: No, my good lord;
Nor wish'd to hold my peace.

DUKE: I wish you now, then;
Pray you take note of it; and when you have
A business for yourself, pray heaven you then be perfect.

LUCIO: I warrant your honour.

DUKE: The warrant's for yourself; take heed to't.

ISABELLA: This gentleman told somewhat of my tale.

LUCIO: Right.

DUKE: It may be right; but you are i' the wrong
To speak before your time. Proceed.

ISABELLA: I went
To this pernicious caitiff deputy.

DUKE: That's somewhat madly spoken.

ISABELLA: Pardon it;
The phrase is to the matter.

DUKE: Mended again. The matter- proceed.

ISABELLA: In brief- to set the needless process by,
How I persuaded, how I pray'd, and kneel'd,
How he refell'd me, and how I replied,
For this was of much length- the vile conclusion
I now begin with grief and shame to utter:
He would not, but by gift of my chaste body
To his concupiscible intemperate lust,
Release my brother; and, after much debatement,
My sisterly remorse confutes mine honour,
And I did yield to him. But the next morn betimes,
His purpose surfeiting, he sends a warrant
For my poor brother's head.

DUKE: This is most likely!

ISABELLA: O that it were as like as it is true!

DUKE: By heaven, fond wretch, thou know'st not what thou speak'st,
Or else thou art suborn'd against his honour
In hateful practice. First, his integrity
Stands without blemish; next, it imports no reason
That with such vehemency he should pursue
Faults proper to himself. If he had so offended,
He would have weigh'd thy brother by himself,

And not have cut him off. Some one hath set you on;
Confess the truth, and say by whose advice
Thou cam'st here to complain.

ISABELLA: And is this all?
Then, O you blessed ministers above,
Keep me in patience; and, with ripened time,
Unfold the evil which is here wrapt up
In countenance! Heaven shield your Grace from woe,
As I, thus wrong'd, hence unbelieved go!

DUKE: I know you'd fain be gone. An officer!
To prison with her! Shall we thus permit
A blasting and a scandalous breath to fall
On him so near us? This needs must be a practice.
Who knew of your intent and coming hither?

ISABELLA: One that I would were here, Friar Lodowick.

DUKE: A ghostly father, belike. Who knows that Lodowick?

LUCIO: My lord, I know him; 'tis a meddling friar.
I do not like the man; had he been lay, my lord,
For certain words he spake against your Grace
In your retirement, I had swing'd him soundly.

DUKE: Words against me? This's a good friar, belike!
And to set on this wretched woman here
Against our substitute! Let this friar be found.

LUCIO: But yesternight, my lord, she and that friar,
I saw them at the prison; a saucy friar,
A very scurvy fellow.

PETER: Blessed be your royal Grace!
I have stood by, my lord, and I have heard
Your royal ear abus'd. First, hath this woman

Most wrongfully accus'd your substitute;
Who is as free from touch or soil with her
As she from one ungot.

DUKE: We did believe no less.
Know you that Friar Lodowick that she speaks of?

PETER: I know him for a man divine and holy;
Not scurvy, nor a temporary meddler,
As he's reported by this gentleman;
And, on my trust, a man that never yet
Did, as he vouches, misreport your Grace.

LUCIO: My lord, most villainously; believe it.

PETER: Well, he in time may come to clear himself;
But at this instant he is sick, my lord,
Of a strange fever. Upon his mere request-
Being come to knowledge that there was complaint
Intended 'gainst Lord Angelo- came I hither
To speak, as from his mouth, what he doth know
Is true and false; and what he, with his oath
And all probation, will make up full clear,
Whensoever he's convented. First, for this woman-
To justify this worthy nobleman,
So vulgarly and personally accus'd-
Her shall you hear disproved to her eyes,
Till she herself confess it.

DUKE: Good friar, let's hear it.
   Exit Isabella Guarded
Do you not smile at this, Lord Angelo?
O heaven, the vanity of wretched fools!
Give us some seats. Come, cousin Angelo;
In this I'll be impartial; be you judge
Of your own cause.
   Enter Mariana Veiled

Is this the witness, friar?
First let her show her face, and after speak.

MARIANA: Pardon, my lord; I will not show my face
Until my husband bid me.

DUKE: What, are you married?

MARIANA: No, my lord.

DUKE: Are you a maid?

MARIANA: No, my lord.

DUKE: A widow, then?

MARIANA: Neither, my lord.

DUKE: Why, you are nothing then; neither maid, widow, nor wife.

LUCIO: My lord, she may be a punk; for many of them are neither
maid, widow, nor wife.

DUKE: Silence that fellow. I would he had some cause
To prattle for himself.

LUCIO: Well, my lord.

MARIANA: My lord, I do confess I ne'er was married,
And I confess, besides, I am no maid.
I have known my husband; yet my husband
Knows not that ever he knew me.

LUCIO: He was drunk, then, my lord; it can be no better.

DUKE: For the benefit of silence, would thou wert so too!

LUCIO: Well, my lord.

DUKE: This is no witness for Lord Angelo.

MARIANA: Now I come to't, my lord:
She that accuses him of fornication,
In self-same manner doth accuse my husband;
And charges him, my lord, with such a time
When I'll depose I had him in mine arms,
With all th' effect of love.

ANGELO: Charges she moe than me?

MARIANA: Not that I know.

DUKE: No? You say your husband.

MARIANA: Why, just, my lord, and that is Angelo,
Who thinks he knows that he ne'er knew my body,
But knows he thinks that he knows Isabel's.

ANGELO: This is a strange abuse. Let's see thy face.

MARIANA: My husband bids me; now I will unmask.
    Unveiling
This is that face, thou cruel Angelo,
Which once thou swor'st was worth the looking on;
This is the hand which, with a vow'd contract,
Was fast belock'd in thine; this is the body
That took away the match from Isabel,
And did supply thee at thy garden-house
In her imagin'd person.

DUKE: Know you this woman?

LUCIO: Carnally, she says.

DUKE: Sirrah, no more.

LUCIO: Enough, my lord.

ANGELO: My lord, I must confess I know this woman;
And five years since there was some speech of marriage
Betwixt myself and her; which was broke off,
Partly for that her promised proportions
Came short of composition; but in chief
For that her reputation was disvalued
In levity. Since which time of five years
I never spake with her, saw her, nor heard from her,
Upon my faith and honour.

MARIANA: Noble Prince,
As there comes light from heaven and words from breath,
As there is sense in truth and truth in virtue,
I am affianc'd this man's wife as strongly
As words could make up vows. And, my good lord,
But Tuesday night last gone, in's garden-house,
He knew me as a wife. As this is true,
Let me in safety raise me from my knees,
Or else for ever be confixed here,
A marble monument!

ANGELO: I did but smile till now.
Now, good my lord, give me the scope of justice;
My patience here is touch'd. I do perceive
These poor informal women are no more
But instruments of some more mightier member
That sets them on. Let me have way, my lord,
To find this practice out.

DUKE: Ay, with my heart;
And punish them to your height of pleasure.
Thou foolish friar, and thou pernicious woman,
Compact with her that's gone, think'st thou thy oaths,

Though they would swear down each particular saint,
Were testimonies against his worth and credit,
That's seal'd in approbation? You, Lord Escalus,
Sit with my cousin; lend him your kind pains
To find out this abuse, whence 'tis deriv'd.
There is another friar that set them on;
Let him be sent for.

PETER: Would lie were here, my lord! For he indeed
Hath set the women on to this complaint.
Your provost knows the place where he abides,
And he may fetch him.

DUKE: Go, do it instantly.
   Exit Provost
And you, my noble and well-warranted cousin,
Whom it concerns to hear this matter forth,
Do with your injuries as seems you best
In any chastisement. I for a while will leave you;
But stir not you till you have well determin'd
Upon these slanderers.

ESCALUS: My lord, we'll do it throughly.
   Exit Duke
Signior Lucio, did not you say you knew that Friar Lodowick to be
a dishonest person?

LUCIO: 'Cucullus non facit monachum': honest in nothing but in his
clothes; and one that hath spoke most villainous speeches of the Duke.

ESCALUS: We shall entreat you to abide here till he come and
enforce them against him. We shall find this friar a notable fellow.

LUCIO: As any in Vienna, on my word.

ESCALUS: Call that same Isabel here once again; I would speak with her.
Exit an Attendant

Pray you, my lord, give me leave to question; you shall see how I'll handle her.

LUCIO: Not better than he, by her own report.

ESCALUS: Say you?

LUCIO: Marry, sir, I think, if you handled her privately, she would sooner confess; perchance, publicly, she'll be asham'd.
  Re-enter Officers with Isabella; and Provost with the Duke in His Friar's Habit

ESCALUS: I will go darkly to work with her.

LUCIO: That's the way; for women are light at midnight.

ESCALUS: Come on, mistress; here's a gentlewoman denies all that you have said.

LUCIO: My lord, here comes the rascal I spoke of, here with the

PROVOST:

ESCALUS: In very good time. Speak not you to him till we call upon you.

LUCIO: Mum.

ESCALUS: Come, sir; did you set these women on to slander Lord Angelo? They have confess'd you did.

DUKE: 'Tis false.

ESCALUS: How! Know you where you are?

DUKE: Respect to your great place! and let the devil
Be sometime honour'd for his burning throne!
Where is the Duke? 'Tis he should hear me speak.

ESCALUS: The Duke's in us; and we will hear you speak;
Look you speak justly.

DUKE: Boldly, at least. But, O, poor souls,
Come you to seek the lamb here of the fox,
Good night to your redress! Is the Duke gone?
Then is your cause gone too. The Duke's unjust
Thus to retort your manifest appeal,
And put your trial in the villain's mouth
Which here you come to accuse.

LUCIO: This is the rascal; this is he I spoke of.

ESCALUS: Why, thou unreverend and unhallowed friar,
Is't not enough thou hast suborn'd these women
To accuse this worthy man, but, in foul mouth,
And in the witness of his proper ear,
To call him villain; and then to glance from him
To th' Duke himself, to tax him with injustice?
Take him hence; to th' rack with him! We'll touze you
Joint by joint, but we will know his purpose.
What, 'unjust'!

DUKE: Be not so hot; the Duke
Dare no more stretch this finger of mine than he
Dare rack his own; his subject am I not,
Nor here provincial. My business in this state
Made me a looker-on here in Vienna,
Where I have seen corruption boil and bubble
Till it o'errun the stew: laws for all faults,
But faults so countenanc'd that the strong statutes
Stand like the forfeits in a barber's shop,
As much in mock as mark.

ESCALUS: Slander to th' state! Away with him to prison!

ANGELO: What can you vouch against him, Signior Lucio?

Is this the man that you did tell us of?

LUCIO: 'Tis he, my lord. Come hither, good-man bald-pate.
Do you know me?

DUKE: I remember you, sir, by the sound of your voice. I met you at
the prison, in the absence of the Duke.

LUCIO: O did you so? And do you remember what you said of the Duke?

DUKE: Most notedly, sir.

LUCIO: Do you so, sir? And was the Duke a fleshmonger, a fool, and
a coward, as you then reported him to be?

DUKE: You must, sir, change persons with me ere you make that my
report; you, indeed, spoke so of him; and much more, much worse.

LUCIO: O thou damnable fellow! Did not I pluck thee by the nose for
thy speeches?

DUKE: I protest I love the Duke as I love myself.

ANGELO: Hark how the villain would close now, after his treasonable
abuses!

ESCALUS: Such a fellow is not to be talk'd withal. Away with him to
prison! Where is the Provost? Away with him to prison! Lay bolts
enough upon him; let him speak no more. Away with those giglets
too, and with the other confederate companion!
  The Provost Lays Bands on the Duke
DUKE: Stay, sir; stay awhile.

ANGELO: What, resists he? Help him, Lucio.

LUCIO: Come, sir; come, sir; come, sir; foh, sir! Why, you
bald-pated lying rascal, you must be hooded, must you? Show your

knave's visage, with a pox to you! Show your sheep-biting face,
and be hang'd an hour! Will't not off?
Pulls off the Friar's Bood and Discovers the Duke

DUKE: Thou art the first knave that e'er mad'st a duke.
First, Provost, let me bail these gentle three.
To Lucio Sneak not away, sir, for the friar and you
Must have a word anon. Lay hold on him.

LUCIO: This may prove worse than hanging.

DUKE: *To Escalus* What you have spoke I pardon; sit you down.
We'll borrow place of him.
To Angelo Sir, by your leave.
Hast thou or word, or wit, or impudence,
That yet can do thee office? If thou hast,
Rely upon it till my tale be heard,
And hold no longer out.

ANGELO: O my dread lord,
I should be guiltier than my guiltiness,
To think I can be undiscernible,
When I perceive your Grace, like pow'r divine,
Hath look'd upon my passes. Then, good Prince,
No longer session hold upon my shame,
But let my trial be mine own confession;
Immediate sentence then, and sequent death,
Is all the grace I beg.

DUKE: Come hither, Mariana.
Say, wast thou e'er contracted to this woman?

ANGELO: I was, my lord.

DUKE: Go, take her hence and marry her instantly.
Do you the office, friar; which consummate,
Return him here again. Go with him, Provost.

Exeunt Angelo, Mariana, Friar Peter, and Provost

ESCALUS: My lord, I am more amaz'd at his dishonour
Than at the strangeness of it.

DUKE: Come hither, Isabel.
Your friar is now your prince. As I was then
Advertising and holy to your business,
Not changing heart with habit, I am still
Attorney'd at your service.

ISABELLA: O, give me pardon,
That I, your vassal have employ'd and pain'd
Your unknown sovereignty.

DUKE: You are pardon'd, Isabel.
And now, dear maid, be you as free to us.
Your brother's death, I know, sits at your heart;
And you may marvel why I obscur'd myself,
Labouring to save his life, and would not rather
Make rash remonstrance of my hidden pow'r
Than let him so be lost. O most kind maid,
It was the swift celerity of his death,
Which I did think with slower foot came on,
That brain'd my purpose. But peace be with him!
That life is better life, past fearing death,
Than that which lives to fear. Make it your comfort,
So happy is your brother.

ISABELLA: I do, my lord.
   Re-enter Angelo, Mariana, Friar Peter, and Provost

DUKE: For this new-married man approaching here,
Whose salt imagination yet hath wrong'd
Your well-defended honour, you must pardon
For Mariana's sake; but as he adjudg'd your brother-
Being criminal in double violation

Of sacred chastity and of promise-breach,
Thereon dependent, for your brother's life-
The very mercy of the law cries out
Most audible, even from his proper tongue,
'An Angelo for Claudio, death for death!'
Haste still pays haste, and leisure answers leisure;
Like doth quit like, and Measure still for Measure.
Then, Angelo, thy fault's thus manifested,
Which, though thou wouldst deny, denies thee vantage.
We do condemn thee to the very block
Where Claudio stoop'd to death, and with like haste.
Away with him!

MARIANA: O my most gracious lord,
I hope you will not mock me with a husband.

DUKE: It is your husband mock'd you with a husband.
Consenting to the safeguard of your honour,
I thought your marriage fit; else imputation,
For that he knew you, might reproach your life,
And choke your good to come. For his possessions,
Although by confiscation they are ours,
We do instate and widow you withal
To buy you a better husband.

MARIANA: O my dear lord,
I crave no other, nor no better man.

DUKE: Never crave him; we are definitive.

MARIANA: Gentle my liege-
  Kneeling

DUKE: You do but lose your labour.
Away with him to death!
To Lucio Now, sir, to you.

MARIANA: O my good lord! Sweet Isabel, take my part;
Lend me your knees, and all my life to come
I'll lend you all my life to do you service.

DUKE: Against all sense you do importune her.
Should she kneel down in mercy of this fact,
Her brother's ghost his paved bed would break,
And take her hence in horror.

MARIANA: Isabel,
Sweet Isabel, do yet but kneel by me;
Hold up your hands, say nothing; I'll speak all.
They say best men moulded out of faults;
And, for the most, become much more the better
For being a little bad; so may my husband.
O Isabel, will you not lend a knee?

DUKE: He dies for Claudio's death.

ISABELLA: *Kneeling* Most bounteous sir,
Look, if it please you, on this man condemn'd,
As if my brother liv'd. I partly think
A due sincerity govern'd his deeds
Till he did look on me; since it is so,
Let him not die. My brother had but justice,
In that he did the thing for which he died;
For Angelo,
His act did not o'ertake his bad intent,
And must be buried but as an intent
That perish'd by the way. Thoughts are no subjects;
Intents but merely thoughts.

MARIANA: Merely, my lord.

DUKE: Your suit's unprofitable; stand up, I say.
I have bethought me of another fault.
Provost, how came it Claudio was beheaded

At an unusual hour?

PROVOST: It was commanded so.

DUKE: Had you a special warrant for the deed?

PROVOST: No, my good lord; it was by private message.

DUKE: For which I do discharge you of your office;
Give up your keys.

PROVOST: Pardon me, noble lord;
I thought it was a fault, but knew it not;
Yet did repent me, after more advice;
For testimony whereof, one in the prison,
That should by private order else have died,
I have reserv'd alive.

DUKE: What's he?

PROVOST: His name is Barnardine.

DUKE: I would thou hadst done so by Claudio.
Go fetch him hither; let me look upon him.
  Exit Provost

ESCALUS: I am sorry one so learned and so wise
As you, Lord Angelo, have still appear'd,
Should slip so grossly, both in the heat of blood
And lack of temper'd judgment afterward.

ANGELO: I am sorry that such sorrow I procure;
And so deep sticks it in my penitent heart
That I crave death more willingly than mercy;
'Tis my deserving, and I do entreat it.
  Re-enter Provost, with Barnardine, Claudio (Muffled) and Juliet

DUKE: Which is that Barnardine?

PROVOST: This, my lord.

DUKE: There was a friar told me of this man.
Sirrah, thou art said to have a stubborn soul,
That apprehends no further than this world,
And squar'st thy life according. Thou'rt condemn'd;
But, for those earthly faults, I quit them all,
And pray thee take this mercy to provide
For better times to come. Friar, advise him;
I leave him to your hand. What muffl'd fellow's that?

PROVOST: This is another prisoner that I sav'd,
Who should have died when Claudio lost his head;
As like almost to Claudio as himself.
   Unmuffles Claudio

DUKE: *To Isabella* If he be like your brother, for his sake
Is he pardon'd; and for your lovely sake,
Give me your hand and say you will be mine,
He is my brother too. But fitter time for that.
By this Lord Angelo perceives he's safe;
Methinks I see a quick'ning in his eye.
Well, Angelo, your evil quits you well.
Look that you love your wife; her worth worth yours.
I find an apt remission in myself;
And yet here's one in place I cannot pardon.
To Lucio You, sirrah, that knew me for a fool, a coward,
One all of luxury, an ass, a madman!
Wherein have I so deserv'd of you
That you extol me thus?

LUCIO: Faith, my lord, I spoke it but according to the trick.
If you will hang me for it, you may; but I had rather it would
please you I might be whipt.

DUKE: Whipt first, sir, and hang'd after.
Proclaim it, Provost, round about the city,
If any woman wrong'd by this lewd fellow-
As I have heard him swear himself there's one
Whom he begot with child, let her appear,
And he shall marry her. The nuptial finish'd,
Let him be whipt and hang'd.

LUCIO: I beseech your Highness, do not marry me to a whore. Your
Highness said even now I made you a duke; good my lord, do not
recompense me in making me a cuckold.

DUKE: Upon mine honour, thou shalt marry her.
Thy slanders I forgive; and therewithal
Remit thy other forfeits. Take him to prison;
And see our pleasure herein executed.

LUCIO: Marrying a punk, my lord, is pressing to death, whipping, and hanging.

DUKE: Slandering a prince deserves it.
   Exeunt Officers with Lucio
She, Claudio, that you wrong'd, look you restore.
Joy to you, Mariana! Love her, Angelo;
I have confess'd her, and I know her virtue.
Thanks, good friend Escalus, for thy much goodness;
There's more behind that is more gratulate.
Thanks, Provost, for thy care and secrecy;
We shall employ thee in a worthier place.
Forgive him, Angelo, that brought you home
The head of Ragozine for Claudio's:
Th' offence pardons itself. Dear Isabel,
I have a motion much imports your good;
Whereto if you'll a willing ear incline,
What's mine is yours, and what is yours is mine.
So, bring us to our palace, where we'll show
What's yet behind that's meet you all should know.
   Exeunt

END

The History of Troilus and Cressida

Dramatis Personae

PRIAM, King of Troy
His sons:
HECTOR
TROILUS
PARIS
DEIPHOBUS
HELENUS
MARGARELON, a bastard son of Priam
 Trojan commanders:
AENEAS
ANTENOR
CALCHAS, a Trojan priest, taking part with the Greeks
PANDARUS, uncle to Cressida
AGAMEMNON, the Greek general
MENELAUS, his brother
Greek commanders:
ACHILLES
AJAX
ULYSSES
NESTOR
DIOMEDES
PATROCLUS
THERSITES, a deformed and scurrilous Greek
ALEXANDER, servant to Cressida
SERVANT to Troilus
SERVANT to Paris
SERVANT to Diomedes
HELEN, wife to Menelaus
ANDROMACHE, wife to Hector
CASSANDRA, daughter to Priam, a prophetess
CRESSIDA, daughter to Calchas
Trojan and Greek Soldiers, and Attendants

SCENE: *Troy and the Greek camp before it*

PROLOGUE

In Troy, there lies the scene. From isles of Greece
The princes orgillous, their high blood chaf'd,
Have to the port of Athens sent their ships
Fraught with the ministers and instruments
Of cruel war. Sixty and nine that wore
Their crownets regal from th' Athenian bay
Put forth toward Phrygia; and their vow is made
To ransack Troy, within whose strong immures
The ravish'd Helen, Menelaus' queen,
With wanton Paris sleeps-and that's the quarrel.
To Tenedos they come,
And the deep-drawing barks do there disgorge
Their war-like fraughtage. Now on Dardan plains
The fresh and yet unbruised Greeks do pitch
Their brave pavilions: Priam's six-gated city,
Dardan, and Tymbria, Helias, Chetas, Troien,
And Antenorides, with massy staples
And corresponsive and fulfilling bolts,
Sperr up the sons of Troy.
Now expectation, tickling skittish spirits
On one and other side, Troyan and Greek,
Sets all on hazard-and hither am I come
A Prologue arm'd, but not in confidence
Of author's pen or actor's voice, but suited
In like conditions as our argument,
To tell you, fair beholders, that our play
Leaps o'er the vaunt and firstlings of those broils,
Beginning in the middle; starting thence away,
To what may be digested in a play.
Like or find fault; do as your pleasures are;
Now good or bad, 'tis but the chance of war.

ACT I. SCENE I. Troy. Before Priam's Palace

Enter Troilus Armed, and Pandarus

TROILUS: Call here my varlet; I'll unarm again.
Why should I war without the walls of Troy
That find such cruel battle here within?
Each Troyan that is master of his heart,
Let him to field; Troilus, alas, hath none!

PANDARUS: Will this gear ne'er be mended?

TROILUS: The Greeks are strong, and skilful to their strength,
Fierce to their skill, and to their fierceness valiant;
But I am weaker than a woman's tear,
Tamer than sleep, fonder than ignorance,
Less valiant than the virgin in the night,
And skilless as unpractis'd infancy.

PANDARUS: Well, I have told you enough of this; for my part,
I'll not meddle nor make no farther. He that will have a cake
out of the wheat must needs tarry the grinding.

TROILUS: Have I not tarried?

PANDARUS: Ay, the grinding; but you must tarry the bolting.

TROILUS: Have I not tarried?

PANDARUS: Ay, the bolting; but you must tarry the leavening.

TROILUS: Still have I tarried.

PANDARUS: Ay, to the leavening; but here's yet in the word
'hereafter' the kneading, the making of the cake, the heating
of the oven, and the baking; nay, you must stay the cooling too,
or you may chance to burn your lips.

TROILUS: Patience herself, what goddess e'er she be,
Doth lesser blench at suff'rance than I do.
At Priam's royal table do I sit;
And when fair Cressid comes into my thoughts-
So, traitor, then she comes when she is thence.

PANDARUS: Well, she look'd yesternight fairer than ever I saw her look, or any woman else.

TROILUS: I was about to tell thee: when my heart,
As wedged with a sigh, would rive in twain,
Lest Hector or my father should perceive me,
I have, as when the sun doth light a storm,
Buried this sigh in wrinkle of a smile.
But sorrow that is couch'd in seeming gladness
Is like that mirth fate turns to sudden sadness.

PANDARUS: An her hair were not somewhat darker than Helen's- well, go to- there were no more comparison between the women. But, for my part, she is my kinswoman; I would not, as they term it, praise her, but I would somebody had heard her talk yesterday, as I did. I will not dispraise your sister Cassandra's wit; but-

TROILUS: O Pandarus! I tell thee, Pandarus-
When I do tell thee there my hopes lie drown'd,
Reply not in how many fathoms deep
They lie indrench'd. I tell thee I am mad
In Cressid's love. Thou answer'st 'She is fair'-
Pourest in the open ulcer of my heart-
Her eyes, her hair, her cheek, her gait, her voice,
Handlest in thy discourse. O, that her hand,
In whose comparison all whites are ink
Writing their own reproach; to whose soft seizure
The cygnet's down is harsh, and spirit of sense
Hard as the palm of ploughman! This thou tell'st me,
As true thou tell'st me, when I say I love her;
But, saying thus, instead of oil and balm,

Thou lay'st in every gash that love hath given me
The knife that made it.

PANDARUS: I speak no more than truth.

TROILUS: Thou dost not speak so much.

PANDARUS: Faith, I'll not meddle in it. Let her be as she is: if
she be fair, 'tis the better for her; an she be not, she has the
mends in her own hands.

TROILUS: Good Pandarus! How now, Pandarus!

PANDARUS: I have had my labour for my travail, ill thought on of
her and ill thought on of you; gone between and between, but
small thanks for my labour.

TROILUS: What, art thou angry, Pandarus? What, with me?

PANDARUS: Because she's kin to me, therefore she's not so fair as
Helen. An she were not kin to me, she would be as fair a Friday
as Helen is on Sunday. But what care I? I care not an she were a
blackamoor; 'tis all one to me.

TROILUS: Say I she is not fair?

PANDARUS: I do not care whether you do or no. She's a fool to stay
behind her father. Let her to the Greeks; and so I'll tell her
the next time I see her. For my part, I'll meddle nor make no
more i' th' matter.

TROILUS: Pandarus!

PANDARUS: Not I.

TROILUS: Sweet Pandarus!

PANDARUS: Pray you, speak no more to me: I will leave all
as I found it, and there an end.
   Exit. Sound alarum

TROILUS: Peace, you ungracious clamours! Peace, rude sounds!
Fools on both sides! Helen must needs be fair,
When with your blood you daily paint her thus.
I cannot fight upon this argument;
It is too starv'd a subject for my sword.
But Pandarus-O gods, how do you plague me!
I cannot come to Cressid but by Pandar;
And he's as tetchy to be woo'd to woo
As she is stubborn-chaste against all suit.
Tell me, Apollo, for thy Daphne's love,
What Cressid is, what Pandar, and what we?
Her bed is India; there she lies, a pearl;
Between our Ilium and where she resides
Let it be call'd the wild and wand'ring flood;
Ourself the merchant, and this sailing Pandar
Our doubtful hope, our convoy, and our bark.
   Alarum. Enter Aeneas

AENEAS: How now, Prince Troilus! Wherefore not afield?

TROILUS: Because not there. This woman's answer sorts,
For womanish it is to be from thence.
What news, Aeneas, from the field to-day?

AENEAS: That Paris is returned home, and hurt.

TROILUS: By whom, Aeneas?

AENEAS: Troilus, by Menelaus.

TROILUS: Let Paris bleed: 'tis but a scar to scorn;
Paris is gor'd with Menelaus' horn.
   Alarum

AENEAS: Hark what good sport is out of town to-day!

TROILUS: Better at home, if 'would I might' were 'may.'
But to the sport abroad. Are you bound thither?

AENEAS: In all swift haste.

TROILUS: Come, go we then together.
  Exeunt

ACT I. SCENE II. Troy. A Street
Enter Cressida and Her Man Alexander

CRESSIDA: Who were those went by?

ALEXANDER: Queen Hecuba and Helen.

CRESSIDA: And whither go they?

ALEXANDER: Up to the eastern tower,
Whose height commands as subject all the vale,
To see the battle. Hector, whose patience
Is as a virtue fix'd, to-day was mov'd.
He chid Andromache, and struck his armourer;
And, like as there were husbandry in war,
Before the sun rose he was harness'd light,
And to the field goes he; where every flower
Did as a prophet weep what it foresaw
In Hector's wrath.

CRESSIDA: What was his cause of anger?

ALEXANDER: The noise goes, this: there is among the Greeks
A lord of Troyan blood, nephew to Hector;
They call him Ajax.

CRESSIDA: Good; and what of him?

ALEXANDER: They say he is a very man per se,
And stands alone.

CRESSIDA: So do all men, unless they are drunk, sick, or have no legs.

ALEXANDER: This man, lady, hath robb'd many beasts of their
particular additions: he is as valiant as a lion, churlish as the
bear, slow as the elephant-a man into whom nature hath so crowded
humours that his valour is crush'd into folly, his folly sauced
with discretion. There is no man hath a virtue that he hath not a
glimpse of, nor any man an attaint but he carries some stain of
it; he is melancholy without cause and merry against the hair; he
hath the joints of every thing; but everything so out of joint
that he is a gouty Briareus, many hands and no use, or purblind
Argus, all eyes and no sight.

CRESSIDA: But how should this man, that makes me smile, make Hector
angry?

ALEXANDER: They say he yesterday cop'd Hector in the battle and
struck him down, the disdain and shame whereof hath ever since
kept Hector fasting and waking.
    Enter Pandarus

CRESSIDA: Who comes here?

ALEXANDER: Madam, your uncle Pandarus.

CRESSIDA: Hector's a gallant man.

ALEXANDER: As may be in the world, lady.

PANDARUS: What's that? What's that?

CRESSIDA: Good morrow, uncle Pandarus.

PANDARUS: Good morrow, cousin Cressid. What do you talk of?- Good morrow, Alexander.-How do you, cousin? When were you at Ilium?

CRESSIDA: This morning, uncle.

PANDARUS: What were you talking of when I came? Was Hector arm'd and gone ere you came to Ilium? Helen was not up, was she?

CRESSIDA: Hector was gone; but Helen was not up.

PANDARUS: E'en so. Hector was stirring early.

CRESSIDA: That were we talking of, and of his anger.

PANDARUS: Was he angry?

CRESSIDA: So he says here.

PANDARUS: True, he was so; I know the cause too; he'll lay about him today, I can tell them that. And there's Troilus will not come far behind him; let them take heed of Troilus, I can tell them that too.

CRESSIDA: What, is he angry too?

PANDARUS: Who, Troilus? Troilus is the better man of the two.

CRESSIDA: O Jupiter! there's no comparison.

PANDARUS: What, not between Troilus and Hector? Do you know a man if you see him?

CRESSIDA: Ay, if I ever saw him before and knew him.

PANDARUS: Well, I say Troilus is Troilus.

CRESSIDA: Then you say as I say, for I am sure he is not Hector.

PANDARUS: No, nor Hector is not Troilus in some degrees.

CRESSIDA: 'Tis just to each of them: he is himself.

PANDARUS: Himself! Alas, poor Troilus! I would he were!

CRESSIDA: So he is.

PANDARUS: Condition I had gone barefoot to India.

CRESSIDA: He is not Hector.

PANDARUS: Himself! no, he's not himself. Would 'a were himself! Well, the gods are above; time must friend or end. Well, Troilus, well! I would my heart were in her body! No, Hector is not a better man than Troilus.

CRESSIDA: Excuse me.

PANDARUS: He is elder.

CRESSIDA: Pardon me, pardon me.

PANDARUS: Th' other's not come to't; you shall tell me another tale when th' other's come to't. Hector shall not have his wit this year.

CRESSIDA: He shall not need it if he have his own.

PANDARUS: Nor his qualities.

CRESSIDA: No matter.

PANDARUS: Nor his beauty.

CRESSIDA: 'Twould not become him: his own's better.

PANDARUS: YOU have no judgment, niece. Helen herself swore th' other day that Troilus, for a brown favour, for so 'tis, I must confess- not brown neither-

CRESSIDA: No, but brown.

PANDARUS: Faith, to say truth, brown and not brown.

CRESSIDA: To say the truth, true and not true.

PANDARUS: She prais'd his complexion above Paris.

CRESSIDA: Why, Paris hath colour enough.

PANDARUS: So he has.

CRESSIDA: Then Troilus should have too much. If she prais'd him above, his complexion is higher than his; he having colour enough, and the other higher, is too flaming praise for a good complexion. I had as lief Helen's golden tongue had commended Troilus for a copper nose.

PANDARUS: I swear to you I think Helen loves him better than Paris.

CRESSIDA: Then she's a merry Greek indeed.

PANDARUS: Nay, I am sure she does. She came to him th' other day into the compass'd window-and you know he has not past three or four hairs on his chin-

CRESSIDA: Indeed a tapster's arithmetic may soon bring his particulars therein to a total.

PANDARUS: Why, he is very young, and yet will he within three pound lift as much as his brother Hector.

CRESSIDA: Is he so young a man and so old a lifter?

PANDARUS: But to prove to you that Helen loves him: she came and puts me her white hand to his cloven chin-

CRESSIDA: Juno have mercy! How came it cloven?

PANDARUS: Why, you know, 'tis dimpled. I think his smiling becomes him better than any man in all Phrygia.

CRESSIDA: O, he smiles valiantly!

PANDARUS: Does he not?

CRESSIDA: O yes, an 'twere a cloud in autumn!

PANDARUS: Why, go to, then! But to prove to you that Helen loves Troilus-

CRESSIDA: Troilus will stand to the proof, if you'll prove it so.

PANDARUS: Troilus! Why, he esteems her no more than I esteem an addle egg.

CRESSIDA: If you love an addle egg as well as you love an idle head, you would eat chickens i' th' shell.

PANDARUS: I cannot choose but laugh to think how she tickled his chin. Indeed, she has a marvell's white hand, I must needs confess.

CRESSIDA: Without the rack.

PANDARUS: And she takes upon her to spy a white hair on his chin.

CRESSIDA: Alas, poor chin! Many a wart is richer.

PANDARUS: But there was such laughing! Queen Hecuba laugh'd that her eyes ran o'er.

CRESSIDA: With millstones.

PANDARUS: And Cassandra laugh'd.

CRESSIDA: But there was a more temperate fire under the pot of her eyes. Did her eyes run o'er too?

PANDARUS: And Hector laugh'd.

CRESSIDA: At what was all this laughing?

PANDARUS: Marry, at the white hair that Helen spied on Troilus' chin.

CRESSIDA: An't had been a green hair I should have laugh'd too.

PANDARUS: They laugh'd not so much at the hair as at his pretty answer.

CRESSIDA: What was his answer?

PANDARUS: Quoth she 'Here's but two and fifty hairs on your chin, and one of them is white.'

CRESSIDA: This is her question.

PANDARUS: That's true; make no question of that. 'Two and fifty hairs,' quoth he 'and one white. That white hair is my father, and all the rest are his sons.' 'Jupiter!' quoth she 'which of these hairs is Paris my husband?' 'The forked one,' quoth he, 'pluck't out and give it him.' But there was such laughing! and Helen so blush'd, and Paris so chaf'd; and all the rest so laugh'd that it pass'd.

CRESSIDA: So let it now; for it has been a great while going by.

PANDARUS: Well, cousin, I told you a thing yesterday; think on't.

CRESSIDA: So I do.

PANDARUS: I'll be sworn 'tis true; he will weep you, and 'twere a man born in April.

CRESSIDA: And I'll spring up in his tears, an 'twere a nettle against May.
  Sound a Retreat

PANDARUS: Hark! they are coming from the field. Shall we stand up here and see them as they pass toward Ilium? Good niece, do, sweet niece Cressida.

CRESSIDA: At your pleasure.

PANDARUS: Here, here, here's an excellent place; here we may see most bravely. I'll tell you them all by their names as they pass by; but mark Troilus above the rest.
  Aeneas Passes

CRESSIDA: Speak not so loud.

PANDARUS: That's Aeneas. Is not that a brave man? He's one of the flowers of Troy, I can tell you. But mark Troilus; you shall see anon.
  Antenor Passes

CRESSIDA: Who's that?

PANDARUS: That's Antenor. He has a shrewd wit, I can tell you; and he's a man good enough; he's one o' th' soundest judgments in Troy, whosoever, and a proper man of person. When comes Troilus? I'll show you Troilus anon. If he see me, you shall see him nod at me.

CRESSIDA: Will he give you the nod?

PANDARUS: You shall see.

CRESSIDA: If he do, the rich shall have more.
Hector Passes

PANDARUS: That's Hector, that, that, look you, that; there's a
fellow! Go thy way, Hector! There's a brave man, niece. O brave
Hector! Look how he looks. There's a countenance! Is't not a
brave man?

CRESSIDA: O, a brave man!

PANDARUS: Is 'a not? It does a man's heart good. Look you what
hacks are on his helmet! Look you yonder, do you see? Look you
there. There's no jesting; there's laying on; take't off who
will, as they say. There be hacks.

CRESSIDA: Be those with swords?

PANDARUS: Swords! anything, he cares not; an the devil come to him,
it's all one. By God's lid, it does one's heart good. Yonder
comes Paris, yonder comes Paris.
Paris Passes
Look ye yonder, niece; is't not a gallant man too, is't not? Why, this is brave
now. Who said he came hurt home to-day? He's not hurt. Why, this will do
Helen's heart good now, ha! Would I could see Troilus now! You shall see
Troilus anon.
Helenus Passes

CRESSIDA: Who's that?

PANDARUS: That's Helenus. I marvel where Troilus is. That's
Helenus. I think he went not forth to-day. That's Helenus.

CRESSIDA: Can Helenus fight, uncle?

PANDARUS: Helenus! no. Yes, he'll fight indifferent well. I marvel
where Troilus is. Hark! do you not hear the people cry 'Troilus'?
Helenus is a priest.

CRESSIDA: What sneaking fellow comes yonder?
Troilus Passes

PANDARUS: Where? yonder? That's Deiphobus. 'Tis Troilus. There's a man, niece. Hem! Brave Troilus, the prince of chivalry!

CRESSIDA: Peace, for shame, peace!

PANDARUS: Mark him; note him. O brave Troilus! Look well upon him, niece; look you how his sword is bloodied, and his helm more hack'd than Hector's; and how he looks, and how he goes! O admirable youth! he never saw three and twenty. Go thy way, Troilus, go thy way. Had I a sister were a grace or a daughter a goddess, he should take his choice. O admirable man! Paris? Paris is dirt to him; and, I warrant, Helen, to change, would give an eye to boot.

CRESSIDA: Here comes more.
Common Soldiers Pass

PANDARUS: Asses, fools, dolts! chaff and bran, chaff and bran! porridge after meat! I could live and die in the eyes of Troilus. Ne'er look, ne'er look; the eagles are gone. Crows and daws, crows and daws! I had rather be such a man as Troilus than Agamemnon and all Greece.

CRESSIDA: There is amongst the Greeks Achilles, a better man than Troilus.

PANDARUS: Achilles? A drayman, a porter, a very camel!

CRESSIDA: Well, well.

PANDARUS: Well, well! Why, have you any discretion? Have you any eyes? Do you know what a man is? Is not birth, beauty, good shape, discourse, manhood, learning, gentleness, virtue, youth, liberality, and such like, the spice and salt that season a man?

CRESSIDA: Ay, a minc'd man; and then to be bak'd with no date in the pie, for then the man's date is out.

PANDARUS: You are such a woman! A man knows not at what ward you lie.

CRESSIDA: Upon my back, to defend my belly; upon my wit, to defend my wiles; upon my secrecy, to defend mine honesty; my mask, to defend my beauty; and you, to defend all these; and at all these wards I lie at, at a thousand watches.

PANDARUS: Say one of your watches.

CRESSIDA: Nay, I'll watch you for that; and that's one of the chiefest of them too. If I cannot ward what I would not have hit, I can watch you for telling how I took the blow; unless it swell past hiding, and then it's past watching

PANDARUS: You are such another!
  Enter Troilus' Boy

BOY: Sir, my lord would instantly speak with you.

PANDARUS: Where?

BOY: At your own house; there he unarms him.

PANDARUS: Good boy, tell him I come.
  Exit Boy
I doubt he be hurt. Fare ye well, good niece.

CRESSIDA: Adieu, uncle.

PANDARUS: I will be with you, niece, by and by.

CRESSIDA: To bring, uncle.

PANDARUS: Ay, a token from Troilus.

CRESSIDA: By the same token, you are a bawd.
   Exit Pandarus
Words, vows, gifts, tears, and love's full sacrifice,
He offers in another's enterprise;
But more in Troilus thousand-fold I see
Than in the glass of Pandar's praise may be,
Yet hold I off. Women are angels, wooing:
Things won are done; joy's soul lies in the doing.
That she belov'd knows nought that knows not this:
Men prize the thing ungain'd more than it is.
That she was never yet that ever knew
Love got so sweet as when desire did sue;
Therefore this maxim out of love I teach:
Achievement is command; ungain'd, beseech.
Then though my heart's content firm love doth bear,
Nothing of that shall from mine eyes appear.
   Exit

ACT I. SCENE III. The Grecian Camp. Before Agamemnon's Tent
Sennet. Enter Agamemnon, Nestor, Ulysses, Diomedes, Menelaus, and Others

AGAMEMNON: Princes,
What grief hath set these jaundies o'er your cheeks?
The ample proposition that hope makes
In all designs begun on earth below
Fails in the promis'd largeness; checks and disasters
Grow in the veins of actions highest rear'd,
As knots, by the conflux of meeting sap,
Infects the sound pine, and diverts his grain
Tortive and errant from his course of growth.
Nor, princes, is it matter new to us
That we come short of our suppose so far
That after seven years' siege yet Troy walls stand;
Sith every action that hath gone before,
Whereof we have record, trial did draw

Bias and thwart, not answering the aim,
And that unbodied figure of the thought
That gave't surmised shape. Why then, you princes,
Do you with cheeks abash'd behold our works
And call them shames, which are, indeed, nought else
But the protractive trials of great Jove
To find persistive constancy in men;
The fineness of which metal is not found
In fortune's love? For then the bold and coward,
The wise and fool, the artist and unread,
The hard and soft, seem all affin'd and kin.
But in the wind and tempest of her frown
Distinction, with a broad and powerful fan,
Puffing at all, winnows the light away;
And what hath mass or matter by itself
Lies rich in virtue and unmingled.

NESTOR: With due observance of thy godlike seat,
Great Agamemnon, Nestor shall apply
Thy latest words. In the reproof of chance
Lies the true proof of men. The sea being smooth,
How many shallow bauble boats dare sail
Upon her patient breast, making their way
With those of nobler bulk!
But let the ruffian Boreas once enrage
The gentle Thetis, and anon behold
The strong-ribb'd bark through liquid mountains cut,
Bounding between the two moist elements
Like Perseus' horse. Where's then the saucy boat,
Whose weak untimber'd sides but even now
Co-rivall'd greatness? Either to harbour fled
Or made a toast for Neptune. Even so
Doth valour's show and valour's worth divide
In storms of fortune; for in her ray and brightness
The herd hath more annoyance by the breeze
Than by the tiger; but when the splitting wind
Makes flexible the knees of knotted oaks,

And flies fled under shade-why, then the thing of courage
As rous'd with rage, with rage doth sympathise,
And with an accent tun'd in self-same key
Retorts to chiding fortune.

ULYSSES: Agamemnon,
Thou great commander, nerve and bone of Greece,
Heart of our numbers, soul and only spirit
In whom the tempers and the minds of all
Should be shut up-hear what Ulysses speaks.
Besides the applause and approbation
The which, *To Agamemnon* most mighty, for thy place and sway,
To Nestor And, thou most reverend, for thy stretch'd-out life,
I give to both your speeches- which were such
As Agamemnon and the hand of Greece
Should hold up high in brass; and such again
As venerable Nestor, hatch'd in silver,
Should with a bond of air, strong as the axle-tree
On which heaven rides, knit all the Greekish ears
To his experienc'd tongue-yet let it please both,
Thou great, and wise, to hear Ulysses speak.

AGAMEMNON: Speak, Prince of Ithaca; and be't of less expect
That matter needless, of importless burden,
Divide thy lips than we are confident,
When rank Thersites opes his mastic jaws,
We shall hear music, wit, and oracle.

ULYSSES: Troy, yet upon his basis, had been down,
And the great Hector's sword had lack'd a master,
But for these instances:
The specialty of rule hath been neglected;
And look how many Grecian tents do stand
Hollow upon this plain, so many hollow factions.
When that the general is not like the hive,
To whom the foragers shall all repair,
What honey is expected? Degree being vizarded,

Th' unworthiest shows as fairly in the mask.
The heavens themselves, the planets, and this centre,
Observe degree, priority, and place,
Insisture, course, proportion, season, form,
Office, and custom, in all line of order;
And therefore is the glorious planet Sol
In noble eminence enthron'd and spher'd
Amidst the other, whose med'cinable eye
Corrects the ill aspects of planets evil,
And posts, like the commandment of a king,
Sans check, to good and bad. But when the planets
In evil mixture to disorder wander,
What plagues and what portents, what mutiny,
What raging of the sea, shaking of earth,
Commotion in the winds! Frights, changes, horrors,
Divert and crack, rend and deracinate,
The unity and married calm of states
Quite from their fixture! O, when degree is shak'd,
Which is the ladder of all high designs,
The enterprise is sick! How could communities,
Degrees in schools, and brotherhoods in cities,
Peaceful commerce from dividable shores,
The primogenity and due of birth,
Prerogative of age, crowns, sceptres, laurels,
But by degree, stand in authentic place?
Take but degree away, untune that string,
And hark what discord follows! Each thing melts
In mere oppugnancy: the bounded waters
Should lift their bosoms higher than the shores,
And make a sop of all this solid globe;
Strength should be lord of imbecility,
And the rude son should strike his father dead;
Force should be right; or, rather, right and wrong-
Between whose endless jar justice resides-
Should lose their names, and so should justice too.
Then everything includes itself in power,
Power into will, will into appetite;

And appetite, an universal wolf,
So doubly seconded with will and power,
Must make perforce an universal prey,
And last eat up himself. Great Agamemnon,
This chaos, when degree is suffocate,
Follows the choking.
And this neglection of degree it is
That by a pace goes backward, with a purpose
It hath to climb. The general's disdain'd
By him one step below, he by the next,
That next by him beneath; so ever step,
Exampl'd by the first pace that is sick
Of his superior, grows to an envious fever
Of pale and bloodless emulation.
And 'tis this fever that keeps Troy on foot,
Not her own sinews. To end a tale of length,
Troy in our weakness stands, not in her strength.

NESTOR: Most wisely hath Ulysses here discover'd
The fever whereof all our power is sick.

AGAMEMNON: The nature of the sickness found, Ulysses,
What is the remedy?

ULYSSES: The great Achilles, whom opinion crowns
The sinew and the forehand of our host,
Having his ear full of his airy fame,
Grows dainty of his worth, and in his tent
Lies mocking our designs; with him Patroclus
Upon a lazy bed the livelong day
Breaks scurril jests;
And with ridiculous and awkward action-
Which, slanderer, he imitation calls-
He pageants us. Sometime, great Agamemnon,
Thy topless deputation he puts on;
And like a strutting player whose conceit
Lies in his hamstring, and doth think it rich

To hear the wooden dialogue and sound
'Twixt his stretch'd footing and the scaffoldage-
Such to-be-pitied and o'er-wrested seeming
He acts thy greatness in; and when he speaks
'Tis like a chime a-mending; with terms unsquar'd,
Which, from the tongue of roaring Typhon dropp'd,
Would seem hyperboles. At this fusty stuff
The large Achilles, on his press'd bed lolling,
From his deep chest laughs out a loud applause;
Cries 'Excellent! 'tis Agamemnon just.
Now play me Nestor; hem, and stroke thy beard,
As he being drest to some oration.'
That's done-as near as the extremest ends
Of parallels, as like Vulcan and his wife;
Yet god Achilles still cries 'Excellent!
'Tis Nestor right. Now play him me, Patroclus,
Arming to answer in a night alarm.'
And then, forsooth, the faint defects of age
Must be the scene of mirth: to cough and spit
And, with a palsy-fumbling on his gorget,
Shake in and out the rivet. And at this sport
Sir Valour dies; cries 'O, enough, Patroclus;
Or give me ribs of steel! I shall split all
In pleasure of my spleen.' And in this fashion
All our abilities, gifts, natures, shapes,
Severals and generals of grace exact,
Achievements, plots, orders, preventions,
Excitements to the field or speech for truce,
Success or loss, what is or is not, serves
As stuff for these two to make paradoxes.

NESTOR: And in the imitation of these twain-
Who, as Ulysses says, opinion crowns
With an imperial voice-many are infect.
Ajax is grown self-will'd and bears his head
In such a rein, in full as proud a place
As broad Achilles; keeps his tent like him;

Makes factious feasts; rails on our state of war
Bold as an oracle, and sets Thersites,
A slave whose gall coins slanders like a mint,
To match us in comparisons with dirt,
To weaken and discredit our exposure,
How rank soever rounded in with danger.

ULYSSES: They tax our policy and call it cowardice,
Count wisdom as no member of the war,
Forestall prescience, and esteem no act
But that of hand. The still and mental parts
That do contrive how many hands shall strike
When fitness calls them on, and know, by measure
Of their observant toil, the enemies' weight-
Why, this hath not a finger's dignity:
They call this bed-work, mapp'ry, closet-war;
So that the ram that batters down the wall,
For the great swinge and rudeness of his poise,
They place before his hand that made the engine,
Or those that with the fineness of their souls
By reason guide his execution.

NESTOR: Let this be granted, and Achilles' horse
Makes many Thetis' sons.
    Tucket

AGAMEMNON: What trumpet? Look, Menelaus.

MENELAUS: From Troy.
    Enter Aeneas

AGAMEMNON: What would you fore our tent?

AENEAS: Is this great Agamemnon's tent, I pray you?

AGAMEMNON: Even this.

AENEAS: May one that is a herald and a prince
Do a fair message to his kingly eyes?

AGAMEMNON: With surety stronger than Achilles' an
Fore all the Greekish heads, which with one voice
Call Agamemnon head and general.

AENEAS: Fair leave and large security. How may
A stranger to those most imperial looks
Know them from eyes of other mortals?

AGAMEMNON: How?

AENEAS: Ay;
I ask, that I might waken reverence,
And bid the cheek be ready with a blush
Modest as Morning when she coldly eyes
The youthful Phoebus.
Which is that god in office, guiding men?
Which is the high and mighty Agamemnon?

AGAMEMNON: This Troyan scorns us, or the men of Troy
Are ceremonious courtiers.

AENEAS: Courtiers as free, as debonair, unarm'd,
As bending angels; that's their fame in peace.
But when they would seem soldiers, they have galls,
Good arms, strong joints, true swords; and, Jove's accord,
Nothing so full of heart. But peace, Aeneas,
Peace, Troyan; lay thy finger on thy lips.
The worthiness of praise distains his worth,
If that the prais'd himself bring the praise forth;
But what the repining enemy commends,
That breath fame blows; that praise, sole pure, transcends.

AGAMEMNON: Sir, you of Troy, call you yourself Aeneas?

AENEAS: Ay, Greek, that is my name.

AGAMEMNON: What's your affair, I pray you?

AENEAS: Sir, pardon; 'tis for Agamemnon's ears.

AGAMEMNON: He hears nought privately that comes from Troy.

AENEAS: Nor I from Troy come not to whisper with him;
I bring a trumpet to awake his ear,
To set his sense on the attentive bent,
And then to speak.

AGAMEMNON: Speak frankly as the wind;
It is not Agamemnon's sleeping hour.
That thou shalt know, Troyan, he is awake,
He tells thee so himself.

AENEAS: Trumpet, blow loud,
Send thy brass voice through all these lazy tents;
And every Greek of mettle, let him know
What Troy means fairly shall be spoke aloud.
    Sound Trumpet
We have, great Agamemnon, here in Troy
A prince called Hector-Priam is his father-
Who in this dull and long-continued truce
Is resty grown; he bade me take a trumpet
And to this purpose speak: Kings, princes, lords!
If there be one among the fair'st of Greece
That holds his honour higher than his ease,
That seeks his praise more than he fears his peril,
That knows his valour and knows not his fear,
That loves his mistress more than in confession
With truant vows to her own lips he loves,
And dare avow her beauty and her worth
In other arms than hers-to him this challenge.
Hector, in view of Troyans and of Greeks,

Shall make it good or do his best to do it:
He hath a lady wiser, fairer, truer,
Than ever Greek did couple in his arms;
And will to-morrow with his trumpet call
Mid-way between your tents and walls of Troy
To rouse a Grecian that is true in love.
If any come, Hector shall honour him;
If none, he'll say in Troy, when he retires,
The Grecian dames are sunburnt and not worth
The splinter of a lance. Even so much.

AGAMEMNON: This shall be told our lovers, Lord Aeneas.
If none of them have soul in such a kind,
We left them all at home. But we are soldiers;
And may that soldier a mere recreant prove
That means not, hath not, or is not in love.
If then one is, or hath, or means to be,
That one meets Hector; if none else, I am he.

NESTOR: Tell him of Nestor, one that was a man
When Hector's grandsire suck'd. He is old now;
But if there be not in our Grecian mould
One noble man that hath one spark of fire
To answer for his love, tell him from me
I'll hide my silver beard in a gold beaver,
And in my vantbrace put this wither'd brawn,
And, meeting him, will tell him that my lady
Was fairer than his grandame, and as chaste
As may be in the world. His youth in flood,
I'll prove this truth with my three drops of blood.

AENEAS: Now heavens forfend such scarcity of youth!

ULYSSES: Amen.

AGAMEMNON: Fair Lord Aeneas, let me touch your hand;
To our pavilion shall I lead you, first.

Achilles shall have word of this intent;
So shall each lord of Greece, from tent to tent.
Yourself shall feast with us before you go,
And find the welcome of a noble foe.
    Exeunt All but Ulysses and Nestor

ULYSSES: Nestor!

NESTOR: What says Ulysses?

ULYSSES: I have a young conception in my brain;
Be you my time to bring it to some shape.

NESTOR: What is't?

ULYSSES: This 'tis:
Blunt wedges rive hard knots. The seeded pride
That hath to this maturity blown up
In rank Achilles must or now be cropp'd
Or, shedding, breed a nursery of like evil
To overbulk us all.

NESTOR: Well, and how?

ULYSSES: This challenge that the gallant Hector sends,
However it is spread in general name,
Relates in purpose only to Achilles.

NESTOR: True. The purpose is perspicuous even as substance
Whose grossness little characters sum up;
And, in the publication, make no strain
But that Achilles, were his brain as barren
As banks of Libya-though, Apollo knows,
'Tis dry enough-will with great speed of judgment,
Ay, with celerity, find Hector's purpose
Pointing on him.

ULYSSES: And wake him to the answer, think you?

NESTOR: Why, 'tis most meet. Who may you else oppose
That can from Hector bring those honours off,
If not Achilles? Though 't be a sportful combat,
Yet in this trial much opinion dwells;
For here the Troyans taste our dear'st repute
With their fin'st palate; and trust to me, Ulysses,
Our imputation shall be oddly pois'd
In this vile action; for the success,
Although particular, shall give a scantling
Of good or bad unto the general;
And in such indexes, although small pricks
To their subsequent volumes, there is seen
The baby figure of the giant mas
Of things to come at large. It is suppos'd
He that meets Hector issues from our choice;
And choice, being mutual act of all our souls,
Makes merit her election, and doth boil,
As 'twere from forth us all, a man distill'd
Out of our virtues; who miscarrying,
What heart receives from hence a conquering part,
To steel a strong opinion to themselves?
Which entertain'd, limbs are his instruments,
In no less working than are swords and bows
Directive by the limbs.

ULYSSES: Give pardon to my speech.
Therefore 'tis meet Achilles meet not Hector.
Let us, like merchants, show our foulest wares
And think perchance they'll sell; if not, the lustre
Of the better yet to show shall show the better,
By showing the worst first. Do not consent
That ever Hector and Achilles meet;
For both our honour and our shame in this
Are dogg'd with two strange followers.

NESTOR: I see them not with my old eyes. What are they?

ULYSSES: What glory our Achilles shares from Hector,
Were he not proud, we all should wear with him;
But he already is too insolent;
And it were better parch in Afric sun
Than in the pride and salt scorn of his eyes,
Should he scape Hector fair. If he were foil'd,
Why, then we do our main opinion crush
In taint of our best man. No, make a lott'ry;
And, by device, let blockish Ajax draw
The sort to fight with Hector. Among ourselves
Give him allowance for the better man;
For that will physic the great Myrmidon,
Who broils in loud applause, and make him fall
His crest, that prouder than blue Iris bends.
If the dull brainless Ajax come safe off,
We'll dress him up in voices; if he fail,
Yet go we under our opinion still
That we have better men. But, hit or miss,
Our project's life this shape of sense assumes-
Ajax employ'd plucks down Achilles' plumes.

NESTOR: Now, Ulysses, I begin to relish thy advice;
And I will give a taste thereof forthwith
To Agamemnon. Go we to him straight.
Two curs shall tame each other: pride alone
Must tarre the mastiffs on, as 'twere their bone.
    Exeunt

ACT II. SCENE I. The Grecian Camp
Enter Ajax and Thersites

AJAX: Thersites!

THERSITES: Agamemnon-how if he had boils full, an over, generally?

AJAX: Thersites!

THERSITES: And those boils did run-say so. Did not the general run then? Were not that a botchy core?

AJAX: Dog!

THERSITES: Then there would come some matter from him; I see none now.

AJAX: Thou bitch-wolf's son, canst thou not hear? Feel, then.
  Strikes Him

THERSITES: The plague of Greece upon thee, thou mongrel beef-witted lord!

AJAX: Speak, then, thou whinid'st leaven, speak. I will beat thee into handsomeness.

THERSITES: I shall sooner rail thee into wit and holiness; but I think thy horse will sooner con an oration than thou learn a prayer without book. Thou canst strike, canst thou? A red murrain o' thy jade's tricks!

AJAX: Toadstool, learn me the proclamation.

THERSITES: Dost thou think I have no sense, thou strikest me thus?

AJAX: The proclamation!

THERSITES: Thou art proclaim'd, a fool, I think.

AJAX: Do not, porpentine, do not; my fingers itch.

THERSITES: I would thou didst itch from head to foot and I had the scratching of thee; I would make thee the loathsomest scab in Greece. When thou art forth in the incursions, thou strikest as slow as another.

AJAX: I say, the proclamation.

THERSITES: Thou grumblest and railest every hour on Achilles; and thou art as full of envy at his greatness as Cerberus is at Proserpina's beauty-ay, that thou bark'st at him.

AJAX: Mistress Thersites!

THERSITES: Thou shouldst strike him.

AJAX: Cobloaf!

THERSITES: He would pun thee into shivers with his fist, as a sailor breaks a biscuit.

AJAX: You whoreson cur!
   Strikes Him

THERSITES: Do, do.

AJAX: Thou stool for a witch!

THERSITES: Ay, do, do; thou sodden-witted lord! Thou hast no more brain than I have in mine elbows; an assinico may tutor thee. You scurvy valiant ass! Thou art here but to thrash Troyans, and thou art bought and sold among those of any wit like a barbarian slave. If thou use to beat me, I will begin at thy heel and tell what thou art by inches, thou thing of no bowels, thou!

AJAX: You dog!

THERSITES: You scurvy lord!

AJAX: You cur!
   Strikes Him

THERSITES: Mars his idiot! Do, rudeness; do, camel; do, do.
Enter Achilles and Patroclus

ACHILLES: Why, how now, Ajax! Wherefore do you thus?
How now, Thersites! What's the matter, man?

THERSITES: You see him there, do you?

ACHILLES: Ay; what's the matter?

THERSITES: Nay, look upon him.

ACHILLES: So I do. What's the matter?

THERSITES: Nay, but regard him well.

ACHILLES: Well! why, so I do.

THERSITES: But yet you look not well upon him; for who some ever
you take him to be, he is Ajax.

ACHILLES: I know that, fool.

THERSITES: Ay, but that fool knows not himself.

AJAX: Therefore I beat thee.

THERSITES: Lo, lo, lo, lo, what modicums of wit he utters! His
evasions have ears thus long. I have bobb'd his brain more than
he has beat my bones. I will buy nine sparrows for a penny, and
his pia mater is not worth the ninth part of a sparrow. This
lord, Achilles, Ajax-who wears his wit in his belly and his guts
in his head-I'll tell you what I say of him.

ACHILLES: What?

THERSITES: I say this Ajax-

Ajax Offers to Strike Him

ACHILLES: Nay, good Ajax.

THERSITES: Has not so much wit-

ACHILLES: Nay, I must hold you.

THERSITES: As will stop the eye of Helen's needle, for whom he comes to fight.

ACHILLES: Peace, fool.

THERSITES: I would have peace and quietness, but the fool will not-he there; that he; look you there.

AJAX: O thou damned cur! I shall-

ACHILLES: Will you set your wit to a fool's?

THERSITES: No, I warrant you, the fool's will shame it.

PATROCLUS: Good words, Thersites.

ACHILLES: What's the quarrel?

AJAX: I bade the vile owl go learn me the tenour of the proclamation, and he rails upon me.

THERSITES: I serve thee not.

AJAX: Well, go to, go to.

THERSITES: I serve here voluntary.

ACHILLES: Your last service was suff'rance; 'twas not voluntary. No man is beaten voluntary. Ajax was here the voluntary, and you as under an impress.

THERSITES: E'en so; a great deal of your wit too lies in your sinews, or else there be liars. Hector shall have a great catch an he knock out either of your brains: 'a were as good crack a fusty nut with no kernel.

ACHILLES: What, with me too, Thersites?

THERSITES: There's Ulysses and old Nestor-whose wit was mouldy ere your grandsires had nails on their toes-yoke you like draught oxen, and make you plough up the wars.

ACHILLES: What, what?

THERSITES: Yes, good sooth. To Achilles, to Ajax, to-

AJAX: I shall cut out your tongue.

THERSITES: 'Tis no matter; I shall speak as much as thou afterwards.

PATROCLUS: No more words, Thersites; peace!

THERSITES: I will hold my peace when Achilles' brach bids me, shall I?

ACHILLES: There's for you, Patroclus.

THERSITES: I will see you hang'd like clotpoles ere I come any more to your tents. I will keep where there is wit stirring, and leave the faction of fools.
    Exit

PATROCLUS: A good riddance.

ACHILLES: Marry, this, sir, is proclaim'd through all our host,

That Hector, by the fifth hour of the sun,
Will with a trumpet 'twixt our tents and Troy,
To-morrow morning, call some knight to arms
That hath a stomach; and such a one that dare
Maintain I know not what; 'tis trash. Farewell.

AJAX: Farewell. Who shall answer him?

ACHILLES: I know not; 'tis put to lott'ry. Otherwise. He knew his man.

AJAX: O, meaning you! I will go learn more of it.
　　Exeunt

ACT II. SCENE II. Troy. Priam's Palace
Enter Priam, Hector, Troilus, Paris, and Helenus

PRIAM: After so many hours, lives, speeches, spent,
Thus once again says Nestor from the Greeks:
'Deliver Helen, and all damage else-
As honour, loss of time, travail, expense,
Wounds, friends, and what else dear that is consum'd
In hot digestion of this cormorant war-
Shall be struck off.' Hector, what say you to't?

HECTOR: Though no man lesser fears the Greeks than I,
As far as toucheth my particular,
Yet, dread Priam,
There is no lady of more softer bowels,
More spongy to suck in the sense of fear,
More ready to cry out 'Who knows what follows?'
Than Hector is. The wound of peace is surety,
Surety secure; but modest doubt is call'd
The beacon of the wise, the tent that searches
To th' bottom of the worst. Let Helen go.
Since the first sword was drawn about this question,
Every tithe soul 'mongst many thousand dismes
Hath been as dear as Helen-I mean, of ours.

If we have lost so many tenths of ours
To guard a thing not ours, nor worth to us,
Had it our name, the value of one ten,
What merit's in that reason which denies
The yielding of her up?

TROILUS: Fie, fie, my brother!
Weigh you the worth and honour of a king,
So great as our dread father's, in a scale
Of common ounces? Will you with counters sum
The past-proportion of his infinite,
And buckle in a waist most fathomless
With spans and inches so diminutive
As fears and reasons? Fie, for godly shame!

HELENUS: No marvel though you bite so sharp at reasons,
You are so empty of them. Should not our father
Bear the great sway of his affairs with reasons,
Because your speech hath none that tells him so?

TROILUS: You are for dreams and slumbers, brother priest;
You fur your gloves with reason. Here are your reasons:
You know an enemy intends you harm;
You know a sword employ'd is perilous,
And reason flies the object of all harm.
Who marvels, then, when Helenus beholds
A Grecian and his sword, if he do set
The very wings of reason to his heels
And fly like chidden Mercury from Jove,
Or like a star disorb'd? Nay, if we talk of reason,
Let's shut our gates and sleep. Manhood and honour
Should have hare hearts, would they but fat their thoughts
With this cramm'd reason. Reason and respect
Make livers pale and lustihood deject.

HECTOR: Brother, she is not worth what she doth, cost
The keeping.

TROILUS: What's aught but as 'tis valued?

HECTOR: But value dwells not in particular will:
It holds his estimate and dignity
As well wherein 'tis precious of itself
As in the prizer. 'Tis mad idolatry
To make the service greater than the god-I
And the will dotes that is attributive
To what infectiously itself affects,
Without some image of th' affected merit.

TROILUS: I take to-day a wife, and my election
Is led on in the conduct of my will;
My will enkindled by mine eyes and ears,
Two traded pilots 'twixt the dangerous shores
Of will and judgment: how may I avoid,
Although my will distaste what it elected,
The wife I chose? There can be no evasion
To blench from this and to stand firm by honour.
We turn not back the silks upon the merchant
When we have soil'd them; nor the remainder viands
We do not throw in unrespective sieve,
Because we now are full. It was thought meet
Paris should do some vengeance on the Greeks;
Your breath with full consent benied his sails;
The seas and winds, old wranglers, took a truce,
And did him service. He touch'd the ports desir'd;
And for an old aunt whom the Greeks held captive
He brought a Grecian queen, whose youth and freshness
Wrinkles Apollo's, and makes stale the morning.
Why keep we her? The Grecians keep our aunt.
Is she worth keeping? Why, she is a pearl
Whose price hath launch'd above a thousand ships,
And turn'd crown'd kings to merchants.
If you'll avouch 'twas wisdom Paris went-
As you must needs, for you all cried 'Go, go'-
If you'll confess he brought home worthy prize-

As you must needs, for you all clapp'd your hands,
And cried 'Inestimable!' -why do you now
The issue of your proper wisdoms rate,
And do a deed that never fortune did-
Beggar the estimation which you priz'd
Richer than sea and land? O theft most base,
That we have stol'n what we do fear to keep!
But thieves unworthy of a thing so stol'n
That in their country did them that disgrace
We fear to warrant in our native place!

CASSANDRA: *Within* Cry, Troyans, cry.

PRIAM: What noise, what shriek is this?

TROILUS: 'Tis our mad sister; I do know her voice.

CASSANDRA: *Within* Cry, Troyans.

HECTOR: It is Cassandra.
  Enter Cassandra, Raving

CASSANDRA: Cry, Troyans, cry. Lend me ten thousand eyes,
And I will fill them with prophetic tears.

HECTOR: Peace, sister, peace.

CASSANDRA: Virgins and boys, mid-age and wrinkled eld,
Soft infancy, that nothing canst but cry,
Add to my clamours. Let us pay betimes
A moiety of that mass of moan to come.
Cry, Troyans, cry. Practise your eyes with tears.
Troy must not be, nor goodly Ilion stand;
Our firebrand brother, Paris, burns us all.
Cry, Troyans, cry, A Helen and a woe!
Cry, cry. Troy burns, or else let Helen go.
  Exit

HECTOR: Now, youthful Troilus, do not these high strains
Of divination in our sister work
Some touches of remorse, or is your blood
So madly hot that no discourse of reason,
Nor fear of bad success in a bad cause,
Can qualify the same?

TROILUS: Why, brother Hector,
We may not think the justness of each act
Such and no other than event doth form it;
Nor once deject the courage of our minds
Because Cassandra's mad. Her brain-sick raptures
Cannot distaste the goodness of a quarrel
Which hath our several honours all engag'd
To make it gracious. For my private part,
I am no more touch'd than all Priam's sons;
And Jove forbid there should be done amongst us
Such things as might offend the weakest spleen
To fight for and maintain.

PARIS: Else might the world convince of levity
As well my undertakings as your counsels;
But I attest the gods, your full consent
Gave wings to my propension, and cut of
All fears attending on so dire a project.
For what, alas, can these my single arms?
What propugnation is in one man's valour
To stand the push and enmity of those
This quarrel would excite? Yet, I protest,
Were I alone to pass the difficulties,
And had as ample power as I have will,
Paris should ne'er retract what he hath done
Nor faint in the pursuit.

PRIAM: Paris, you speak
Like one besotted on your sweet delights.
You have the honey still, but these the gall;

So to be valiant is no praise at all.

PARIS: Sir, I propose not merely to myself
The pleasures such a beauty brings with it;
But I would have the soil of her fair rape
Wip'd off in honourable keeping her.
What treason were it to the ransack'd queen,
Disgrace to your great worths, and shame to me,
Now to deliver her possession up
On terms of base compulsion! Can it be
That so degenerate a strain as this
Should once set footing in your generous bosoms?
There's not the meanest spirit on our party
Without a heart to dare or sword to draw
When Helen is defended; nor none so noble
Whose life were ill bestow'd or death unfam'd
Where Helen is the subject. Then, I say,
Well may we fight for her whom we know well
The world's large spaces cannot parallel.

HECTOR: Paris and Troilus, you have both said well;
And on the cause and question now in hand
Have gloz'd, but superficially; not much
Unlike young men, whom Aristode thought
Unfit to hear moral philosophy.
The reasons you allege do more conduce
To the hot passion of distemp'red blood
Than to make up a free determination
'Twixt right and wrong; for pleasure and revenge
Have ears more deaf than adders to the voice
Of any true decision. Nature craves
All dues be rend'red to their owners. Now,
What nearer debt in all humanity
Than wife is to the husband? If this law
Of nature be corrupted through affection;
And that great minds, of partial indulgence
To their benumbed wills, resist the same;

There is a law in each well-order'd nation
To curb those raging appetites that are
Most disobedient and refractory.
If Helen, then, be wife to Sparta's king-
As it is known she is-these moral laws
Of nature and of nations speak aloud
To have her back return'd. Thus to persist
In doing wrong extenuates not wrong,
But makes it much more heavy. Hector's opinion
Is this, in way of truth. Yet, ne'er the less,
My spritely brethren, I propend to you
In resolution to keep Helen still;
For 'tis a cause that hath no mean dependence
Upon our joint and several dignities.

TROILUS: Why, there you touch'd the life of our design.
Were it not glory that we more affected
Than the performance of our heaving spleens,
I would not wish a drop of Troyan blood
Spent more in her defence. But, worthy Hector,
She is a theme of honour and renown,
A spur to valiant and magnanimous deeds,
Whose present courage may beat down our foes,
And fame in time to come canonize us;
For I presume brave Hector would not lose
So rich advantage of a promis'd glory
As smiles upon the forehead of this action
For the wide world's revenue.

HECTOR: I am yours,
You valiant offspring of great Priamus.
I have a roisting challenge sent amongst
The dull and factious nobles of the Greeks
Will strike amazement to their drowsy spirits.
I was advertis'd their great general slept,
Whilst emulation in the army crept.
This, I presume, will wake him.

Exeunt

ACT II. SCENE III. The Grecian Camp. Before the Tent of Achilles
Enter Thersites, Solus

THERSITES: How now, Thersites! What,
lost in the labyrinth of thy fury? Shall the
elephant Ajax carry it thus? He beats me, and
I rail at him. O worthy satisfaction! Would it
were otherwise: that I could beat him, whilst he
rail'd at me! 'Sfoot, I'll learn to conjure and raise
devils, but I'll see some issue of my spiteful
execrations. Then there's Achilles, a rare engineer!
If Troy be not taken till these two undermine it,
the walls will stand till they fall of themselves.
O thou great thunder-darter of Olympus,
forget that thou art Jove, the king of gods, and,
Mercury, lose all the serpentine craft of thy caduceus,
if ye take not that little little less-than-little
wit from them that they have! which short-arm'd
ignorance itself knows is so abundant scarce, it will
not in circumvention deliver a fly from a spider
without drawing their massy irons and cutting the web.
After this, the vengeance on the whole camp! or,
rather, the Neapolitan bone-ache! for that,
methinks, is the curse depending on those that
war for a placket. I have said my prayers; and
devil Envy say 'Amen.' What ho! my Lord Achilles!
    Enter Patroclus

PATROCLUS: Who's there? Thersites! Good Thersites, come in and
rail.

THERSITES: If I could 'a rememb'red a gilt counterfeit, thou
wouldst not have slipp'd out of my contemplation; but it is no
matter; thyself upon thyself! The common curse of mankind, folly
and ignorance, be thine in great revenue! Heaven bless thee from

a tutor, and discipline come not near thee! Let thy blood be thy direction till thy death. Then if she that lays thee out says thou art a fair corse, I'll be sworn and sworn upon't she never shrouded any but lazars. Amen. Where's Achilles?

PATROCLUS: What, art thou devout? Wast thou in prayer?

THERSITES: Ay, the heavens hear me!

PATROCLUS: Amen.
  Enter Achilles

ACHILLES: Who's there?

PATROCLUS: Thersites, my lord.

ACHILLES: Where, where? O, where? Art thou come? Why, my cheese, my digestion, why hast thou not served thyself in to my table so many meals? Come, what's Agamemnon?

THERSITES: Thy commander, Achilles. Then tell me, Patroclus, what's Achilles?

PATROCLUS: Thy lord, Thersites. Then tell me, I pray thee, what's Thersites?

THERSITES: Thy knower, Patroclus. Then tell me, Patroclus, what art thou?

PATROCLUS: Thou must tell that knowest.

ACHILLES: O, tell, tell,

THERSITES: I'll decline the whole question. Agamemnon commands Achilles; Achilles is my lord; I am Patroclus' knower; and Patroclus is a fool.

PATROCLUS: You rascal!

THERSITES: Peace, fool! I have not done.

ACHILLES: He is a privileg'd man. Proceed, Thersites.

THERSITES: Agamemnon is a fool; Achilles is a fool; Thersites is a fool; and, as aforesaid, Patroclus is a fool.

ACHILLES: Derive this; come.

THERSITES: Agamemnon is a fool to offer to command Achilles; Achilles is a fool to be commanded of Agamemnon; Thersites is a fool to serve such a fool; and this Patroclus is a fool positive.

PATROCLUS: Why am I a fool?

THERSITES: Make that demand of the Creator. It suffices me thou art. Look you, who comes here?

ACHILLES: Come, Patroclus, I'll speak with nobody. Come in with me,

THERSITES: Here is such patchery, such juggling, and such knavery. All the argument is a whore and a cuckold-a good quarrel to draw emulous factions and bleed to death upon. Now the dry serpigo on the subject, and war and lechery confound all!
Exit
Enter Agamemnon, Ulysses, Nestor, Diomedes, Ajax, and Calchas

AGAMEMNON: Where is Achilles?

PATROCLUS: Within his tent; but ill-dispos'd, my lord.

AGAMEMNON: Let it be known to him that we are here.
He shent our messengers; and we lay by
Our appertainings, visiting of him.
Let him be told so; lest, perchance, he think

We dare not move the question of our place
Or know not what we are.

PATROCLUS: I shall say so to him.
Exit

ULYSSES: We saw him at the opening of his tent.
He is not sick.

AJAX: Yes, lion-sick, sick of proud heart. You may call it
melancholy, if you will favour the man; but, by my head, 'tis
pride. But why, why? Let him show us a cause. A word, my lord.
Takes Agamemnon Aside

NESTOR: What moves Ajax thus to bay at him?

ULYSSES: Achilles hath inveigled his fool from him.

NESTOR: Who, Thersites?

ULYSSES: He.

NESTOR: Then will Ajax lack matter, if he have lost his argument

ULYSSES: No; you see he is his argument that has his argument-
Achilles.

NESTOR: All the better; their fraction is more our wish than their
faction. But it was a strong composure a fool could disunite!

ULYSSES: The amity that wisdom knits not, folly may easily untie.
Re-enter Patroclus
Here comes Patroclus.

NESTOR: No Achilles with him.

ULYSSES: The elephant hath joints, but none for courtesy; his legs are legs for necessity, not for flexure.

PATROCLUS: Achilles bids me say he is much sorry
If any thing more than your sport and pleasure
Did move your greatness and this noble state
To call upon him; he hopes it is no other
But for your health and your digestion sake,
An after-dinner's breath.

AGAMEMNON: Hear you, Patroclus.
We are too well acquainted with these answers;
But his evasion, wing'd thus swift with scorn,
Cannot outfly our apprehensions.
Much attribute he hath, and much the reason
Why we ascribe it to him. Yet all his virtues,
Not virtuously on his own part beheld,
Do in our eyes begin to lose their gloss;
Yea, like fair fruit in an unwholesome dish,
Are like to rot untasted. Go and tell him
We come to speak with him; and you shall not sin
If you do say we think him over-proud
And under-honest, in self-assumption greater
Than in the note of judgment; and worthier than himself
Here tend the savage strangeness he puts on,
Disguise the holy strength of their command,
And underwrite in an observing kind
His humorous predominance; yea, watch
His pettish lunes, his ebbs, his flows, as if
The passage and whole carriage of this action
Rode on his tide. Go tell him this, and ad
That if he overhold his price so much
We'll none of him, but let him, like an engine
Not portable, lie under this report:
Bring action hither; this cannot go to war.
A stirring dwarf we do allowance give
Before a sleeping giant. Tell him so.

PATROCLUS: I shall, and bring his answer presently.
  Exit

AGAMEMNON: In second voice we'll not be satisfied;
We come to speak with him. Ulysses, enter you.
  Exit Ulysses

AJAX: What is he more than another?

AGAMEMNON: No more than what he thinks he is.

AJAX: Is he so much? Do you not think he thinks himself a better
man than I am?

AGAMEMNON: No question.

AJAX: Will you subscribe his thought and say he is?

AGAMEMNON: No, noble Ajax; you are as strong, as valiant, as wise,
no less noble, much more gentle, and altogether more tractable.

AJAX: Why should a man be proud? How doth pride grow? I know not
what pride is.

AGAMEMNON: Your mind is the clearer, Ajax, and your virtues the
fairer. He that is proud eats up himself. Pride is his own glass,
his own trumpet, his own chronicle; and whatever praises itself
but in the deed devours the deed in the praise.
  Re-enter Ulysses

AJAX: I do hate a proud man as I do hate the engend'ring of toads.

NESTOR: *Aside* And yet he loves himself: is't not strange?

ULYSSES: Achilles will not to the field to-morrow.

AGAMEMNON: What's his excuse?

ULYSSES: He doth rely on none;
But carries on the stream of his dispose,
Without observance or respect of any,
In will peculiar and in self-admission.

AGAMEMNON: Why will he not, upon our fair request,
Untent his person and share the air with us?

ULYSSES: Things small as nothing, for request's sake only,
He makes important; possess'd he is with greatness,
And speaks not to himself but with a pride
That quarrels at self-breath. Imagin'd worth
Holds in his blood such swol'n and hot discourse
That 'twixt his mental and his active parts
Kingdom'd Achilles in commotion rages,
And batters down himself. What should I say?
He is so plaguy proud that the death tokens of it
Cry 'No recovery.'

AGAMEMNON: Let Ajax go to him.
Dear lord, go you and greet him in his tent.
'Tis said he holds you well; and will be led
At your request a little from himself.

ULYSSES: O Agamemnon, let it not be so!
We'll consecrate the steps that Ajax makes
When they go from Achilles. Shall the proud lord
That bastes his arrogance with his own seam
And never suffers matter of the world
Enter his thoughts, save such as doth revolve
And ruminate himself-shall he be worshipp'd
Of that we hold an idol more than he?
No, this thrice-worthy and right valiant lord
Shall not so stale his palm, nobly acquir'd,
Nor, by my will, assubjugate his merit,
As amply titled as Achilles is,
By going to Achilles.

That were to enlard his fat-already pride,
And add more coals to Cancer when he burns
With entertaining great Hyperion.
This lord go to him! Jupiter forbid,
And say in thunder 'Achilles go to him.'

NESTOR: *Aside* O, this is well! He rubs the vein of him.

DIOMEDES: *Aside* And how his silence drinks up this applause!

AJAX: If I go to him, with my armed fist I'll pash him o'er the face.

AGAMEMNON: O, no, you shall not go.

AJAX: An 'a be proud with me I'll pheeze his pride.
Let me go to him.

ULYSSES: Not for the worth that hangs upon our quarrel.

AJAX: A paltry, insolent fellow!

NESTOR: *Aside* How he describes himself!

AJAX: Can he not be sociable?

ULYSSES: *Aside* The raven chides blackness.

AJAX: I'll let his humours blood.

AGAMEMNON: *Aside* He will be the physician that should be the patient.

AJAX: An all men were a my mind-

ULYSSES: *Aside* Wit would be out of fashion.

AJAX: 'A should not bear it so, 'a should eat's words first.
Shall pride carry it?

NESTOR: *Aside* An 'twould, you'd carry half.

ULYSSES: *Aside* 'A would have ten shares.

AJAX: I will knead him, I'll make him supple.

NESTOR: *Aside* He's not yet through warm. Force him with praises;
pour in, pour in; his ambition is dry.

ULYSSES: *To Agamemnon* My lord, you feed too much on this dislike.

NESTOR: Our noble general, do not do so.

DIOMEDES: You must prepare to fight without Achilles.

ULYSSES: Why 'tis this naming of him does him harm.
Here is a man-but 'tis before his face;
I will be silent.

NESTOR: Wherefore should you so?
He is not emulous, as Achilles is.

ULYSSES: Know the whole world, he is as valiant.

AJAX: A whoreson dog, that shall palter with us thus!
Would he were a Troyan!

NESTOR: What a vice were it in Ajax now-

ULYSSES: If he were proud.

DIOMEDES: Or covetous of praise.

ULYSSES: Ay, or surly borne.

DIOMEDES: Or strange, or self-affected.

ULYSSES: Thank the heavens, lord, thou art of sweet composure
Praise him that gat thee, she that gave thee suck;
Fam'd be thy tutor, and thy parts of nature
Thrice-fam'd beyond, beyond all erudition;
But he that disciplin'd thine arms to fight-
Let Mars divide eternity in twain
And give him half; and, for thy vigour,
Bull-bearing Milo his addition yield
To sinewy Ajax. I will not praise thy wisdom,
Which, like a bourn, a pale, a shore, confines
Thy spacious and dilated parts. Here's Nestor,
Instructed by the antiquary times-
He must, he is, he cannot but be wise;
But pardon, father Nestor, were your days
As green as Ajax' and your brain so temper'd,
You should not have the eminence of him,
But be as Ajax.

AJAX: Shall I call you father?

NESTOR: Ay, my good son.

DIOMEDES: Be rul'd by him, Lord Ajax.

ULYSSES: There is no tarrying here; the hart Achilles
Keeps thicket. Please it our great general
To call together all his state of war;
Fresh kings are come to Troy. To-morrow
We must with all our main of power stand fast;
And here's a lord-come knights from east to west
And cull their flower, Ajax shall cope the best.

AGAMEMNON: Go we to council. Let Achilles sleep.
Light boats sail swift, though greater hulks draw deep.
   Exeunt

ACT III. SCENE I. Troy. Priam's Palace

Music Sounds Within. Enter Pandarus and a Servant

PANDARUS: Friend, you-pray you, a word. Do you not follow the young Lord Paris?

SERVANT: Ay, sir, when he goes before me.

PANDARUS: You depend upon him, I mean?

SERVANT: Sir, I do depend upon the lord.

PANDARUS: You depend upon a notable gentleman; I must needs praise him.

SERVANT: The lord be praised!

PANDARUS: You know me, do you not?

SERVANT: Faith, sir, superficially.

PANDARUS: Friend, know me better: I am the Lord Pandarus.

SERVANT: I hope I shall know your honour better.

PANDARUS: I do desire it.

SERVANT: You are in the state of grace.

PANDARUS: Grace! Not so, friend; honour and lordship are my titles. What music is this?

SERVANT: I do but partly know, sir; it is music in parts.

PANDARUS: Know you the musicians?

SERVANT: Wholly, sir.

PANDARUS: Who play they to?

SERVANT: To the hearers, sir.

PANDARUS: At whose pleasure, friend?

SERVANT: At mine, sir, and theirs that love music.

PANDARUS: Command, I mean, friend.

SERVANT: Who shall I command, sir?

PANDARUS: Friend, we understand not one another: I am to courtly, and thou art too cunning. At whose request do these men play?

SERVANT: That's to't, indeed, sir. Marry, sir, at the request of Paris my lord, who is there in person; with him the mortal Venus, the heart-blood of beauty, love's invisible soul-

PANDARUS: Who, my cousin, Cressida?

SERVANT: No, sir, Helen. Could not you find out that by her attributes?

PANDARUS: It should seem, fellow, that thou hast not seen the Lady

CRESSIDA: I come to speak with Paris from the Prince Troilus; I will make a complimental assault upon him, for my business seethes.

SERVANT: Sodden business! There's a stew'd phrase indeed!
  Enter Paris and Helen, Attended

PANDARUS: Fair be to you, my lord, and to all this fair company! Fair desires, in all fair measure, fairly guide them- especially to you, fair queen! Fair thoughts be your fair pillow.

HELEN: Dear lord, you are full of fair words.

PANDARUS: You speak your fair pleasure, sweet queen. Fair prince, here is good broken music.

PARIS: You have broke it, cousin; and by my life, you shall make it whole again; you shall piece it out with a piece of your performance.

HELEN: He is full of harmony.

PANDARUS: Truly, lady, no.

HELEN: O, sir-

PANDARUS: Rude, in sooth; in good sooth, very rude.

PARIS: Well said, my lord. Well, you say so in fits.

PANDARUS: I have business to my lord, dear queen. My lord, will you vouchsafe me a word?

HELEN: Nay, this shall not hedge us out. We'll hear you sing, certainly-

PANDARUS: Well sweet queen, you are pleasant with me. But, marry, thus, my lord: my dear lord and most esteemed friend, your brother Troilus-

HELEN: My Lord Pandarus, honey-sweet lord-

PANDARUS: Go to, sweet queen, go to-commends himself most affectionately to you-

HELEN: You shall not bob us out of our melody. If you do, our melancholy upon your head!

PANDARUS: Sweet queen, sweet queen; that's a sweet queen, i' faith.

HELEN: And to make a sweet lady sad is a sour offence.

PANDARUS: Nay, that shall not serve your turn; that shall it not, in truth, la. Nay, I care not for such words; no, no. -And, my lord, he desires you that, if the King call for him at supper, you will make his excuse.

HELEN: My Lord Pandarus!

PANDARUS: What says my sweet queen, my very very sweet queen?

PARIS: What exploit's in hand? Where sups he to-night?

HELEN: Nay, but, my lord-

PANDARUS: What says my sweet queen?-My cousin will fall out with you.

HELEN: You must not know where he sups.

PARIS: I'll lay my life, with my disposer Cressida.

PANDARUS: No, no, no such matter; you are wide. Come, your disposer is sick.

PARIS: Well, I'll make's excuse.

PANDARUS: Ay, good my lord. Why should you say Cressida? No, your poor disposer's sick.

PARIS: I spy.

PANDARUS: You spy! What do you spy?-Come, give me an instrument.

Now, sweet queen.

HELEN: Why, this is kindly done.

PANDARUS: My niece is horribly in love with a thing you have, sweet Queen.

HELEN: She shall have it, my lord, if it be not my Lord Paris.

PANDARUS: He! No, she'll none of him; they two are twain.

HELEN: Falling in, after falling out, may make them three.

PANDARUS: Come, come. I'll hear no more of this; I'll sing you a song now.

HELEN: Ay, ay, prithee now. By my troth, sweet lord, thou hast a fine forehead.

PANDARUS: Ay, you may, you may.

HELEN: Let thy song be love. This love will undo us all. O Cupid, Cupid, Cupid!

PANDARUS: Love! Ay, that it shall, i' faith.

PARIS: Ay, good now, love, love, nothing but love.

PANDARUS: In good troth, it begins so.
  Sings
Love, love, nothing but love, still love, still more!
    For, oh, love's bow
    Shoots buck and doe;
    The shaft confounds
    Not that it wounds,
But tickles still the sore.
These lovers cry, O ho, they die!

Yet that which seems the wound to kill
Doth turn O ho! to ha! ha! he!
    So dying love lives still.
O ho! a while, but ha! ha! ha!
O ho! groans out for ha! ha! ha!-hey ho!

HELEN: In love, i' faith, to the very tip of the nose.

PARIS: He eats nothing but doves, love; and that breeds hot blood, and hot blood begets hot thoughts, and hot thoughts beget hot deeds, and hot deeds is love.

PANDARUS: Is this the generation of love: hot blood, hot thoughts, and hot deeds? Why, they are vipers. Is love a generation of vipers? Sweet lord, who's a-field today?

PARIS: Hector, Deiphobus, Helenus, Antenor, and all the gallantry of Troy. I would fain have arm'd to-day, but my Nell would not have it so. How chance my brother Troilus went not?

HELEN: He hangs the lip at something. You know all, Lord Pandarus.

PANDARUS: Not I, honey-sweet queen. I long to hear how they spend to-day. You'll remember your brother's excuse?

PARIS: To a hair.

PANDARUS: Farewell, sweet queen.

HELEN: Commend me to your niece.

PANDARUS: I will, sweet queen.
    Exit. Sound a retreat

PARIS: They're come from the field. Let us to Priam's hall
To greet the warriors. Sweet Helen, I must woo you
To help unarm our Hector. His stubborn buckles,

With these your white enchanting fingers touch'd,
Shall more obey than to the edge of steel
Or force of Greekish sinews; you shall do more
Than all the island kings-disarm great Hector.

HELEN: 'Twill make us proud to be his servant, Paris;
Yea, what he shall receive of us in duty
Gives us more palm in beauty than we have,
Yea, overshines ourself.

PARIS: Sweet, above thought I love thee.
Exeunt

ACT III. SCENE II. Troy. Pandarus' Orchard
Enter Pandarus and Troilus' Boy, Meeting

PANDARUS: How now! Where's thy master? At my cousin Cressida's?

BOY: No, sir; he stays for you to conduct him thither.
Enter Troilus

PANDARUS: O, here he comes. How now, how now!

TROILUS: Sirrah, walk off.
Exit Boy

PANDARUS: Have you seen my cousin?

TROILUS: No, Pandarus. I stalk about her door
Like a strange soul upon the Stygian banks
Staying for waftage. O, be thou my Charon,
And give me swift transportance to these fields
Where I may wallow in the lily beds
Propos'd for the deserver! O gentle Pandar,
From Cupid's shoulder pluck his painted wings,
And fly with me to Cressid!

PANDARUS: Walk here i' th' orchard, I'll bring her straight.
Exit

TROILUS: I am giddy; expectation whirls me round.
Th' imaginary relish is so sweet
That it enchants my sense; what will it be
When that the wat'ry palate tastes indeed
Love's thrice-repured nectar? Death, I fear me;
Swooning destruction; or some joy too fine,
Too subtle-potent, tun'd too sharp in sweetness,
For the capacity of my ruder powers.
I fear it much; and I do fear besides
That I shall lose distinction in my joys;
As doth a battle, when they charge on heaps
The enemy flying.
Re-enter Pandarus

PANDARUS: She's making her ready, she'll come straight; you must be
witty now. She does so blush, and fetches her wind so short, as
if she were fray'd with a sprite. I'll fetch her. It is the
prettiest villain; she fetches her breath as short as a new-ta'en
sparrow.
Exit

TROILUS: Even such a passion doth embrace my bosom.
My heart beats thicker than a feverous pulse,
And all my powers do their bestowing lose,
Like vassalage at unawares encount'ring
The eye of majesty.
Re-enter Pandarus with Cressida

PANDARUS: Come, come, what need you blush? Shame's a baby.-Here she
is now; swear the oaths now to her that you have sworn to me.-
What, are you gone again? You must be watch'd ere you be made
tame, must you? Come your ways, come your ways; an you draw
backward, we'll put you i' th' fills.-Why do you not speak to
her?-Come, draw this curtain and let's see your picture.

Alas the day, how loath you are to offend daylight! An 'twere
dark, you'd close sooner. So, so; rub on, and kiss the mistress
How now, a kiss in fee-farm! Build there, carpenter; the air is
sweet. Nay, you shall fight your hearts out ere I part you. The
falcon as the tercel, for all the ducks i' th' river. Go to, go to.

TROILUS: You have bereft me of all words, lady.

PANDARUS: Words pay no debts, give her deeds; but she'll bereave
you o' th' deeds too, if she call your activity in question.
What, billing again? Here's 'In witness whereof the parties
interchangeably.' Come in, come in; I'll go get a fire.
  Exit

CRESSIDA: Will you walk in, my lord?

TROILUS: O Cressid, how often have I wish'd me thus!

CRESSIDA: Wish'd, my lord! The gods grant-O my lord!

TROILUS: What should they grant? What makes this pretty abruption?
What too curious dreg espies my sweet lady in the fountain of our love?

CRESSIDA: More dregs than water, if my fears have eyes.

TROILUS: Fears make devils of cherubims; they never see truly.

CRESSIDA: Blind fear, that seeing reason leads, finds safer footing
than blind reason stumbling without fear. To fear the worst oft
cures the worse.

TROILUS: O, let my lady apprehend no fear! In all Cupid's pageant
there is presented no monster.

CRESSIDA: Nor nothing monstrous neither?

TROILUS: Nothing, but our undertakings when we vow to weep seas,

live in fire, cat rocks, tame tigers; thinking it harder for our
mistress to devise imposition enough than for us to undergo any
difficulty imposed. This is the monstruosity in love, lady, that
the will is infinite, and the execution confin'd; that the desire
is boundless, and the act a slave to limit.

CRESSIDA: They say all lovers swear more performance than they are
able, and yet reserve an ability that they never perform; vowing
more than the perfection of ten, and discharging less than the
tenth part of one. They that have the voice of lions and the act
of hares, are they not monsters?

TROILUS: Are there such? Such are not we. Praise us as we are
tasted, allow us as we prove; our head shall go bare till merit
crown it. No perfection in reversion shall have a praise in
present. We will not name desert before his birth; and, being
born, his addition shall be humble. Few words to fair faith:
Troilus shall be such to Cressid as what envy can say worst shall
be a mock for his truth; and what truth can speak truest not
truer than Troilus.

CRESSIDA: Will you walk in, my lord?
  Re-enter Pandarus

PANDARUS: What, blushing still? Have you not done talking yet?

CRESSIDA: Well, uncle, what folly I commit, I dedicate to you.

PANDARUS: I thank you for that; if my lord get a boy of you, you'll
give him me. Be true to my lord; if he flinch, chide me for it.

TROILUS: You know now your hostages: your uncle's word and my firm
faith.

PANDARUS: Nay, I'll give my word for her too: our kindred, though
they be long ere they are wooed, they are constant being won;
they are burs, I can tell you; they'll stick where they are thrown.

CRESSIDA: Boldness comes to me now and brings me heart.
Prince Troilus, I have lov'd you night and day
For many weary months.

TROILUS: Why was my Cressid then so hard to win?

CRESSIDA: Hard to seem won; but I was won, my lord,
With the first glance that ever-pardon me.
If I confess much, you will play the tyrant.
I love you now; but till now not so much
But I might master it. In faith, I lie;
My thoughts were like unbridled children, grown
Too headstrong for their mother. See, we fools!
Why have I blabb'd? Who shall be true to us,
When we are so unsecret to ourselves?
But, though I lov'd you well, I woo'd you not;
And yet, good faith, I wish'd myself a man,
Or that we women had men's privilege
Of speaking first. Sweet, bid me hold my tongue,
For in this rapture I shall surely speak
The thing I shall repent. See, see, your silence,
Cunning in dumbness, from my weakness draws
My very soul of counsel. Stop my mouth.

TROILUS: And shall, albeit sweet music issues thence.

PANDARUS: Pretty, i' faith.

CRESSIDA: My lord, I do beseech you, pardon me;
'Twas not my purpose thus to beg a kiss.
I am asham'd. O heavens! what have I done?
For this time will I take my leave, my lord.

TROILUS: Your leave, sweet Cressid!

PANDARUS: Leave! An you take leave till to-morrow morning-

CRESSIDA: Pray you, content you.

TROILUS: What offends you, lady?

CRESSIDA: Sir, mine own company.

TROILUS: You cannot shun yourself.

CRESSIDA: Let me go and try.
I have a kind of self resides with you;
But an unkind self, that itself will leave
To be another's fool. I would be gone.
Where is my wit? I know not what I speak.

TROILUS: Well know they what they speak that speak so wisely.

CRESSIDA: Perchance, my lord, I show more craft than love;
And fell so roundly to a large confession
To angle for your thoughts; but you are wise-
Or else you love not; for to be wise and love
Exceeds man's might; that dwells with gods above.

TROILUS: O that I thought it could be in a woman-
As, if it can, I will presume in you-
To feed for aye her lamp and flames of love;
To keep her constancy in plight and youth,
Outliving beauty's outward, with a mind
That doth renew swifter than blood decays!
Or that persuasion could but thus convince me
That my integrity and truth to you
Might be affronted with the match and weight
Of such a winnowed purity in love.
How were I then uplifted! but, alas,
I am as true as truth's simplicity,
And simpler than the infancy of truth.

CRESSIDA: In that I'll war with you.

TROILUS: O virtuous fight,
When right with right wars who shall be most right!
True swains in love shall in the world to come
Approve their truth by Troilus, when their rhymes,
Full of protest, of oath, and big compare,
Want similes, truth tir'd with iteration-
As true as steel, as plantage to the moon,
As sun to day, as turtle to her mate,
As iron to adamant, as earth to th' centre-
Yet, after all comparisons of truth,
As truth's authentic author to be cited,
'As true as Troilus' shall crown up the verse
And sanctify the numbers.

CRESSIDA: Prophet may you be!
If I be false, or swerve a hair from truth,
When time is old and hath forgot itself,
When waterdrops have worn the stones of Troy,
And blind oblivion swallow'd cities up,
And mighty states characterless are grated
To dusty nothing-yet let memory
From false to false, among false maids in love,
Upbraid my falsehood when th' have said 'As false
As air, as water, wind, or sandy earth,
As fox to lamb, or wolf to heifer's calf,
Pard to the hind, or stepdame to her son'-
Yea, let them say, to stick the heart of falsehood,
'As false as Cressid.'

PANDARUS: Go to, a bargain made; seal it, seal it; I'll be the
witness. Here I hold your hand; here my cousin's. If ever you
prove false one to another, since I have taken such pains to
bring you together, let all pitiful goers- between be call'd to
the world's end after my name-call them all Pandars; let all
constant men be Troiluses, all false women Cressids, and all
brokers between Pandars. Say 'Amen.'

TROILUS: Amen.

CRESSIDA: Amen.

PANDARUS: Amen. Whereupon I will show you a chamber
and a bed; which bed, because it shall not speak of your
pretty encounters, press it to death. Away!
And Cupid grant all tongue-tied maidens here,
Bed, chamber, pander, to provide this gear!
   Exeunt

ACT III. SCENE III. The Greek Camp

*Flourish. Enter Agamemnon, Ulysses, Diomedes, Nestor, Ajax, Menelaus, and
Calchas*

CALCHAS: Now, Princes, for the service I have done,
Th' advantage of the time prompts me aloud
To call for recompense. Appear it to your mind
That, through the sight I bear in things to come,
I have abandon'd Troy, left my possession,
Incurr'd a traitor's name, expos'd myself
From certain and possess'd conveniences
To doubtful fortunes, sequest'ring from me all
That time, acquaintance, custom, and condition,
Made tame and most familiar to my nature;
And here, to do you service, am become
As new into the world, strange, unacquainted-
I do beseech you, as in way of taste,
To give me now a little benefit
Out of those many regist'red in promise,
Which you say live to come in my behalf.

AGAMEMNON: What wouldst thou of us, Troyan? Make demand.

CALCHAS: You have a Troyan prisoner call'd Antenor,
Yesterday took; Troy holds him very dear.
Oft have you-often have you thanks therefore-

Desir'd my Cressid in right great exchange,
Whom Troy hath still denied; but this Antenor,
I know, is such a wrest in their affairs
That their negotiations all must slack
Wanting his manage; and they will almost
Give us a prince of blood, a son of Priam,
In change of him. Let him be sent, great Princes,
And he shall buy my daughter; and her presence
Shall quite strike off all service I have done
In most accepted pain.

AGAMEMNON: Let Diomedes bear him,
And bring us Cressid hither. Calchas shall have
What he requests of us. Good Diomed,
Furnish you fairly for this interchange;
Withal, bring word if Hector will to-morrow
Be answer'd in his challenge. Ajax is ready.

DIOMEDES: This shall I undertake; and 'tis a burden
Which I am proud to bear.
  Exeunt Diomedes and Calchas
  Achilles and Patroclus Stand in Their Tent

ULYSSES: Achilles stands i' th' entrance of his tent.
Please it our general pass strangely by him,
As if he were forgot; and, Princes all,
Lay negligent and loose regard upon him.
I will come last. 'Tis like he'll question me
Why such unplausive eyes are bent, why turn'd on him?
If so, I have derision med'cinable
To use between your strangeness and his pride,
Which his own will shall have desire to drink.
It may do good. Pride hath no other glass
To show itself but pride; for supple knees
Feed arrogance and are the proud man's fees.

AGAMEMNON: We'll execute your purpose, and put on

A form of strangeness as we pass along.
So do each lord; and either greet him not,
Or else disdainfully, which shall shake him more
Than if not look'd on. I will lead the way.

ACHILLES: What comes the general to speak with me?
You know my mind. I'll fight no more 'gainst Troy.

AGAMEMNON: What says Achilles? Would he aught with us?

NESTOR: Would you, my lord, aught with the general?

ACHILLES: No.

NESTOR: Nothing, my lord.

AGAMEMNON: The better.
    Exeunt Agamemnon and Nestor

ACHILLES: Good day, good day.

MENELAUS: How do you? How do you?
    Exit

ACHILLES: What, does the cuckold scorn me?

AJAX: How now, Patroclus?

ACHILLES: Good morrow, Ajax.

AJAX: Ha?

ACHILLES: Good morrow.

AJAX: Ay, and good next day too.
    Exit

ACHILLES: What mean these fellows? Know they not Achilles?

PATROCLUS: They pass by strangely. They were us'd to bend,
To send their smiles before them to Achilles,
To come as humbly as they us'd to creep
To holy altars.

ACHILLES: What, am I poor of late?
'Tis certain, greatness, once fall'n out with fortune,
Must fall out with men too. What the declin'd is,
He shall as soon read in the eyes of others
As feel in his own fall; for men, like butterflies,
Show not their mealy wings but to the summer;
And not a man for being simply man
Hath any honour, but honour for those honours
That are without him, as place, riches, and favour,
Prizes of accident, as oft as merit;
Which when they fall, as being slippery standers,
The love that lean'd on them as slippery too,
Doth one pluck down another, and together
Die in the fall. But 'tis not so with me:
Fortune and I are friends; I do enjoy
At ample point all that I did possess
Save these men's looks; who do, methinks, find out
Something not worth in me such rich beholding
As they have often given. Here is Ulysses.
I'll interrupt his reading.
How now, Ulysses!

ULYSSES: Now, great Thetis' son!

ACHILLES: What are you reading?

ULYSSES: A strange fellow here
Writes me that man-how dearly ever parted,
How much in having, or without or in-
Cannot make boast to have that which he hath,

Nor feels not what he owes, but by reflection;
As when his virtues shining upon others
Heat them, and they retort that heat again
To the first giver.

ACHILLES: This is not strange, Ulysses.
The beauty that is borne here in the face
The bearer knows not, but commends itself
To others' eyes; nor doth the eye itself-
That most pure spirit of sense-behold itself,
Not going from itself; but eye to eye opposed
Salutes each other with each other's form;
For speculation turns not to itself
Till it hath travell'd, and is mirror'd there
Where it may see itself. This is not strange at all.

ULYSSES: I do not strain at the position-
It is familiar-but at the author's drift;
Who, in his circumstance, expressly proves
That no man is the lord of anything,
Though in and of him there be much consisting,
Till he communicate his parts to others;
Nor doth he of himself know them for aught
Till he behold them formed in th' applause
Where th' are extended; who, like an arch, reverb'rate
The voice again; or, like a gate of steel
Fronting the sun, receives and renders back
His figure and his heat. I was much rapt in this;
And apprehended here immediately
Th' unknown Ajax. Heavens, what a man is there!
A very horse that has he knows not what!
Nature, what things there are
Most abject in regard and dear in use!
What things again most dear in the esteem
And poor in worth! Now shall we see to-morrow-
An act that very chance doth throw upon him-
Ajax renown'd. O heavens, what some men do,

While some men leave to do!
How some men creep in skittish Fortune's-hall,
Whiles others play the idiots in her eyes!
How one man eats into another's pride,
While pride is fasting in his wantonness!
To see these Grecian lords!-why, even already
They clap the lubber Ajax on the shoulder,
As if his foot were on brave Hector's breast,
And great Troy shrinking.

ACHILLES: I do believe it; for they pass'd by me
As misers do by beggars-neither gave to me
Good word nor look. What, are my deeds forgot?

ULYSSES: Time hath, my lord, a wallet at his back,
Wherein he puts alms for oblivion,
A great-siz'd monster of ingratitudes.
Those scraps are good deeds past, which are devour'd
As fast as they are made, forgot as soon
As done. Perseverance, dear my lord,
Keeps honour bright. To have done is to hang
Quite out of fashion, like a rusty mail
In monumental mock'ry. Take the instant way;
For honour travels in a strait so narrow -
Where one but goes abreast. Keep then the path,
For emulation hath a thousand sons
That one by one pursue; if you give way,
Or hedge aside from the direct forthright,
Like to an ent'red tide they all rush by
And leave you hindmost;
Or, like a gallant horse fall'n in first rank,
Lie there for pavement to the abject rear,
O'er-run and trampled on. Then what they do in present,
Though less than yours in past, must o'ertop yours;
For Time is like a fashionable host,
That slightly shakes his parting guest by th' hand;
And with his arms out-stretch'd, as he would fly,

Grasps in the corner. The welcome ever smiles,
And farewell goes out sighing. O, let not virtue seek
Remuneration for the thing it was;
For beauty, wit,
High birth, vigour of bone, desert in service,
Love, friendship, charity, are subjects all
To envious and calumniating Time.
One touch of nature makes the whole world kin-
That all with one consent praise new-born gawds,
Though they are made and moulded of things past,
And give to dust that is a little gilt
More laud than gilt o'er-dusted.
The present eye praises the present object.
Then marvel not, thou great and complete man,
That all the Greeks begin to worship Ajax,
Since things in motion sooner catch the eye
Than what stirs not. The cry went once on thee,
And still it might, and yet it may again,
If thou wouldst not entomb thyself alive
And case thy reputation in thy tent,
Whose glorious deeds but in these fields of late
Made emulous missions 'mongst the gods themselves,
And drave great Mars to faction.

ACHILLES: Of this my privacy
I have strong reasons.

ULYSSES: But 'gainst your privacy
The reasons are more potent and heroical.
'Tis known, Achilles, that you are in love
With one of Priam's daughters.

ACHILLES: Ha! known!

ULYSSES: Is that a wonder?
The providence that's in a watchful state
Knows almost every grain of Plutus' gold;

Finds bottom in th' uncomprehensive deeps;
Keeps place with thought, and almost, like the gods,
Do thoughts unveil in their dumb cradles.
There is a mystery-with whom relation
Durst never meddle-in the soul of state,
Which hath an operation more divine
Than breath or pen can give expressure to.
All the commerce that you have had with Troy
As perfectly is ours as yours, my lord;
And better would it fit Achilles much
To throw down Hector than Polyxena.
But it must grieve young Pyrrhus now at home,
When fame shall in our island sound her trump,
And all the Greekish girls shall tripping sing
'Great Hector's sister did Achilles win;
But our great Ajax bravely beat down him.'
Farewell, my lord. I as your lover speak.
The fool slides o'er the ice that you should break.
   Exit

PATROCLUS: To this effect, Achilles, have I mov'd you.
A woman impudent and mannish grown
Is not more loath'd than an effeminate man
In time of action. I stand condemn'd for this;
They think my little stomach to the war
And your great love to me restrains you thus.
Sweet, rouse yourself; and the weak wanton Cupid
Shall from your neck unloose his amorous fold,
And, like a dew-drop from the lion's mane,
Be shook to airy air.

ACHILLES: Shall Ajax fight with Hector?

PATROCLUS: Ay, and perhaps receive much honour by him.

ACHILLES: I see my reputation is at stake;
My fame is shrewdly gor'd.

PATROCLUS: O, then, beware:
Those wounds heal ill that men do give themselves;
Omission to do what is necessary
Seals a commission to a blank of danger;
And danger, like an ague, subtly taints
Even then when they sit idly in the sun.

ACHILLES: Go call Thersites hither, sweet Patroclus.
I'll send the fool to Ajax, and desire him
T' invite the Troyan lords, after the combat,
To see us here unarm'd. I have a woman's longing,
An appetite that I am sick withal,
To see great Hector in his weeds of peace;
To talk with him, and to behold his visage,
Even to my full of view.
    Enter Thersites
A labour sav'd!

THERSITES: A wonder!

ACHILLES: What?

THERSITES: Ajax goes up and down the field asking for himself.

ACHILLES: How so?

THERSITES: He must fight singly to-morrow with Hector, and is so
prophetically proud of an heroical cudgelling that he raves in
saying nothing.

ACHILLES: How can that be?

THERSITES: Why, 'a stalks up and down like a peacock-a stride and a
stand; ruminaies like an hostess that hath no arithmetic but her
brain to set down her reckoning, bites his lip with a politic
regard, as who should say 'There were wit in this head, an
'twould out'; and so there is; but it lies as coldly in him as

fire in a flint, which will not show without knocking. The man's
undone for ever; for if Hector break not his neck i' th' combat,
he'll break't himself in vainglory. He knows not me. I said 'Good
morrow, Ajax'; and he replies 'Thanks, Agamemnon.' What think you
of this man that takes me for the general? He's grown a very land
fish, languageless, a monster. A plague of opinion! A man may
wear it on both sides, like leather jerkin.

ACHILLES: Thou must be my ambassador to him, Thersites.

THERSITES: Who, I? Why, he'll answer nobody; he professes not
answering. Speaking is for beggars: he wears his tongue in's
arms. I will put on his presence. Let Patroclus make his demands
to me, you shall see the pageant of Ajax.

ACHILLES: To him, Patroclus. Tell him I humbly desire the valiant
Ajax to invite the most valorous Hector to come unarm'd to my
tent; and to procure safe conduct for his person of the
magnanimous and most illustrious six-or-seven-times-honour'd
Captain General of the Grecian army, et cetera, Agamemnon. Do
this.

PATROCLUS: Jove bless great Ajax!

THERSITES: Hum!

PATROCLUS: I come from the worthy Achilles—

THERSITES: Ha!

PATROCLUS: Who most humbly desires you to invite Hector to his tent—

THERSITES: Hum!

PATROCLUS: And to procure safe conduct from Agamemnon.

THERSITES: Agamemnon!

PATROCLUS: Ay, my lord.

THERSITES: Ha!

PATROCLUS: What you say to't?

THERSITES: God buy you, with all my heart.

PATROCLUS: Your answer, sir.

THERSITES: If to-morrow be a fair day, by eleven of the clock it will go one way or other. Howsoever, he shall pay for me ere he has me.

PATROCLUS: Your answer, sir.

THERSITES: Fare ye well, with all my heart.

ACHILLES: Why, but he is not in this tune, is he?

THERSITES: No, but he's out a tune thus. What music will be in him when Hector has knock'd out his brains I know not; but, I am sure, none; unless the fiddler Apollo get his sinews to make catlings on.

ACHILLES: Come, thou shalt bear a letter to him straight.

THERSITES: Let me carry another to his horse; for that's the more capable creature.

ACHILLES: My mind is troubled, like a fountain stirr'd;
And I myself see not the bottom of it.
    Exeunt Achilles and Patroclus

THERSITES: Would the fountain of your mind were clear again, that I might water an ass at it. I had rather be a tick in a sheep than such a valiant ignorance.
    Exit

ACT IV. SCENE I. Troy. A Street

Enter, at One Side, Aeneas, and Servant with a Torch; at Another, Paris, Deiphobus, Antenor, Diomedes the Grecian, and Others, with Torches

PARIS: See, ho! Who is that there?

DEIPHOBUS: It is the Lord Aeneas.

AENEAS: Is the Prince there in person?
Had I so good occasion to lie long
As you, Prince Paris, nothing but heavenly business
Should rob my bed-mate of my company.

DIOMEDES: That's my mind too. Good morrow, Lord Aeneas.

PARIS: A valiant Greek, Aeneas -take his hand:
Witness the process of your speech, wherein
You told how Diomed, a whole week by days,
Did haunt you in the field.

AENEAS: Health to you, valiant sir,
During all question of the gentle truce;
But when I meet you arm'd, as black defiance
As heart can think or courage execute.

DIOMEDES: The one and other Diomed embraces.
Our bloods are now in calm; and so long health!
But when contention and occasion meet,
By Jove, I'll play the hunter for thy life
With all my force, pursuit, and policy.

AENEAS: And thou shalt hunt a lion, that will fly
With his face backward. In humane gentleness,
Welcome to Troy! now, by Anchises' life,
Welcome indeed! By Venus' hand I swear
No man alive can love in such a sort
The thing he means to kill, more excellently.

DIOMEDES: We sympathise. Jove let Aeneas live,
If to my sword his fate be not the glory,
A thousand complete courses of the sun!
But in mine emulous honour let him die
With every joint a wound, and that to-morrow!

AENEAS: We know each other well.

DIOMEDES: We do; and long to know each other worse.

PARIS: This is the most despiteful'st gentle greeting
The noblest hateful love, that e'er I heard of.
What business, lord, so early?

AENEAS: I was sent for to the King; but why, I know not.

PARIS: His purpose meets you: 'twas to bring this Greek
To Calchas' house, and there to render him,
For the enfreed Antenor, the fair Cressid.
Let's have your company; or, if you please,
Haste there before us. I constantly believe-
Or rather call my thought a certain knowledge-
My brother Troilus lodges there to-night.
Rouse him and give him note of our approach,
With the whole quality wherefore; I fear
We shall be much unwelcome.

AENEAS: That I assure you:
Troilus had rather Troy were borne to Greece
Than Cressid borne from Troy.

PARIS: There is no help;
The bitter disposition of the time
Will have it so. On, lord; we'll follow you.

AENEAS: Good morrow, all.
  Exit with servant

PARIS: And tell me, noble Diomed-faith, tell me true,
Even in the soul of sound good-fellowship-
Who in your thoughts deserves fair Helen best,
Myself or Menelaus?

DIOMEDES: Both alike:
He merits well to have her that doth seek her,
Not making any scruple of her soilure,
With such a hell of pain and world of charge;
And you as well to keep her that defend her,
Not palating the taste of her dishonour,
With such a costly loss of wealth and friends.
He like a puling cuckold would drink up
The lees and dregs of a flat tamed piece;
You, like a lecher, out of whorish loins
Are pleas'd to breed out your inheritors.
Both merits pois'd, each weighs nor less nor more;
But he as he, the heavier for a whore.

PARIS: You are too bitter to your country-woman.

DIOMEDES: She's bitter to her country. Hear me, Paris:
For every false drop in her bawdy veins
A Grecian's life hath sunk; for every scruple
Of her contaminated carrion weight
A Troyan hath been slain; since she could speak,
She hath not given so many good words breath
As for her Greeks and Troyans suff'red death.

PARIS: Fair Diomed, you do as chapmen do,
Dispraise the thing that you desire to buy;
But we in silence hold this virtue well:
We'll not commend what we intend to sell.
Here lies our way.
   Exeunt

ACT IV. SCENE II. Troy. The Court of Pandarus' House

Enter Troilus and Cressida

TROILUS: Dear, trouble not yourself; the morn is cold.

CRESSIDA: Then, sweet my lord, I'll call mine uncle down;
He shall unbolt the gates.

TROILUS: Trouble him not;
To bed, to bed! Sleep kill those pretty eyes,
And give as soft attachment to thy senses
As infants' empty of all thought!

CRESSIDA: Good morrow, then.

TROILUS: I prithee now, to bed.

CRESSIDA: Are you aweary of me?

TROILUS: O Cressida! but that the busy day,
Wak'd by the lark, hath rous'd the ribald crows,
And dreaming night will hide our joys no longer,
I would not from thee.

CRESSIDA: Night hath been too brief.

TROILUS: Beshrew the witch! with venomous wights she stays
As tediously as hell, but flies the grasps of love
With wings more momentary-swift than thought.
You will catch cold, and curse me.

CRESSIDA: Prithee tarry.
You men will never tarry.
O foolish Cressid! I might have still held off,
And then you would have tarried. Hark! there's one up.

PANDARUS: *Within* What's all the doors open here?

TROILUS: It is your uncle.
Enter Pandarus

CRESSIDA: A pestilence on him! Now will he be mocking.
I shall have such a life!

PANDARUS: How now, how now! How go maidenheads?
Here, you maid! Where's my cousin Cressid?

CRESSIDA: Go hang yourself, you naughty mocking uncle.
You bring me to do, and then you flout me too.

PANDARUS: To do what? to do what? Let her say what.
What have I brought you to do?

CRESSIDA: Come, come, beshrew your heart! You'll ne'er be good,
Nor suffer others.

PANDARUS: Ha, ha! Alas, poor wretch! a poor capocchia! hast not
slept to-night? Would he not, a naughty man, let it sleep? A
bugbear take him!

CRESSIDA: Did not I tell you? Would he were knock'd i' th' head!
One Knocks
Who's that at door? Good uncle, go and see.
My lord, come you again into my chamber.
You smile and mock me, as if I meant naughtily.

TROILUS: Ha! ha!

CRESSIDA: Come, you are deceiv'd, I think of no such thing.
Knock How earnestly they knock! Pray you come in:
I would not for half Troy have you seen here.
Exeunt Troilus and Cressida

PANDARUS: Who's there? What's the matter? Will you beat down the
door? How now? What's the matter?

Enter Aeneas

AENEAS: Good morrow, lord, good morrow.

PANDARUS: Who's there? My lord Aeneas? By my troth,
I knew you not. What news with you so early?

AENEAS: Is not Prince Troilus here?

PANDARUS: Here! What should he do here?

AENEAS: Come, he is here, my lord; do not deny him.
It doth import him much to speak with me.

PANDARUS: Is he here, say you? It's more than I know, I'll be
sworn. For my own part, I came in late. What should he do here?

AENEAS: Who!-nay, then. Come, come, you'll do him wrong ere you are
ware; you'll be so true to him to be false to him. Do not you
know of him, but yet go fetch him hither; go.
    Re-enter Troilus

TROILUS: How now! What's the matter?

AENEAS: My lord, I scarce have leisure to salute you,
My matter is so rash. There is at hand
Paris your brother, and Deiphobus,
The Grecian Diomed, and our Antenor
Deliver'd to us; and for him forthwith,
Ere the first sacrifice, within this hour,
We must give up to Diomedes' hand
The Lady Cressida.

TROILUS: Is it so concluded?

AENEAS: By Priam, and the general state of Troy.
They are at hand and ready to effect it.

TROILUS: How my achievements mock me!
I will go meet them; and, my lord Aeneas,
We met by chance; you did not find me here.

AENEAS: Good, good, my lord, the secrets of neighbour Pandar
Have not more gift in taciturnity.
   Exeunt Troilus and Aeneas

PANDARUS: Is't possible? No sooner got but lost? The devil take
Antenor! The young prince will go mad. A plague upon Antenor! I
would they had broke's neck.
   Re-enter Cressida

CRESSIDA: How now! What's the matter? Who was here?

PANDARUS: Ah, ah!

CRESSIDA: Why sigh you so profoundly? Where's my lord? Gone? Tell
me, sweet uncle, what's the matter?

PANDARUS: Would I were as deep under the earth as I am above!

CRESSIDA: O the gods! What's the matter?

PANDARUS: Pray thee, get thee in. Would thou hadst ne'er been born!
I knew thou wouldst be his death! O, poor gentleman! A plague
upon Antenor!

CRESSIDA: Good uncle, I beseech you, on my knees I beseech you,
what's the matter?

PANDARUS: Thou must be gone, wench, thou must be gone; thou art
chang'd for Antenor; thou must to thy father, and be gone from

TROILUS: 'Twill be his death; 'twill be his bane; he cannot bear it.

CRESSIDA: O you immortal gods! I will not go.

PANDARUS: Thou must.

CRESSIDA: I will not, uncle. I have forgot my father;
I know no touch of consanguinity,
No kin, no love, no blood, no soul so near me
As the sweet Troilus. O you gods divine,
Make Cressid's name the very crown of falsehood,
If ever she leave Troilus! Time, force, and death,
Do to this body what extremes you can,
But the strong base and building of my love
Is as the very centre of the earth,
Drawing all things to it. I'll go in and weep-

PANDARUS: Do, do.

CRESSIDA: Tear my bright hair, and scratch my praised cheeks,
Crack my clear voice with sobs and break my heart,
With sounding 'Troilus.' I will not go from Troy.
   Exeunt

ACT IV. SCENE III. Troy. A Street Before Pandarus' House
Enter Paris, Troilus, Aeneas, Deiphobus, Antenor, and Diomedes

PARIS: It is great morning; and the hour prefix'd
For her delivery to this valiant Greek
Comes fast upon. Good my brother Troilus,
Tell you the lady what she is to do
And haste her to the purpose.

TROILUS: Walk into her house.
I'll bring her to the Grecian presently;
And to his hand when I deliver her,
Think it an altar, and thy brother Troilus
A priest, there off'ring to it his own heart.
   Exit

PARIS: I know what 'tis to love,

And would, as I shall pity, I could help!
Please you walk in, my lords.
Exeunt

ACT IV. SCENE IV. Troy. Pandarus' House
Enter Pandarus and Cressida

PANDARUS: Be moderate, be moderate.

CRESSIDA: Why tell you me of moderation?
The grief is fine, full, perfect, that I taste,
And violenteth in a sense as strong
As that which causeth it. How can I moderate it?
If I could temporize with my affections
Or brew it to a weak and colder palate,
The like allayment could I give my grief.
My love admits no qualifying dross;
No more my grief, in such a precious loss.
Enter Troilus

PANDARUS: Here, here, here he comes. Ah, sweet ducks!

CRESSIDA: O Troilus! Troilus!
Embracing Him

PANDARUS: What a pair of spectacles is here! Let me embrace too. 'O
heart,' as the goodly saying is,
  O heart, heavy heart,
  Why sigh'st thou without breaking?
where he answers again
  Because thou canst not ease thy smart
  By friendship nor by speaking.
There was never a truer rhyme. Let us cast away nothing, for we
may live to have need of such a verse. We see it, we see it. How
now, lambs!

TROILUS: Cressid, I love thee in so strain'd a purity

That the bless'd gods, as angry with my fancy,
More bright in zeal than the devotion which
Cold lips blow to their deities, take thee from me.

CRESSIDA: Have the gods envy?

PANDARUS: Ay, ay, ay; 'tis too plain a case.

CRESSIDA: And is it true that I must go from Troy?

TROILUS: A hateful truth.

CRESSIDA: What, and from Troilus too?

TROILUS: From Troy and Troilus.

CRESSIDA: Is't possible?

TROILUS: And suddenly; where injury of chance
Puts back leave-taking, justles roughly by
All time of pause, rudely beguiles our lips
Of all rejoindure, forcibly prevents
Our lock'd embrasures, strangles our dear vows
Even in the birth of our own labouring breath.
We two, that with so many thousand sighs
Did buy each other, must poorly sell ourselves
With the rude brevity and discharge of one.
Injurious time now with a robber's haste
Crams his rich thievery up, he knows not how.
As many farewells as be stars in heaven,
With distinct breath and consign'd kisses to them,
He fumbles up into a loose adieu,
And scants us with a single famish'd kiss,
Distasted with the salt of broken tears.

AENEAS: *Within* My lord, is the lady ready?

TROILUS: Hark! you are call'd. Some say the Genius so
Cries 'Come' to him that instantly must die.
Bid them have patience; she shall come anon.

PANDARUS: Where are my tears? Rain, to lay this wind, or my heart
will be blown up by th' root?
  Exit

CRESSIDA: I must then to the Grecians?

TROILUS: No remedy.

CRESSIDA: A woeful Cressid 'mongst the merry Greeks!
When shall we see again?

TROILUS: Hear me, my love. Be thou but true of heart-

CRESSIDA: I true! how now! What wicked deem is this?

TROILUS: Nay, we must use expostulation kindly,
For it is parting from us.
I speak not 'Be thou true' as fearing thee,
For I will throw my glove to Death himself
That there's no maculation in thy heart;
But 'Be thou true' say I to fashion in
My sequent protestation: be thou true,
And I will see thee.

CRESSIDA: O, you shall be expos'd, my lord, to dangers
As infinite as imminent! But I'll be true.

TROILUS: And I'll grow friend with danger. Wear this sleeve.

CRESSIDA: And you this glove. When shall I see you?

TROILUS: I will corrupt the Grecian sentinels
To give thee nightly visitation.

But yet be true.

CRESSIDA: O heavens! 'Be true' again!

TROILUS: Hear why I speak it, love.
The Grecian youths are full of quality;
They're loving, well compos'd with gifts of nature,
And flowing o'er with arts and exercise.
How novelties may move, and parts with person,
Alas, a kind of godly jealousy,
Which I beseech you call a virtuous sin,
Makes me afeard.

CRESSIDA: O heavens! you love me not.

TROILUS: Die I a villain, then!
In this I do not call your faith in question
So mainly as my merit. I cannot sing,
Nor heel the high lavolt, nor sweeten talk,
Nor play at subtle games-fair virtues all,
To which the Grecians are most prompt and pregnant;
But I can tell that in each grace of these
There lurks a still and dumb-discoursive devil
That tempts most cunningly. But be not tempted.

CRESSIDA: Do you think I will?

TROILUS: No.
But something may be done that we will not;
And sometimes we are devils to ourselves,
When we will tempt the frailty of our powers,
Presuming on their changeful potency.

AENEAS: *Within* Nay, good my lord!

TROILUS: Come, kiss; and let us part.

PARIS: *Within* Brother Troilus!

TROILUS: Good brother, come you hither;
And bring Aeneas and the Grecian with you.

CRESSIDA: My lord, will you be true?

TROILUS: Who, I? Alas, it is my vice, my fault!
Whiles others fish with craft for great opinion,
I with great truth catch mere simplicity;
Whilst some with cunning gild their copper crowns,
With truth and plainness I do wear mine bare.
   Enter Aeneas, Paris, Antenor, Deiphobus, and Diomedes
Fear not my truth: the moral of my wit
Is 'plain and true'; there's all the reach of it.
Welcome, Sir Diomed! Here is the lady
Which for Antenor we deliver you;
At the port, lord, I'll give her to thy hand,
And by the way possess thee what she is.
Entreat her fair; and, by my soul, fair Greek,
If e'er thou stand at mercy of my sword,
Name Cressid, and thy life shall be as safe
As Priam is in Ilion.

DIOMEDES: Fair Lady Cressid,
So please you, save the thanks this prince expects.
The lustre in your eye, heaven in your cheek,
Pleads your fair usage; and to Diomed
You shall be mistress, and command him wholly.

TROILUS: Grecian, thou dost not use me courteously
To shame the zeal of my petition to the
In praising her. I tell thee, lord of Greece,
She is as far high-soaring o'er thy praises
As thou unworthy to be call'd her servant.
I charge thee use her well, even for my charge;
For, by the dreadful Pluto, if thou dost not,

Though the great bulk Achilles be thy guard,
I'll cut thy throat.

DIOMEDES: O, be not mov'd, Prince Troilus.
Let me be privileg'd by my place and message
To be a speaker free: when I am hence
I'll answer to my lust. And know you, lord,
I'll nothing do on charge: to her own worth
She shall be priz'd. But that you say 'Be't so,'
I speak it in my spirit and honour, 'No.'

TROILUS: Come, to the port. I'll tell thee, Diomed,
This brave shall oft make thee to hide thy head.
Lady, give me your hand; and, as we walk,
To our own selves bend we our needful talk.
    Exeunt Troilus, Cressida, and Diomedes Sound Trumpet

PARIS: Hark! Hector's trumpet.

AENEAS: How have we spent this morning!
The Prince must think me tardy and remiss,
That swore to ride before him to the field.

PARIS: 'Tis Troilus' fault. Come, come to field with him.

DEIPHOBUS: Let us make ready straight.

AENEAS: Yea, with a bridegroom's fresh alacrity
Let us address to tend on Hector's heels.
The glory of our Troy doth this day lie
On his fair worth and single chivalry.
    Exeunt

ACT IV. SCENE V. The Grecian Camp. Lists Set out

Enter Ajax, Armed; Agamemnon, Achilles, Patroclus, Menelaus, Ulysses, Nestor, and Others

AGAMEMNON: Here art thou in appointment fresh and fair,
Anticipating time with starting courage.
Give with thy trumpet a loud note to Troy,
Thou dreadful Ajax, that the appalled air
May pierce the head of the great combatant,
And hale him hither.

AJAX: Thou, trumpet, there's my purse.
Now crack thy lungs and split thy brazen pipe;
Blow, villain, till thy sphered bias cheek
Out-swell the colic of puff Aquilon'd.
Come, stretch thy chest, and let thy eyes spout blood:
Thou blowest for Hector.
   Trumpet Sounds

ULYSSES: No trumpet answers.

ACHILLES: 'Tis but early days.
   Enter Diomedes, with Cressida

AGAMEMNON: Is not yond Diomed, with Calchas' daughter?

ULYSSES: 'Tis he, I ken the manner of his gait:
He rises on the toe. That spirit of his
In aspiration lifts him from the earth.

AGAMEMNON: Is this the lady Cressid?

DIOMEDES: Even she.

AGAMEMNON: Most dearly welcome to the Greeks, sweet lady.

NESTOR: Our general doth salute you with a kiss.

ULYSSES: Yet is the kindness but particular;
'Twere better she were kiss'd in general.

NESTOR: And very courtly counsel: I'll begin.
So much for Nestor.

ACHILLES: I'll take that winter from your lips, fair lady.
Achilles bids you welcome.

MENELAUS: I had good argument for kissing once.

PATROCLUS: But that's no argument for kissing now;
For thus popp'd Paris in his hardiment,
And parted thus you and your argument.

ULYSSES: O deadly gall, and theme of all our scorns!
For which we lose our heads to gild his horns.

PATROCLUS: The first was Menelaus' kiss; this, mine-
    Kisses Her Again
Patroclus kisses you.

MENELAUS: O, this is trim!

PATROCLUS: Paris and I kiss evermore for him.

MENELAUS: I'll have my kiss, sir. Lady, by your leave.

CRESSIDA: In kissing, do you render or receive?

PATROCLUS: Both take and give.

CRESSIDA: I'll make my match to live,
The kiss you take is better than you give;
Therefore no kiss.

MENELAUS: I'll give you boot; I'll give you three for one.

CRESSIDA: You are an odd man; give even or give none.

MENELAUS: An odd man, lady? Every man is odd.

CRESSIDA: No, Paris is not; for you know 'tis true
That you are odd, and he is even with you.

MENELAUS: You fillip me o' th' head.

CRESSIDA: No, I'll be sworn.

ULYSSES: It were no match, your nail against his horn.
May I, sweet lady, beg a kiss of you?

CRESSIDA: You may.

ULYSSES: I do desire it.

CRESSIDA: Why, beg then.

ULYSSES: Why then, for Venus' sake give me a kiss
When Helen is a maid again, and his.

CRESSIDA: I am your debtor; claim it when 'tis due.

ULYSSES: Never's my day, and then a kiss of you.

DIOMEDES: Lady, a word. I'll bring you to your father.
  Exit with Cressida

NESTOR: A woman of quick sense.

ULYSSES: Fie, fie upon her!
There's language in her eye, her cheek, her lip,
Nay, her foot speaks; her wanton spirits look out
At every joint and motive of her body.
O these encounters so glib of tongue

That give a coasting welcome ere it comes,
And wide unclasp the tables of their thoughts
To every ticklish reader! Set them down
For sluttish spoils of opportunity,
And daughters of the game.
    Trumpet Within

ALL: The Troyans' trumpet.
    Enter Hector, Armed; Aeneas, Troilus, Paris, Helenus, and Other Trojans, with Attendants

AGAMEMNON: Yonder comes the troop.

AENEAS: Hail, all the state of Greece! What shall be done
To him that victory commands? Or do you purpose
A victor shall be known? Will you the knights
Shall to the edge of all extremity
Pursue each other, or shall they be divided
By any voice or order of the field?
Hector bade ask.

AGAMEMNON: Which way would Hector have it?

AENEAS: He cares not; he'll obey conditions.

ACHILLES: 'Tis done like Hector; but securely done,
A little proudly, and great deal misprizing
The knight oppos'd.

AENEAS: If not Achilles, sir,
What is your name?

ACHILLES: If not Achilles, nothing.

AENEAS: Therefore Achilles. But whate'er, know this:
In the extremity of great and little
Valour and pride excel themselves in Hector;

The one almost as infinite as all,
The other blank as nothing. Weigh him well,
And that which looks like pride is courtesy.
This Ajax is half made of Hector's blood;
In love whereof half Hector stays at home;
Half heart, half hand, half Hector comes to seek
This blended knight, half Troyan and half Greek.

ACHILLES: A maiden battle then? O, I perceive you!
Re-enter Diomedes

AGAMEMNON: Here is Sir Diomed. Go, gentle knight,
Stand by our Ajax. As you and Lord Eneas
Consent upon the order of their fight,
So be it; either to the uttermost,
Or else a breath. The combatants being kin
Half stints their strife before their strokes begin.
Ajax and Hector Enter the Lists

ULYSSES: They are oppos'd already.

AGAMEMNON: What Troyan is that same that looks so heavy?

ULYSSES: The youngest son of Priam, a true knight;
Not yet mature, yet matchless; firm of word;
Speaking in deeds and deedless in his tongue;
Not soon provok'd, nor being provok'd soon calm'd;
His heart and hand both open and both free;
For what he has he gives, what thinks he shows,
Yet gives he not till judgment guide his bounty,
Nor dignifies an impair thought with breath;
Manly as Hector, but more dangerous;
For Hector in his blaze of wrath subscribes
To tender objects, but he in heat of action
Is more vindicative than jealous love.
They call him Troilus, and on him erect
A second hope as fairly built as Hector.

Thus says Aeneas, one that knows the youth
Even to his inches, and, with private soul,
Did in great Ilion thus translate him to me.
   Alarum. Hector and Ajax Fight

AGAMEMNON: They are in action.

NESTOR: Now, Ajax, hold thine own!

TROILUS: Hector, thou sleep'st;
Awake thee.

AGAMEMNON: His blows are well dispos'd. There, Ajax!
   Trumpets Cease

DIOMEDES: You must no more.

AENEAS: Princes, enough, so please you.

AJAX: I am not warm yet; let us fight again.

DIOMEDES: As Hector pleases.

HECTOR: Why, then will I no more.
Thou art, great lord, my father's sister's son,
A cousin-german to great Priam's seed;
The obligation of our blood forbids
A gory emulation 'twixt us twain:
Were thy commixtion Greek and Troyan so
That thou could'st say 'This hand is Grecian all,
And this is Troyan; the sinews of this leg
All Greek, and this all Troy; my mother's blood
Runs on the dexter cheek, and this sinister
Bounds in my father's'; by Jove multipotent,
Thou shouldst not bear from me a Greekish member
Wherein my sword had not impressure made
Of our rank feud; but the just gods gainsay

That any drop thou borrow'dst from thy mother,
My sacred aunt, should by my mortal sword
Be drained! Let me embrace thee, Ajax.
By him that thunders, thou hast lusty arms;
Hector would have them fall upon him thus.
Cousin, all honour to thee!

AJAX: I thank thee, Hector.
Thou art too gentle and too free a man.
I came to kill thee, cousin, and bear hence
A great addition earned in thy death.

HECTOR: Not Neoptolemus so mirable,
On whose bright crest Fame with her loud'st Oyes
Cries 'This is he' could promise to himself
A thought of added honour torn from Hector.

AENEAS: There is expectance here from both the sides
What further you will do.

HECTOR: We'll answer it:
The issue is embracement. Ajax, farewell.

AJAX: If I might in entreaties find success,
As seld I have the chance, I would desire
My famous cousin to our Grecian tents.

DIOMEDES: 'Tis Agamemnon's wish; and great Achilles
Doth long to see unarm'd the valiant Hector.

HECTOR: Aeneas, call my brother Troilus to me,
And signify this loving interview
To the expecters of our Troyan part;
Desire them home. Give me thy hand, my cousin;
I will go eat with thee, and see your knights.
   Agamemnon and the Rest of the Greeks Come Forward

AJAX: Great Agamemnon comes to meet us here.

HECTOR: The worthiest of them tell me name by name;
But for Achilles, my own searching eyes
Shall find him by his large and portly size.

AGAMEMNON:Worthy all arms! as welcome as to one
That would be rid of such an enemy.
But that's no welcome. Understand more clear,
What's past and what's to come is strew'd with husks
And formless ruin of oblivion;
But in this extant moment, faith and troth,
Strain'd purely from all hollow bias-drawing,
Bids thee with most divine integrity,
From heart of very heart, great Hector, welcome.

HECTOR: I thank thee, most imperious Agamemnon.

AGAMEMNON: *To Troilus* My well-fam'd lord of Troy, no less to you.

MENELAUS: Let me confirm my princely brother's greeting.
You brace of warlike brothers, welcome hither.

HECTOR: Who must we answer?

AENEAS: The noble Menelaus.

HECTOR: O you, my lord? By Mars his gauntlet, thanks!
Mock not that I affect the untraded oath;
Your quondam wife swears still by Venus' glove.
She's well, but bade me not commend her to you.

MENELAUS: Name her not now, sir; she's a deadly theme.

HECTOR: O, pardon; I offend.

NESTOR: I have, thou gallant Troyan, seen thee oft,

Labouring for destiny, make cruel way
Through ranks of Greekish youth; and I have seen thee,
As hot as Perseus, spur thy Phrygian steed,
Despising many forfeits and subduements,
When thou hast hung thy advanced sword i' th' air,
Not letting it decline on the declined;
That I have said to some my standers-by
'Lo, Jupiter is yonder, dealing life!'
And I have seen thee pause and take thy breath,
When that a ring of Greeks have hemm'd thee in,
Like an Olympian wrestling. This have I seen;
But this thy countenance, still lock'd in steel,
I never saw till now. I knew thy grandsire,
And once fought with him. He was a soldier good,
But, by great Mars, the captain of us all,
Never like thee. O, let an old man embrace thee;
And, worthy warrior, welcome to our tents.

AENEAS: 'Tis the old Nestor.

HECTOR: Let me embrace thee, good old chronicle,
That hast so long walk'd hand in hand with time.
Most reverend Nestor, I am glad to clasp thee.

NESTOR: I would my arms could match thee in contention
As they contend with thee in courtesy.

HECTOR: I would they could.

NESTOR: Ha!
By this white beard, I'd fight with thee to-morrow.
Well, welcome, welcome! I have seen the time.

ULYSSES: I wonder now how yonder city stands,
When we have here her base and pillar by us.

HECTOR: I know your favour, Lord Ulysses, well.

Ah, sir, there's many a Greek and Troyan dead,
Since first I saw yourself and Diomed
In Ilion on your Greekish embassy.

ULYSSES: Sir, I foretold you then what would ensue.
My prophecy is but half his journey yet;
For yonder walls, that pertly front your town,
Yond towers, whose wanton tops do buss the clouds,
Must kiss their own feet.

HECTOR: I must not believe you.
There they stand yet; and modestly I think
The fall of every Phrygian stone will cost
A drop of Grecian blood. The end crowns all;
And that old common arbitrator, Time,
Will one day end it.

ULYSSES: So to him we leave it.
Most gentle and most valiant Hector, welcome.
After the General, I beseech you next
To feast with me and see me at my tent.

ACHILLES: I shall forestall thee, Lord Ulysses, thou!
Now, Hector, I have fed mine eyes on thee;
I have with exact view perus'd thee, Hector,
And quoted joint by joint.

HECTOR: Is this Achilles?

ACHILLES: I am Achilles.

HECTOR: Stand fair, I pray thee; let me look on thee.

ACHILLES: Behold thy fill.

HECTOR: Nay, I have done already.

ACHILLES: Thou art too brief. I will the second time,
As I would buy thee, view thee limb by limb.

HECTOR: O, like a book of sport thou'lt read me o'er;
But there's more in me than thou understand'st.
Why dost thou so oppress me with thine eye?

ACHILLES: Tell me, you heavens, in which part of his body
Shall I destroy him? Whether there, or there, or there?
That I may give the local wound a name,
And make distinct the very breach whereout
Hector's great spirit flew. Answer me, heavens.

HECTOR: It would discredit the blest gods, proud man,
To answer such a question. Stand again.
Think'st thou to catch my life so pleasantly
As to prenominate in nice conjecture
Where thou wilt hit me dead?

ACHILLES: I tell thee yea.

HECTOR: Wert thou an oracle to tell me so,
I'd not believe thee. Henceforth guard thee well;
For I'll not kill thee there, nor there, nor there;
But, by the forge that stithied Mars his helm,
I'll kill thee everywhere, yea, o'er and o'er.
You wisest Grecians, pardon me this brag.
His insolence draws folly from my lips;
But I'll endeavour deeds to match these words,
Or may I never-

AJAX: Do not chafe thee, cousin;
And you, Achilles, let these threats alone
Till accident or purpose bring you to't.
You may have every day enough of Hector,
If you have stomach. The general state, I fear,
Can scarce entreat you to be odd with him.

HECTOR: I pray you let us see you in the field;
We have had pelting wars since you refus'd
The Grecians' cause.

ACHILLES: Dost thou entreat me, Hector?
To-morrow do I meet thee, fell as death;
To-night all friends.

HECTOR: Thy hand upon that match.

AGAMEMNON: First, all you peers of Greece, go to my tent;
There in the full convive we; afterwards,
As Hector's leisure and your bounties shall
Concur together, severally entreat him.
Beat loud the tambourines, let the trumpets blow,
That this great soldier may his welcome know.
    Exeunt All but Troilus and Ulysses

TROILUS: My Lord Ulysses, tell me, I beseech you,
In what place of the field doth Calchas keep?

ULYSSES: At Menelaus' tent, most princely Troilus.
There Diomed doth feast with him to-night,
Who neither looks upon the heaven nor earth,
But gives all gaze and bent of amorous view
On the fair Cressid.

TROILUS: Shall I, sweet lord, be bound to you so much,
After we part from Agamemnon's tent,
To bring me thither?

ULYSSES: You shall command me, sir.
As gentle tell me of what honour was
This Cressida in Troy? Had she no lover there
That wails her absence?

TROILUS: O, sir, to such as boasting show their scars

A mock is due. Will you walk on, my lord?
She was belov'd, she lov'd; she is, and doth;
But still sweet love is food for fortune's tooth.
Exeunt

ACT V. SCENE I. The Grecian Camp. Before the Tent of Achilles
Enter Achilles and Patroclus

ACHILLES: I'll heat his blood with Greekish wine to-night,
Which with my scimitar I'll cool to-morrow.
Patroclus, let us feast him to the height.

PATROCLUS: Here comes Thersites.
Enter Thersites

ACHILLES: How now, thou core of envy!
Thou crusty batch of nature, what's the news?

THERSITES: Why, thou picture of what thou seemest, and idol of
idiot worshippers, here's a letter for thee.

ACHILLES: From whence, fragment?

THERSITES: Why, thou full dish of fool, from Troy.

PATROCLUS: Who keeps the tent now?

THERSITES: The surgeon's box or the patient's wound.

PATROCLUS: Well said, Adversity! and what needs these tricks?

THERSITES: Prithee, be silent, boy; I profit not by thy talk; thou
art said to be Achilles' male varlet.

PATROCLUS: Male varlet, you rogue! What's that?

THERSITES: Why, his masculine whore. Now, the rotten diseases of

the south, the guts-griping ruptures, catarrhs, loads o' gravel
in the back, lethargies, cold palsies, raw eyes, dirt-rotten
livers, wheezing lungs, bladders full of imposthume, sciaticas,
limekilns i' th' palm, incurable bone-ache, and the rivelled fee-
simple of the tetter, take and take again such preposterous
discoveries!

PATROCLUS: Why, thou damnable box of envy, thou, what meanest thou
to curse thus?

THERSITES: Do I curse thee?

PATROCLUS: Why, no, you ruinous butt; you whoreson
indistinguishable cur, no.

THERSITES: No! Why art thou, then, exasperate, thou idle immaterial
skein of sleid silk, thou green sarcenet flap for a sore eye,
thou tassel of a prodigal's purse, thou? Ah, how the poor world is
pest'red with such water-flies-diminutives of nature!

PATROCLUS: Out, gall!

THERSITES: Finch egg!

ACHILLES: My sweet Patroclus, I am thwarted quite
From my great purpose in to-morrow's battle.
Here is a letter from Queen Hecuba,
A token from her daughter, my fair love,
Both taxing me and gaging me to keep
An oath that I have sworn. I will not break it.
Fall Greeks; fail fame; honour or go or stay;
My major vow lies here, this I'll obey.
Come, come, Thersites, help to trim my tent;
This night in banqueting must all be spent.
Away, Patroclus!
    Exit with Patroclus

THERSITES: With too much blood and too little brain these two may run mad; but, if with too much brain and to little blood they do, I'll be a curer of madmen. Here's Agamemnon, an honest fellow enough, and one that loves quails, but he has not so much brain as ear-wax; and the goodly transformation of Jupiter there, his brother, the bull, the primitive statue and oblique memorial of cuckolds, a thrifty shoeing-horn in a chain, hanging at his brother's leg-to what form but that he is, should wit larded with malice, and malice forced with wit, turn him to? To an ass, were nothing: he is both ass and ox. To an ox, were nothing: he is both ox and ass. To be a dog, a mule, a cat, a fitchew, a toad, a lizard, an owl, a put-tock, or a herring without a roe, I would not care; but to be Menelaus, I would conspire against destiny. Ask me not what I would be, if I were not Thersites; for I care not to be the louse of a lazar, so I were not Menelaus. Hey-day! sprites and fires!

Enter Hector, Troilus, Ajax, Agamemnon, Ulysses, Nestor, Menelaus, and Diomedes, with Lights

AGAMEMNON: We go wrong, we go wrong.

AJAX: No, yonder 'tis;
There, where we see the lights.

HECTOR: I trouble you.

AJAX: No, not a whit.
Re-enter Achilles

ULYSSES: Here comes himself to guide you.

ACHILLES: Welcome, brave Hector; welcome, Princes all.

AGAMEMNON: So now, fair Prince of Troy, I bid good night;
Ajax commands the guard to tend on you.

HECTOR: Thanks, and good night to the Greeks' general.

MENELAUS: Good night, my lord.

HECTOR: Good night, sweet Lord Menelaus.

THERSITES: Sweet draught! 'Sweet' quoth 'a?
Sweet sink, sweet sewer!

ACHILLES: Good night and welcome, both at once, to those
That go or tarry.

AGAMEMNON: Good night.
  Exeunt Agamemnon and Menelaus

ACHILLES: Old Nestor tarries; and you too, Diomed,
Keep Hector company an hour or two.

DIOMEDES: I cannot, lord; I have important business,
The tide whereof is now. Good night, great Hector.

HECTOR: Give me your hand.

ULYSSES: *Aside to Troilus* Follow his torch; he goes to
Calchas' tent; I'll keep you company.

TROILUS: Sweet sir, you honour me.

HECTOR: And so, good night.
  Exit Diomedes; Ulysses and Troilus Following

ACHILLES: Come, come, enter my tent.
  Exeunt All but Thersites

THERSITES: That same Diomed's a false-hearted rogue, a most unjust
knave; I will no more trust him when he leers than I will a
serpent when he hisses. He will spend his mouth and promise, like
Brabbler the hound; but when he performs, astronomers foretell
it: it is prodigious, there will come some change; the sun

borrows of the moon when Diomed keeps his word. I will rather leave to see Hector than not to dog him. They say he keeps a Troyan drab, and uses the traitor Calchas' tent. I'll after. Nothing but lechery! All incontinent varlets!

Exit

ACT V. SCENE II. The Grecian Camp. Before Calchas' Tent

Enter Diomedes

DIOMEDES: What, are you up here, ho? Speak.

CALCHAS: *Within* Who calls?

DIOMEDES: Diomed. Calchas, I think. Where's your daughter?

CALCHAS: *Within* She comes to you.
Enter Troilus and Ulysses, at a Distance; after Them Thersites.

ULYSSES: Stand Where the Torch May Not Discover Us.
Enter Cressida

TROILUS: Cressid comes forth to him.

DIOMEDES: How now, my charge!

CRESSIDA: Now, my sweet guardian! Hark, a word with you.
Whispers

TROILUS: Yea, so familiar!

ULYSSES: She will sing any man at first sight.

THERSITES: And any man may sing her, if he can take her cliff; she's noted.

DIOMEDES: Will you remember?

CRESSIDA: Remember? Yes.

DIOMEDES: Nay, but do, then;
And let your mind be coupled with your words.

TROILUS: What shall she remember?

ULYSSES: List!

CRESSIDA: Sweet honey Greek, tempt me no more to folly.

THERSITES: Roguery!

DIOMEDES: Nay, then-

CRESSIDA: I'll tell you what-

DIOMEDES: Fo, fo! come, tell a pin; you are a forsworn-

CRESSIDA: In faith, I cannot. What would you have me do?

THERSITES: A juggling trick, to be secretly open.

DIOMEDES: What did you swear you would bestow on me?

CRESSIDA: I prithee, do not hold me to mine oath;
Bid me do anything but that, sweet Greek.

DIOMEDES: Good night.

TROILUS: Hold, patience!

ULYSSES: How now, Troyan!

CRESSIDA: Diomed!

DIOMEDES: No, no, good night; I'll be your fool no more.

TROILUS: Thy better must.

CRESSIDA: Hark! a word in your ear.

TROILUS: O plague and madness!

ULYSSES: You are moved, Prince; let us depart, I pray,
Lest your displeasure should enlarge itself
To wrathful terms. This place is dangerous;
The time right deadly; I beseech you, go.

TROILUS: Behold, I pray you.

ULYSSES: Nay, good my lord, go off;
You flow to great distraction; come, my lord.

TROILUS: I prithee stay.

ULYSSES: You have not patience; come.

TROILUS: I pray you, stay; by hell and all hell's torments,
I will not speak a word.

DIOMEDES: And so, good night.

CRESSIDA: Nay, but you part in anger.

TROILUS: Doth that grieve thee? O withered truth!

ULYSSES: How now, my lord?

TROILUS: By Jove, I will be patient.

CRESSIDA: Guardian! Why, Greek!

DIOMEDES: Fo, fo! adieu! you palter.

CRESSIDA: In faith, I do not. Come hither once again.

ULYSSES: You shake, my lord, at something; will you go?
You will break out.

TROILUS: She strokes his cheek.

ULYSSES: Come, come.

TROILUS: Nay, stay; by Jove, I will not speak a word:
There is between my will and all offences
A guard of patience. Stay a little while.

THERSITES: How the devil luxury, with his fat rump and potato
finger, tickles these together! Fry, lechery, fry!

DIOMEDES: But will you, then?

CRESSIDA: In faith, I will, lo; never trust me else.

DIOMEDES: Give me some token for the surety of it.

CRESSIDA: I'll fetch you one.
  Exit

ULYSSES: You have sworn patience.

TROILUS: Fear me not, my lord;
I will not be myself, nor have cognition
Of what I feel. I am all patience.
  Re-enter Cressida

THERSITES: Now the pledge; now, now, now!

CRESSIDA: Here, Diomed, keep this sleeve.

TROILUS: O beauty! where is thy faith?

ULYSSES: My lord!

TROILUS: I will be patient; outwardly I will.

CRESSIDA: You look upon that sleeve; behold it well.
He lov'd me-O false wench!-Give't me again.

DIOMEDES: Whose was't?

CRESSIDA: It is no matter, now I ha't again.
I will not meet with you to-morrow night.
I prithee, Diomed, visit me no more.

THERSITES: Now she sharpens. Well said, whetstone.

DIOMEDES: I shall have it.

CRESSIDA: What, this?

DIOMEDES: Ay, that.

CRESSIDA: O all you gods! O pretty, pretty pledge!
Thy master now lies thinking on his bed
Of thee and me, and sighs, and takes my glove,
And gives memorial dainty kisses to it,
As I kiss thee. Nay, do not snatch it from me;
He that takes that doth take my heart withal.

DIOMEDES: I had your heart before; this follows it.

TROILUS: I did swear patience.

CRESSIDA: You shall not have it, Diomed; faith, you shall not;
I'll give you something else.

DIOMEDES: I will have this. Whose was it?

CRESSIDA: It is no matter.

DIOMEDES: Come, tell me whose it was.

CRESSIDA: 'Twas one's that lov'd me better than you will.
But, now you have it, take it.

DIOMEDES: Whose was it?

CRESSIDA: By all Diana's waiting women yond,
And by herself, I will not tell you whose.

DIOMEDES: To-morrow will I wear it on my helm,
And grieve his spirit that dares not challenge it.

TROILUS: Wert thou the devil and wor'st it on thy horn,
It should be challeng'd.

CRESSIDA: Well, well, 'tis done, 'tis past; and yet it is not;
I will not keep my word.

DIOMEDES: Why, then farewell;
Thou never shalt mock Diomed again.

CRESSIDA: You shall not go. One cannot speak a word
But it straight starts you.

DIOMEDES: I do not like this fooling.

THERSITES: Nor I, by Pluto; but that that likes not you
Pleases me best.

DIOMEDES: What, shall I come? The hour-

CRESSIDA: Ay, come-O Jove! Do come. I shall be plagu'd.

DIOMEDES: Farewell till then.

CRESSIDA: Good night. I prithee come.
  Exit Diomedes
Troilus, farewell! One eye yet looks on thee;
But with my heart the other eye doth see.
Ah, poor our sex! this fault in us I find,
The error of our eye directs our mind.
What error leads must err; O, then conclude,
Minds sway'd by eyes are full of turpitude.
  Exit

THERSITES: A proof of strength she could not publish more,
Unless she said 'My mind is now turn'd whore.'

ULYSSES: All's done, my lord.

TROILUS: It is.

ULYSSES: Why stay we, then?

TROILUS: To make a recordation to my soul
Of every syllable that here was spoke.
But if I tell how these two did coact,
Shall I not lie in publishing a truth?
Sith yet there is a credence in my heart,
An esperance so obstinately strong,
That doth invert th' attest of eyes and ears;
As if those organs had deceptious functions
Created only to calumniate.
Was Cressid here?

ULYSSES: I cannot conjure, Troyan.

TROILUS: She was not, sure.

ULYSSES: Most sure she was.

TROILUS: Why, my negation hath no taste of madness.

ULYSSES: Nor mine, my lord. Cressid was here but now.

TROILUS: Let it not be believ'd for womanhood.
Think, we had mothers; do not give advantage
To stubborn critics, apt, without a theme,
For depravation, to square the general sex
By Cressid's rule. Rather think this not Cressid.

ULYSSES: What hath she done, Prince, that can soil our mothers?

TROILUS: Nothing at all, unless that this were she.

THERSITES: Will 'a swagger himself out on's own eyes?

TROILUS: This she? No; this is Diomed's Cressida.
If beauty have a soul, this is not she;
If souls guide vows, if vows be sanctimonies,
If sanctimony be the god's delight,
If there be rule in unity itself,
This was not she. O madness of discourse,
That cause sets up with and against itself!
Bifold authority! where reason can revolt
Without perdition, and loss assume all reason
Without revolt: this is, and is not, Cressid.
Within my soul there doth conduce a fight
Of this strange nature, that a thing inseparate
Divides more wider than the sky and earth;
And yet the spacious breadth of this division
Admits no orifex for a point as subtle
As Ariachne's broken woof to enter.
Instance, O instance! strong as Pluto's gates:
Cressid is mine, tied with the bonds of heaven.
Instance, O instance! strong as heaven itself:
The bonds of heaven are slipp'd, dissolv'd, and loos'd;
And with another knot, five-finger-tied,

The fractions of her faith, orts of her love,
The fragments, scraps, the bits, and greasy relics
Of her o'er-eaten faith, are bound to Diomed.

ULYSSES: May worthy Troilus be half-attach'd
With that which here his passion doth express?

TROILUS: Ay, Greek; and that shall be divulged well
In characters as red as Mars his heart
Inflam'd with Venus. Never did young man fancy
With so eternal and so fix'd a soul.
Hark, Greek: as much as I do Cressid love,
So much by weight hate I her Diomed.
That sleeve is mine that he'll bear on his helm;
Were it a casque compos'd by Vulcan's skill
My sword should bite it. Not the dreadful spout
Which shipmen do the hurricano call,
Constring'd in mass by the almighty sun,
Shall dizzy with more clamour Neptune's ear
In his descent than shall my prompted sword
Falling on Diomed.

THERSITES: He'll tickle it for his concupy.

TROILUS: O Cressid! O false Cressid! false, false, false!
Let all untruths stand by thy stained name,
And they'll seem glorious.

ULYSSES: O, contain yourself;
Your passion draws ears hither.
  Enter Aeneas

AENEAS: I have been seeking you this hour, my lord.
Hector, by this, is arming him in Troy;
Ajax, your guard, stays to conduct you home.

TROILUS: Have with you, Prince. My courteous lord, adieu.

Fairwell, revolted fair!-and, Diomed,
Stand fast and wear a castle on thy head.

ULYSSES: I'll bring you to the gates.

TROILUS: Accept distracted thanks.
  Exeunt Troilus, Aeneas. And Ulysses

THERSITES: Would I could meet that rogue
Diomed! I would croak like a raven; I would
bode, I would bode. Patroclus will give me
anything for the intelligence of this whore;
the parrot will not do more for an almond than
he for a commodious drab. Lechery, lechery!
Still wars and lechery! Nothing else holds fashion.
A burning devil take them!
  Exit

ACT V. SCENE III. Troy. Before Priam's Palace
Enter Hector and Andromache

ANDROMACHE: When was my lord so much ungently temper'd
To stop his ears against admonishment?
Unarm, unarm, and do not fight to-day.

HECTOR: You train me to offend you; get you in.
By all the everlasting gods, I'll go.

ANDROMACHE: My dreams will, sure, prove ominous to the day.

HECTOR: No more, I say.
  Enter Cassandra

CASSANDRA: Where is my brother Hector?

ANDROMACHE: Here, sister, arm'd, and bloody in intent.
Consort with me in loud and dear petition,

Pursue we him on knees; for I have dreamt
Of bloody turbulence, and this whole night
Hath nothing been but shapes and forms of slaughter.

CASSANDRA: O, 'tis true!

HECTOR: Ho! bid my trumpet sound.

CASSANDRA: No notes of sally, for the heavens, sweet brother!

HECTOR: Be gone, I say. The gods have heard me swear.

CASSANDRA: The gods are deaf to hot and peevish vows;
They are polluted off'rings, more abhorr'd
Than spotted livers in the sacrifice.

ANDROMACHE: O, be persuaded! Do not count it holy
To hurt by being just. It is as lawful,
For we would give much, to use violent thefts
And rob in the behalf of charity.

CASSANDRA: It is the purpose that makes strong the vow;
But vows to every purpose must not hold.
Unarm, sweet Hector.

HECTOR: Hold you still, I say.
Mine honour keeps the weather of my fate.
Life every man holds dear; but the dear man
Holds honour far more precious dear than life.
   Enter Troilus
How now, young man! Mean'st thou to fight to-day?

ANDROMACHE: Cassandra, call my father to persuade.
   Exit Cassandra

HECTOR: No, faith, young Troilus; doff thy harness, youth;
I am to-day i' th' vein of chivalry.

Let grow thy sinews till their knots be strong,
And tempt not yet the brushes of the war.
Unarm thee, go; and doubt thou not, brave boy,
I'll stand to-day for thee and me and Troy.

TROILUS: Brother, you have a vice of mercy in you
Which better fits a lion than a man.

HECTOR: What vice is that, good Troilus?
Chide me for it.

TROILUS: When many times the captive Grecian falls,
Even in the fan and wind of your fair sword,
You bid them rise and live.

HECTOR: O, 'tis fair play!

TROILUS: Fool's play, by heaven, Hector.

HECTOR: How now! how now!

TROILUS: For th' love of all the gods,
Let's leave the hermit Pity with our mother;
And when we have our armours buckled on,
The venom'd vengeance ride upon our swords,
Spur them to ruthful work, rein them from ruth!

HECTOR: Fie, savage, fie!

TROILUS: Hector, then 'tis wars.

HECTOR: Troilus, I would not have you fight to-day.

TROILUS: Who should withhold me?
Not fate, obedience, nor the hand of Mars
Beck'ning with fiery truncheon my retire;
Not Priamus and Hecuba on knees,

Their eyes o'ergalled with recourse of tears;
Nor you, my brother, with your true sword drawn,
Oppos'd to hinder me, should stop my way,
But by my ruin.

   Re-enter Cassandra, with Priam

CASSANDRA: Lay hold upon him, Priam, hold him fast;
He is thy crutch; now if thou lose thy stay,
Thou on him leaning, and all Troy on thee,
Fall all together.

PRIAM: Come, Hector, come, go back.
Thy wife hath dreamt; thy mother hath had visions;
Cassandra doth foresee; and I myself
Am like a prophet suddenly enrapt
To tell thee that this day is ominous.
Therefore, come back.

HECTOR: Aeneas is a-field;
And I do stand engag'd to many Greeks,
Even in the faith of valour, to appear
This morning to them.

PRIAM: Ay, but thou shalt not go.

HECTOR: I must not break my faith.
You know me dutiful; therefore, dear sir,
Let me not shame respect; but give me leave
To take that course by your consent and voice
Which you do here forbid me, royal Priam.

CASSANDRA: O Priam, yield not to him!

ANDROMACHE: Do not, dear father.

HECTOR: Andromache, I am offended with you.
Upon the love you bear me, get you in.

Exit Andromache

TROILUS: This foolish, dreaming, superstitious girl
Makes all these bodements.

CASSANDRA: O, farewell, dear Hector!
Look how thou diest. Look how thy eye turns pale.
Look how thy wounds do bleed at many vents.
Hark how Troy roars; how Hecuba cries out;
How poor Andromache shrills her dolours forth;
Behold distraction, frenzy, and amazement,
Like witless antics, one another meet,
And all cry, Hector! Hector's dead! O Hector!

TROILUS: Away, away!

CASSANDRA: Farewell!-yet, soft! Hector, I take my leave.
Thou dost thyself and all our Troy deceive.
     Exit

HECTOR: You are amaz'd, my liege, at her exclaim.
Go in, and cheer the town; we'll forth, and fight,
Do deeds worth praise and tell you them at night.

PRIAM: Farewell. The gods with safety stand about thee!
     Exeunt Severally Priam and Hector. Alarums

TROILUS: They are at it, hark! Proud Diomed, believe,
I come to lose my arm or win my sleeve.
     Enter Pandarus

PANDARUS: Do you hear, my lord? Do you hear?

TROILUS: What now?

PANDARUS: Here's a letter come from yond poor girl.

TROILUS: Let me read.

PANDARUS: A whoreson tisick, a whoreson rascally tisick so troubles
me, and the foolish fortune of this girl, and what one thing,
what another, that I shall leave you one o' th's days; and I have
a rheum in mine eyes too, and such an ache in my bones that
unless a man were curs'd I cannot tell what to think on't. What
says she there?

TROILUS: Words, words, mere words, no matter from the heart;
Th' effect doth operate another way.
   Tearing the Letter
Go, wind, to wind, there turn and change together.
My love with words and errors still she feeds,
But edifies another with her deeds.
   Exeunt Severally

ACT V. SCENE IV. The Plain Between Troy and the Grecian Camp
Enter Thersites. Excursions

THERSITES: Now they are clapper-clawing one
another; I'll go look on. That dissembling abominable
varlet, Diomed, has got that same scurvy doting
foolish young knave's sleeve of Troy there in his helm.
I would fain see them meet, that that same young Troyan
ass that loves the whore there might send that Greekish
whoremasterly villain with the sleeve back to the
dissembling luxurious drab of a sleeve-less errand.
A th' t'other side, the policy of those crafty swearing
rascals-that stale old mouse-eaten dry cheese,
Nestor, and that same dog-fox, Ulysses -is not
prov'd worth a blackberry. They set me up, in policy,
that mongrel cur, Ajax, against that dog of as bad a kind,
Achilles; and now is the cur, Ajax prouder than the cur
Achilles, and will not arm to-day; whereupon the
Grecians begin to proclaim barbarism, and policy grows
into an ill opinion.

Enter Diomedes, Troilus Following
Soft! here comes sleeve, and t'other.

TROILUS: Fly not; for shouldst thou take the river Styx
I would swim after.

DIOMEDES: Thou dost miscall retire.
I do not fly; but advantageous care
Withdrew me from the odds of multitude.
Have at thee.

THERSITES: Hold thy whore, Grecian; now for thy whore,
Troyan-now the sleeve, now the sleeve!
    Exeunt Troilus and Diomedes Fighting
    Enter Hector

HECTOR: What art thou, Greek? Art thou for Hector's match?
Art thou of blood and honour?

THERSITES: No, no-I am a rascal; a scurvy railing knave; a very
filthy rogue.

HECTOR: I do believe thee. Live.
    Exit

THERSITES: God-a-mercy, that thou wilt believe me; but a plague
break thy neck for frighting me! What's become of the wenching
rogues? I think they have swallowed one another. I would laugh at
that miracle. Yet, in a sort, lechery eats itself. I'll seek
them.
    Exit

ACT V. SCENE V. Another Part of the Plain
Enter Diomedes and a Servant

DIOMEDES: Go, go, my servant, take thou Troilus' horse;
Present the fair steed to my lady Cressid.

Fellow, commend my service to her beauty;
Tell her I have chastis'd the amorous Troyan,
And am her knight by proof.

SERVANT: I go, my lord.
Exit
Enter Agamemnon

AGAMEMNON: Renew, renew! The fierce Polydamus
Hath beat down enon; bastard Margarelon
Hath Doreus prisoner,
And stands colossus-wise, waving his beam,
Upon the pashed corses of the kings
Epistrophus and Cedius. Polixenes is slain;
Amphimacus and Thoas deadly hurt;
Patroclus ta'en, or slain; and Palamedes
Sore hurt and bruis'd. The dreadful Sagittary
Appals our numbers. Haste we, Diomed,
To reinforcement, or we perish all.
Enter Nestor

NESTOR: Go, bear Patroclus' body to Achilles,
And bid the snail-pac'd Ajax arm for shame.
There is a thousand Hectors in the field;
Now here he fights on Galathe his horse,
And there lacks work; anon he's there afoot,
And there they fly or die, like scaled sculls
Before the belching whale; then is he yonder,
And there the strawy Greeks, ripe for his edge,
Fall down before him like the mower's swath.
Here, there, and everywhere, he leaves and takes;
Dexterity so obeying appetite
That what he will he does, and does so much
That proof is call'd impossibility.
Enter Ulysses

ULYSSES: O, courage, courage, courage, Princes! Great

Achilles Is arming, weeping, cursing, vowing vengeance.
Patroclus' wounds have rous'd his drowsy blood,
Together with his mangled Myrmidons,
That noseless, handless, hack'd and chipp'd, come to
him, Crying on Hector. Ajax hath lost a friend
And foams at mouth, and he is arm'd and at it,
Roaring for Troilus; who hath done to-day
Mad and fantastic execution,
Engaging and redeeming of himself
With such a careless force and forceless care
As if that luck, in very spite of cunning,
Bade him win all.
  Enter Ajax

AJAX: Troilus! thou coward Troilus!
  Exit

DIOMEDES: Ay, there, there.

NESTOR: So, so, we draw together.
  Exit
  Enter Achilles

ACHILLES: Where is this Hector?
Come, come, thou boy-queller, show thy face;
Know what it is to meet Achilles angry.
Hector! where's Hector? I will none but Hector.
  Exeunt

ACT V. SCENE VI. Another Part of the Plain
  Enter Ajax

AJAX: Troilus, thou coward Troilus, show thy head.
  Enter Diomedes

DIOMEDES: Troilus, I say! Where's Troilus?

AJAX: What wouldst thou?

DIOMEDES: I would correct him.

AJAX: Were I the general, thou shouldst have my office
Ere that correction. Troilus, I say! What, Troilus!
  Enter Troilus

TROILUS: O traitor Diomed! Turn thy false face, thou traitor,
And pay thy life thou owest me for my horse.

DIOMEDES: Ha! art thou there?

AJAX: I'll fight with him alone. Stand, Diomed.

DIOMEDES: He is my prize. I will not look upon.

TROILUS: Come, both, you cogging Greeks; have at you
  Exeunt Fighting
  Enter Hector

HECTOR: Yea, Troilus? O, well fought, my youngest brother!
  Enter Achilles

ACHILLES: Now do I see thee, ha! Have at thee, Hector!

HECTOR: Pause, if thou wilt.

ACHILLES: I do disdain thy courtesy, proud Troyan.
Be happy that my arms are out of use;
My rest and negligence befriends thee now,
But thou anon shalt hear of me again;
Till when, go seek thy fortune.
  Exit

HECTOR: Fare thee well.
I would have been much more a fresher man,

Had I expected thee.
Re-enter Troilus
How now, my brother!

TROILUS: Ajax hath ta'en Aeneas. Shall it be?
No, by the flame of yonder glorious heaven,
He shall not carry him; I'll be ta'en too,
Or bring him off. Fate, hear me what I say:
I reck not though thou end my life to-day.
Exit
Enter One in Armour

HECTOR: Stand, stand, thou Greek; thou art a goodly mark.
No? wilt thou not? I like thy armour well;
I'll frush it and unlock the rivets all
But I'll be master of it. Wilt thou not, beast, abide?
Why then, fly on; I'll hunt thee for thy hide.
Exeunt

ACT V. SCENE VII. Another Part of the Plain
Enter Achilles, with Myrmidons

ACHILLES: Come here about me, you my Myrmidons;
Mark what I say. Attend me where I wheel;
Strike not a stroke, but keep yourselves in breath;
And when I have the bloody Hector found,
Empale him with your weapons round about;
In fellest manner execute your arms.
Follow me, sirs, and my proceedings eye.
It is decreed Hector the great must die.
Exeunt
Enter Menelaus and Paris, Fighting; Then Thersites

THERSITES: The cuckold and the cuckold-maker are at it. Now, bull!
now, dog! 'Loo, Paris, 'loo! now my double-horn'd Spartan! 'loo,
Paris, 'loo! The bull has the game. Ware horns, ho!
Exeunt Paris and Menelaus

Enter Margarelon

MARGARELON: Turn, slave, and fight.

THERSITES: What art thou?

MARGARELON: A bastard son of Priam's.

THERSITES: I am a bastard too; I love bastards. I am a bastard
begot, bastard instructed, bastard in mind, bastard in valour, in
everything illegitimate. One bear will not bite another, and
wherefore should one bastard? Take heed, the quarrel's most
ominous to us: if the son of a whore fight for a whore, he tempts
judgment. Farewell, bastard.
Exit

MARGARELON: The devil take thee, coward!
Exit

ACT V. SCENE VIII. Another Part of the Plain
Enter Hector

HECTOR: Most putrified core so fair without,
Thy goodly armour thus hath cost thy life.
Now is my day's work done; I'll take good breath:
Rest, sword; thou hast thy fill of blood and death!
Disarms
Enter Achilles and His Myrmidons

ACHILLES: Look, Hector, how the sun begins to set;
How ugly night comes breathing at his heels;
Even with the vail and dark'ning of the sun,
To close the day up, Hector's life is done.

HECTOR: I am unarm'd; forego this vantage, Greek.

ACHILLES: Strike, fellows, strike; this is the man I seek.

Hector Falls
So, Ilion, fall thou next! Come, Troy, sink down;
Here lies thy heart, thy sinews, and thy bone.
On, Myrmidons, and cry you an amain
'Achilles hath the mighty Hector slain.'
   A Retreat Sounded
Hark! a retire upon our Grecian part.

MYRMIDON: The Troyan trumpets sound the like, my lord.

ACHILLES: The dragon wing of night o'erspreads the earth
And, stickler-like, the armies separates.
My half-supp'd sword, that frankly would have fed,
Pleas'd with this dainty bait, thus goes to bed.
   Sheathes His Sword
Come, tie his body to my horse's tail;
Along the field I will the Troyan trail. *Exeunt*

ACT V. SCENE IX. Another Part of the Plain
   Sound Retreat. Shout. Enter Agamemnon, Ajax, Menelaus, Nestor, Diomedes, and the Rest, Marching

AGAMEMNON: Hark! hark! what shout is this?

NESTOR: Peace, drums!

SOLDIERS: *Within* Achilles! Achilles! Hector's slain. Achilles!

DIOMEDES: The bruit is Hector's slain, and by Achilles.

AJAX: If it be so, yet bragless let it be;
Great Hector was as good a man as he.

AGAMEMNON: March patiently along. Let one be sent
To pray Achilles see us at our tent.
If in his death the gods have us befriended;
Great Troy is ours, and our sharp wars are ended.

Exeunt

ACT V. SCENE X. Another Part of the Plain
Enter Aeneas, Paris, Antenor, and Deiphobus

AENEAS: Stand, ho! yet are we masters of the field.
Never go home; here starve we out the night.
  Enter Troilus

TROILUS: Hector is slain.

ALL: Hector! The gods forbid!

TROILUS: He's dead, and at the murderer's horse's tail,
In beastly sort, dragg'd through the shameful field.
Frown on, you heavens, effect your rage with speed.
Sit, gods, upon your thrones, and smile at Troy.
I say at once let your brief plagues be mercy,
And linger not our sure destructions on.

AENEAS: My lord, you do discomfort all the host.

TROILUS: You understand me not that tell me so.
I do not speak of flight, of fear of death,
But dare all imminence that gods and men
Address their dangers in. Hector is gone.
Who shall tell Priam so, or Hecuba?
Let him that will a screech-owl aye be call'd
Go in to Troy, and say there 'Hector's dead.'
There is a word will Priam turn to stone;
Make wells and Niobes of the maids and wives,
Cold statues of the youth; and, in a word,
Scare Troy out of itself. But, march away;
Hector is dead; there is no more to say.
Stay yet. You vile abominable tents,
Thus proudly pight upon our Phrygian plains,
Let Titan rise as early as he dare,

I'll through and through you. And, thou great-siz'd coward,
No space of earth shall sunder our two hates;
I'll haunt thee like a wicked conscience still,
That mouldeth goblins swift as frenzy's thoughts.
Strike a free march to Troy. With comfort go;
Hope of revenge shall hide our inward woe.
    Enter Pandarus

PANDARUS: But hear you, hear you!

TROILUS: Hence, broker-lackey. Ignominy and shame
Pursue thy life and live aye with thy name!
    Exeunt All but Pandarus

PANDARUS: A goodly medicine for my aching bones! world! world! thus
is the poor agent despis'd! traitors and bawds, how earnestly are
you set a work, and how ill requited! Why should our endeavour be
so lov'd, and the performance so loathed? What verse for it? What
instance for it? Let me see-
    Full merrily the humble-bee doth sing
    Till he hath lost his honey and his sting;
    And being once subdu'd in armed trail,
    Sweet honey and sweet notes together fail.
Good traders in the flesh, set this in your painted
cloths. As many as be here of pander's hall,
Your eyes, half out, weep out at Pandar's fall;
Or, if you cannot weep, yet give some groans,
Though not for me, yet for your aching bones.
Brethren and sisters of the hold-door trade,
Some two months hence my will shall here be made.
It should be now, but that my fear is this,
Some galled goose of Winchester would hiss.
Till then I'll sweat and seek about for eases,
And at that time bequeath you my diseases.
    Exit

END